AFTERNOON AT
THE COUNTRY CLUB

Todd had been an easy conquest. She'd given him a kiss for the nice check he contributed to the charity drive. There was a couch in his office, which they had used. She hadn't even undressed, had just dropped her panty hose on the floor, and lifted her skirt, and that had been that. It was far more real, talking to Grace about it, than it had been at the time.

Grace--social leader, bored wife, rich, beautiful, pampered--said, "I'm still ahead of you. Tell you what--I'll give you my next prospective lover." They both laughed.

After lunch they drank coffee, strong and black. How did I ever get into this? Marguerite thought. But she knew how--and that she didn't want out. She had everything now--a rich husband, a respected place in the community, a new lover whenever she was in the mood. What else could any woman want?

MARGUERITE TANNER

ELIZABETH
NELL
DUBUS

LEISURE BOOKS 🐘 **NEW YORK CITY**

A LEISURE BOOK

Published by

Nordon Publications, Inc.
Two Park Avenue
New York, N.Y. 10016

CHAPTER ONE

The walls of the elevator rose steep and smooth around her; the elevator rose steeply and smoothly in its shaft. The silk of her dress was smooth: it fell against her lightly, barely touching her slip, her panties, her bra. A small sound rose in her, not smoothly, but abruptly. It rose and then popped from her; it seemed to be a sound that should be followed by something else, but she could think of nothing to say.

The elevator car stopped, and the other people stood, waiting. She waited with them. When the car began to move, she looked at the lighted panel and saw that this was her floor; she pushed the stop button. While the people around her looked at her, she pushed the floor button and stood, waiting for the car to move back down. She didn't like getting off elevators alone, seeing long corridors with closed doors.

Dr. Forrester's waiting room was small with two chairs and a table piled with magazines. A sign said: Please be seated. No receptionist. No nurse. Quiet. Such quiet. How could she talk against such quiet; what would she have to say that would be worth breaking that quiet?

Perhaps the silk dress wasn't right. A pantsuit, maybe. Hell. What did she care what she wore? But a psychiatrist, wouldn't he notice? Of course, he would. He would notice everything. She took out her compact, the gold one George had given her on her last birthday. It had a matching cigarette case and lighter, each in its own soft flannel bag to keep it from getting scratched in her purse. She looked in the mirror and touched lipstick to her mouth. Her mouth was too big, she thought, every time she made it up. And the chin beneath was rather square, a firm chin that somehow belied the rest of her face. Her nose was all right—straight, not too long. And her eyes were really fine, large, hazel; they were her best feature. And she used them, looking directly at other people, willing them to look at her, into her eyes. Men liked her hair. She wore it longer than the current fashion, the only item in her appearance that wasn't taken from the pages of *Vogue* or *Harper's Bazaar*. But men liked it. They liked to push their hands through the dark silk of her hair; they liked to lift it and kiss her neck. She wouldn't cut it, no matter what her hairdresser said.

A door opened and she looked up to see a tall man in a soft-blue suit.

"Mrs. Tanner?" He held the door open, she got up and moved toward him.

"I'm Marguerite Tanner," she said. Just lately, when she said that name, people made a sign of recognition.

Dr. Forrester held the door wider and motioned her in. She walked ahead of him down a short hall, with a desk set in an alcove. There was another open door. She went in.

6

She felt shaking sobs rise in her. She stood in the center of the room, felt them rise, and forced them back. She would talk, she would make sounds with the air that was trapped in her lungs and wanted to break from her as cries of . . . grief . . . loss . . . nothing.

There was a wide desk, with a leather-and-wood armchair beside it. She moved to the chair and sat, fumbled in her purse for a cigarette, lit it just as Dr. Forrester brought a lighted match to it.

"I feel like an idiot, that's what's the matter. I mean, why I'm acting like this."

"You didn't say much on the phone. When you called for an appointment. I wasn't sure . . ."

"I'm not sure, either. I got your name from Joan Spiller. You know Joan? Or will you even say if you know Joan? Probably not. Even though she tells people at evey bridge table in town all about it. So I got your name from Joan. I didn't call her up and ask her, I just remembered. And I thought anyone who could put up with Joan could surely put up with me. But I don't know what there is to put up with. I'm really a happy person. I have problems, I guess. Who doesn't? But money—well, I have money. And all that, you know—husband, children, the stuff the ladies' magazines write about. I don't know why I said that about the ladies' magazines. Like I don't believe it. Well, there's nothing to believe, is there? Anyway.

"Sometimes in the morning, when I get up, there's this feeling I have. I don't know what kind of feeling it is. Like maybe before you go to the dentist. Or like I used to feel right at the end of a pregnancy. You look at your stomach and it's all blown up, and there's a baby in there, and you think, how in the hell is all that going to get out of me? And the first time, you really don't know, so maybe the feeling

7

is pretty bad. But after that, you do know. So it's worse. Anyway, I feel kind of like that. Does that make sense? If it does, I wish you'd tell me. No, it won't make any difference, even if you do tell me it's all right. Because I know it's not. Are you counting how many cigarettes I smoke?

"Joan says the dumbest things about you. Joan blames everything on her mother. What makes it so bad is that her mother lives right in this town, and we all see her all the time. I think that's really ugly of Joan. But maybe that's why she's seeing you. Oh, hell. Look, would it do any good to talk about my mother? She really is just a very ordinary mother. Well, she did raise me by herself. With my grandparents. In Grand View, Texas—a little place in East Texas. No one knows where it is. My father died when I was four. So we moved there. From Houston."

CHAPTER TWO

Memory. She was asleep, deep in the covers, her stuffed rabbit held close, one long pink ear tickling up under her chin. Silent sleep, deep sleep. The cold air of November wrapped around her head, wrapped around the tiny bit of her face that reached up above the covers. Then noise beginning to come into the cold, to wrap around her head, too, until it found her ear, and went in, and was registered first as just loudness and then, as she struggled awake, became words, became her mother and daddy having a fight.

She knew how they would look, standing opposite each other. Her father was tall, with big hands and a head of thick blond, almost white, hair. Her mother was not tall; she was small all over, small and pretty with black curly hair, dark eyes, light cream skin. The light cream skin stained red when her mother was angry or upset. It would be red now, the blood rising in her mother's cheeks as the words rose in her throat.

Her father was talking, more than talking, shouting. "Damn fool! What am I supposed to do about this, will you tell me that?"

Her mother talking, not as loud, but still clear. "There's nothing to do about it. Except have it, and take care of it."

"You can have it. You can take care of it. Just leave me out of it."

"Steve, you act like it's all my fault."

"It'll be your fault if you have it. You can go to that woman, the one the Mexican whores go to. She'll fix you up."

"I won't do that."

"So you won't do that. Just like you wouldn't do it before, so we had Marguerite."

"It hasn't been bad, having Marguerite."

"You can say that. All you do is stay home and fool with her. I guess that's fun, at least women do it, they seem to like it. I'm the one who has to go out and get the money to pay for it all. And after buying the shoes, my God, she outgrows them every few months, and the clothes and all the rest of it—shit, is that your idea of what to spend money on? It didn't use to be. When I met you, down in that little shit of a town, you were a lot of fun. Pretty. All over pretty. Now, Christ, you'll get all blown up again. I'll lie on you and feel your stomach pushing me away, the damn baby trying to mess things up before it's even born. And then there'll be two to take care of, two outgrowing everything. Hell, where's the fun we were going to have? And money—what a hell of a way to spend money!"

"You make good money."

"You know what? That's right. I do make good money. And I'll bet if I leave Houston, go some place else, there'll be work there, too. And pretty girls who see to it that they don't get pregnant, and no smelly babies that cry in the night and puke on your clean shirt."

"What are you talking about, Steve, what do you mean, go some place else? You don't mean that, you wouldn't go off and leave me . . ."

"The hell I wouldn't! I told you how I wanted this to be. I wanted it to be you and me, no one else, because we know how to have fun. You're a damn good woman to go to bed with—I guess none better. But you messed it up once, and now you're messing it up again, and I've had it. I'm up to my neck in it, so I'm pulling out. You can do what you want about it—go back to those good parents of yours. They'll be real happy; they can say I told you so because they never wanted you to marry me, and it looks like they were right."

"I'll never go back there." Her mother's voice sounded different now, it sounded the way Marguerite sounded when she had hurt herself and was crying and talking through the crying. She hoped her mother wasn't crying. Grownups weren't supposed to cry. They were supposed to help little children stop crying. If a grownup cried, who helped her to stop?

"I guess you will. Not much else you can do, is there?"

"Steve, don't you feel bad about doing this? Walking out on me?"

"What's to feel bad about? We made a bargain and you didn't live up to it. No kids, we said. Fun, we said. Who whispered in my ear, kissing my neck, blowing chills down me? Don't use anything, you said. It makes it better for you without, you said. It's safe. It's okay. Remember that?"

"Most of the time it was." Her mother wasn't crying now, if she had been crying. But there was a tiredness in her, and in what she said; she sounded the way she did at the end of a day of scrubbing woodwork and polishing window glass in their apartment.

"Most of the time! That's a good one! Well, twice it wasn't. So first there was Marguerite and now another one. Just how long did you intend for this to go on?"

"Most married people have children. I don't see that it's such a crime."

"I never wanted to be like most married people. I only married you because I was crazy for you, crazy for your tits and your cunt and all the rest of it. If you'd gone along with it, I would have just lived with you—never married you at all."

"I might as well as never have married you. It's ending up the same way, anyway."

"Maybe so. I figured you were good for longer than this, though. If there hadn't been the children. I figured you were nineteen when I married you. With any luck, you'd be good-looking for what—fifteen years? So that wouldn't have been a bad run."

"Fifteen years! I've only had a third of that."

"Better for you, maybe. You're still young enough to catch another man. Grand View's probably crawling with men who'd even take on your two kids to go to bed with you. But you better figure some way to let 'em know what hot stuff you are. Want me to give you a letter?"

"You bastard." Marguerite had liked it better when her mother was louder. Now her quiet voice seemed to cut through the air like steel, bearing the words on a shaft of cold hardness. "You bastard." A bastard was something bad, something very bad to make her mother sound that way. A bastard was daddy, daddy was a bastard, a bastard was bad, daddy was bad, you bastard.

12

"No need to get ugly." Her father sounded cheerful. She was never afraid of her father when he sounded like that; usually, he would buy her an ice cream cone or play horsie with her. "You're in luck. I just got paid and I'm feeling generous. I'll give you half my pay, that'll give you enough to take a bus to Grand View."

"I'm not going to Grand View."

"Suit yourself. What time is it? One-thirty? There're worse times to leave home, I guess. I'll just clear out now. No need to hang around, is there? Unless you'd like one more time, huh? Just a little something to remember?"

"I've got all the memories of you I'll ever need," her mother said.

"You'll be a hell of a long time finding anybody who can do it to you like I can. You'll be remembering me when some poor jerk is fucking you and doing a damn lousy job of it."

"That's your only claim to being a man. And even that doesn't make you a man. You're just a dirty little boy."

"Dirty, huh? You've never said stop. You've gone along with everything I ever wanted to do."

"Oh, get out! Pack your things and get the hell out!"

A line of light then, growing wider. The shape of her father coming into the room, moving past the cot she slept on, going around the double bed to the chest on the other side of the room, opening drawers. Looking into the light, through the open door that had let it in, she saw her mother, sitting in a rocking chair, her black curls falling around her face. She wanted to go to her mother and hang on to her, wanted to make sure her mother would not leave, too. It might not be bad to have her father gone. Mother was different when her father wasn't home; they cut out paper dolls and colored red-and-green-and-blue

13

pictures when her father wasn't home. Now he would leave for somewhere and they would play all the time.

There was nothing to watch but her mother sitting in the rocking chair, black curls falling around her face. The rocking chair moved back and forth, her mother's small body moved with it, gently rocking, her head nodding with the movement. Watching the soft movement, hearing the click of the rockers as they went over the edge of the rug and hit the floor, Marguerite rocked back to sleep.

When she woke the next morning she knew that her father was gone, but she did not know how she knew it. Her mother was asleep, arm thrown up over her head, the cover dragging away from her. Marguerite went into the living room and pulled the string hanging from the window shade. The shade flew up, up to the top of the window, and the world outside was framed in the cracked enamel molding of the window.

It was gray, all gray. The building across the alley, gray and tall with only a door at the very bottom, no windows at all. The sky above the building, the concrete that floored the alley—all gray. The light was gray too; as it reached past the raised shade, past the windowsill and into the room it did not so much light up the darkness as soften it to a paler shadow. The light did not touch the furniture in the room and lift the colors into visibility. It seemed to settle around the furniture, the grayness having a peculiar quality of burying the plum-colored sofa and the light-green chairs in grayness, of highlighting only the veil of cigarette ash that lay on the small magazine table.

Marguerite felt cold in the early light; she climbed up on the sofa and pulled her flannel gown around her feet, tucking herself into the warmth. One of her mother's magazines was on the sofa; Marguerite picked it up and

14

turned the pages, looking at the pictures of pretty ladies in bathing suits and evening gowns, of handsome men in funny black suits with long coats and white bow ties. The people in the pictures were movie stars. They all lived in a place called Hollywood, they had a lot of money and they went to birthday parties every day and ate all the ice cream they wanted. One of the ladies was named Loretta Young. Marguerite had heard Cissy, her mother's best friend, say that her mother looked just like Loretta Young, and now Marguerite held the magazine to the gray light coming from the window and tried to see her mother's face in the shiny gray-and-black-and-white picture on the page.

There was a little moaning sound from the bedroom; it seemed to drift in with the gray light, it was all the sound there was in the world. It was her mother, her mother making that sad moaning sound. Listening to it, Marguerite cried, tears falling and blotting on the magazine page before her. Then the bed squeaked, the sharp sound cutting off the moan; it was like a switch being thrown, so quickly did the moaning stop.

"Marguerite? Baby, are you crying?" Her mother was in the doorway, pulling a pink quilted robe around her, her feet sliding out of the soft pink slippers. She moved quickly to the sofa, leaned over, picked Marguerite up. There was a smell of old perfume on her neck. Smelling it made Marguerite think of how pretty her mother looked when she was all dressed up, how she would stand at the mirror when she was finished dressing, pressing the green bulb on the end of her perfume atomizer, and being veiled in a fine mist of sweet scent.

"Don't cry," her mother said. "We'll have breakfast, and then we'll do something fun. We'll go see Cissy. You like to see Cissy, she'll still be in bed and we'll wake her up, and she'll fuss, but then she'll laugh and we'll all have a good time."

They ate breakfast: corn flakes with thin slices of banana, toast with apple butter. Marguerite's mother dressed slowly, settling her shiny white slip over her head and smoothing it over her body, patting the stomach that lay flat beneath the soft sheen of the material. She sat at her dressing table a long while, putting on the makeup that made of her face not quite a mask and yet something much different from the way she looked when she first got up in the morning. Made up, she did look like Loretta Young, looked like she should be in one of the magazines in a bathing suit or a long gown with fur all around the edges.

They stood on a corner waiting for the bus that would take them to Cissy's. Her mother had pulled a wool beret tight over Marguerite's ears, the wool kept out some of the whine of the November wind, but over the wind Marguerite could hear her mother talking, talking not to Marguerite but to herself or to someone yet unseen. "Terrible neighborhood, anyway. We'll be well out of it. I'll talk to Cissy. She will know what to do; she's always got good ideas. There's a way out of this. I'm just not seeing it."

Cissy lived in a downtown hotel, in a large room that was more of a sitting room than a bedroom; the bed was in an alcove, and could be hidden by tall wine-colored draperies that slid on a long brass rod across the opening. Another alcove held a small sink and a refrigerator and a hot plate. Cissy's refrigerator usually had things like olives and peanuts and cherries and Cokes; it was a much better refrigerator than the one at home, with its ordinary

16

supply of milk and eggs and sliced lunch meat.

Marguerite's mother knocked a long time before they could finally hear Cissy answer.

"We're waking her up," Marguerite's mother whispered, and she held Marguerite's hand tightly in hers.

"Good God! Who is it at this hour?" Cissy said, opening the door on the chain and peering through the crack. "My God, Phyllis, what are you doing out so early, you and the kid?" She shut the door so that she could loose the chain. They heard the rattling of the chain, and then the door opened wide, and Cissy stood there in her Japanese kimono with the huge yellow chrysanthemums all over it and with her blond hair piled high. "Well, Lord! Come in, come in. It's early for a visit, but I guess you've been up for hours, with the kid and all. You want coffee? Let me make coffee. God, what time is it, anyway?"

"Only nine-thirty. I know it's too early, but Cissy, I needed to see you. I thought I couldn't wait. Something bad's happened; Steve's left me." The words rushed out of her mother's mouth, there was a kind of rattling sound about them, like the chain when it left the lock. The words were hard and bright like the chain. Steve's left me, that was what Marguerite knew, but did not want to know that she knew.

"Phyllis, my God. When? Left? Just left? The bastard. Look, take off your coat, okay? Sit down. I've got to have coffee; let me put on the water. Look, Marguerite, Aunt Cissy's going to fix you a nice Coke and maybe some cookies, a tea party, and you can get up in my bed with some colors and be all comfy, okay?"

Cissy pulled the wine-colored curtains and switched on the lamp next to the bed. The lamp was shaped like a poodle, a white poodle with a blue ribbon tied around its neck. The shaft of the lamp went down through the poodle's back, and the shade was made of pink eyelet ruffles. Marguerite loved the lamp. She loved to take a piece of tissue and carefully dust the poodle, getting into all the ripples of china that made his fur curls, spitting on her finger, and rubbing the spit on the poodle to make him shine.

She opened the coloring book to a picture of a poodle and began to color the ribbon around his neck blue. Over the soft rub of the crayon against the paper she could hear Cissy and her mother talking. Her mother's voice had a special sound to it now, the sound it always got when she talked to Cissy. It wasn't the same way she sounded when she was talking to the landlady, or even to her husband, but then Cissy was her mother's very best friend.

"I hated to wake you up, Cissy, I know your last show wasn't 'til one this morning, and you probably were out after that, I know that. But I've been awake all night. Well, Steve left around two, not much night left then. I may have finally gone off around six, I just had to talk to you."

"Want a doughnut with that coffee? They're fresh; I bought them before I came in. Okay, now what brought this on? I know things haven't been too good, but nothing bad enough to make him take off, so what?"

"I told him I'm pregnant."

"Jesus! That was dumb."

"Telling him? He'd find out—"

"Getting pregnant. You know how Steve feels."

"You can talk. Okay, I slipped up. Are you taking Steve's side? Because if you are, I'm not listening."

"I'm not taking Steve's side. I think he's a louse. I just meant it's no surprise he got mad. Hell, he didn't want Marguerite, didn't you tell me that?"

18

"He doesn't want anything that gets in the way of his having fun."

"You think he's gone for good?"

"Sure. This has been coming on, anyway. You know Steve, he's restless; he likes a good time. I think he was tired of me, wanted someone—I don't know, younger, flashier."

"You're only twenty-four."

"You know what I mean. You always look pretty, you don't even have to make your bed up, the hotel maid does that. There's something about doing housework. It makes you feel like you smell of dust and greasy dishes all the time. How can a man feel romantic about a girl who scrubs his toilet?"

"So the big question is what are you going to do?"

"I don't know. I don't know."

"Did he leave you any money? Because I've got some. I've had a few little presents lately. You can have—"

"He left me half his pay."

"Enough to get home on?"

"Home? You mean Grand View?"

"Isn't that what you're going to have to do?"

"I don't want to do that. I can't do that."

Now her mother sounded different, stronger; her voice had been soft, coming in just under Cissy's. Now it was opposite Cissy's, the same strong weight. Marguerite crept to the end of the bed, crayon in her hand. She looked between the curtains and saw them sitting on Cissy's favorite pink chairs, a low marble table between them. Marguerite liked to look at Cissy and her mother together, Cissy was blond and pretty, her mother was dark-haired and pretty; they made a pretty world, where nothing bad could happen. Cissy got up to get more coffee. Her silk robe swished as she walked; it made a pretty sound, helping to make a pretty, pretty world.

"But if you don't go home, what then?"

"I could get a job."

"A job! That wouldn't last long. Soon as you start showing, you'd be fired. And what about Marguerite? Who'd take care of her, if you worked?"

"My landlady keeps her for me. When Steve and I went out."

"She'd have to be paid."

"I work for her. I do her ironing, things like that."

"So you'd work all day and then come home and work for her at night."

"You're not very encouraging."

"Look, the worst thing, I mean the very worst thing, that can happen to a woman is to be left with kids to support and no way to do it. What kind of job could you get, anyway? You don't type, do you?"

"I thought a store clerk, or a waitress."

"Yeah, there's really big money in that." Cissy moved to her mother, leaned over and pulled her to her. "God, kid, I'm sorry. I'm sorry. But there's no use in lying to you. You're in a real fix, and I don't think there's a damn thing you can do but go home."

"I used to feel sorry for you, did you know that, Cissy? I'd be with Steve, sitting on the sofa, close, cuddling, listening to the radio, and the rest of the world not even there. And I'd think of you, all dressed up, beautiful, but showing it to a room full of people who don't care about you at all, who keep on eating while you sing, who if they pay attention to you at all do it because they want to take you to bed. And I'd think, poor Cissy. She really doesn't have anything at all. And now look at us. At me."

20

"I'm not interested in my life looking better because yours has gone to pot. We've got to get you straightened out. Look, maybe your folks could send you money, if you're that dead-set against going home."

"They couldn't afford to do anything like that. Even if they could, they probably wouldn't. Anyway, they don't have it. Dad's a high school principal in little old town that would fit into one corner of Houston and never be noticed. He can't send me money."

"Will it be that bad, going home?"

"I left there thankful that I'd never have to live there again. You come from San Antonio; it's not like Grand View. Everybody knows everybody's business. There're certain people who've set themselves up as the ruling class or some such thing. They think they know how everyone should act, and they damn well let you know it if you don't measure up. My father's the principal, so that makes him respectable, but he doesn't have any money, so that makes him a target for their rules. Oh, what's the use? Steve's right, we left there telling ourselves we were going to have fun the rest of our lives. You've read about Scott and Zelda Fitzgerald, well, I think we were going to be the poor man's Fitzgeralds, only there's no nanny to take care of Marguerite, I couldn't stay out dancing 'til three and still nurse her."

"I wish I could come up with something else."

"I guess I should be glad I have a home to go back to. Mother and Dad aren't bad. Mother won't even say I told you so, though, of course, she did. She's too much of a Christian to allow herself to be spiteful. But I'll be back in her house—I'll be a daughter again. Do you have any idea of how hard it is to be a daughter when you've been a wife?"

"Call them right now. Get it over with. And then I'll get dressed, and we'll go out and have a really good lunch. And maybe do a little shopping. We'll have ourselves a real good time. And I tell you what, I met a couple of men in from Austin last night, nice men. No, Phyllis, they really are. And they're calling me later. They want a party after the show tonight. So you come to the show, and then afterward we'll all go out. We'll put Marguerite to bed here; I'll get one of the maids to watch her. A last fling, okay?"

"Okay." Her mother's face looked old with the makeup, the black lines of her eyebrows, the red lines of her lips; underneath was the young and unmarked face of the early morning. Her mother looked like Cissy with the makeup on. Marguerite thought that perhaps she liked her mother better in the early morning, when her face was still all the things it yet could be.

They went to a Mexican restaurant for lunch. Her mother and Cissy drank something that looked like water from tiny glasses. They drank it in a funny way, they held the tiny glass in one hand, and a piece of cut lime in the other between thumb and forefinger. In the web of flesh between the thumb and the hand they poured salt: they licked the salt, sucked the limes, and then swallowed the clear liquid, laughing the whole time. There were many tiny glasses, and Cissy and her mother laughed a lot. When the food came, they ate their tacos and tamales with their fingers, licking the spicy sauce, now drinking Mexican beer from small brown bottles.

"I'm sozzled," her mother said, and leaned back in her chair and laughed.

"Me, too. What we need is a nap." They went back to the hotel, riding in a taxi that smelled of closed-in cigarettes. Her mother opened the window and leaned her head into the rush of clear air, air that was still gray with the clouds of the November afternoon. In Cissy's room, they took off their dresses and reached under their slips to take off bras, panties, and hose. Their slips draped close to their bodies, the electricity of the silk holding the slips over the curving flesh; when Cissy leaned over, Marguerite could see her full breasts, the small nipples at the end.

She colored while they slept. Later they dressed again, her mother putting on one of Cissy's spangly dresses. It made her look all new again, her body in the sheath of shining cloth matched the face she drew onto her features. They kissed Marguerite goodnight and went out in a wave of fresh perfume. Marguerite remembered the smell of her mother's perfume that morning. Morning was far away, the gray light in the gray apartment was far away; now there was only the pink light through the shade on the poodle, there was only the smooth satin of Cissy's sheets.

When she heard voices she curled deeper into the covers to get away from them. One was her mother's voice; she didn't want to hear it, because if she heard it, she would have to wake up to hear what her mother was saying, and she didn't want to wake up. But then she heard a man's voice, it didn't sound like her father's voice, but maybe he had a frog in his throat. He used to tell Marguerite that sometimes, though he never said how the frog got in or how it got out. She looked through a crack in the curtains; as she had thought, it was not her father, but a man she had not seen before. She saw what her mother was doing and thought it was funny; her mother was undressing under her slip the way she had before her nap.

She was folding the clothes she took off very carefully, she had set her borrowed dancing pumps on the floor, heel to heel and very neat. She was not looking at the man while she did all this, not until she had found a hanger and put Cissy's dress on it did she turn around. Then she stood there, looking at the man.

He walked over to her mother, he was tall, as tall as her daddy. As he got near her mother, he was so much bigger that Marguerite could not see her mother anymore. Then she heard a soft sound, it must be her mother that made the sound—the man was too big to have made such a little noise. The man moved. Marguerite could see her mother now. She no longer had the slip on, it was lying at her feet, crumpled, not neat like the other clothes her mother had taken off. The man was holding her mother, his arms stretched out in front of him, one hand on either side of her mother's breasts. Now her mother was looking at the man, she was smiling and she had her head held back, so that the black curls were high on her forehead.

"What are you waiting for?" her mother said, and when she said that the man picked her up and carried her to the sofa and laid her down on it. And then he undressed, but he was not neat. He let his clothes fall every which way on the floor. When he was all undressed, he sat on the edge of the sofa and began to rub his hands on her mother, and to kiss her, not just on her mouth as Marguerite had seen her daddy do, but on her breasts and her stomach. And then the man moved her mother so that her mother was sitting on him, her legs out on either side of him.

It was strange to look at her mother and the man, to hear the sounds they made. Marguerite picked up the red crayon that lay with the other crayons and tumbled in the bedclothes with her coloring book. She took the red

24

crayon firmly in her fist, and slipped off the bed, and made long red lines on the wall of the alcove. The lines were long and red; they grew under the thrust of her crayon and stood out against the creamy white of the alcove wall. She made many, many lines, until the crayon broke. Then she climbed up into the bed and pulled the covers up over her head and slept again.

She woke with the nearness of her mother around her. Her mother's face was dark with sleep. She could see nothing in it. She was hungry, and she padded off to the little kitchen, where she found a bag of doughnuts, and, in the refrigerator, a bottle of milk. She found a cup and poured the milk into it, the glide of milk going all down the sides of the bottle to make a circle of white on the kitchen table. She carried her doughnut and milk into the big room, where Cissy slept on the sofa. There were sheets on the sofa now, and blankets. Marguerite could not see her mother on the sofa anymore, she saw only Cissy, her mouth slightly open, her short blond lashes lying gently on her cheeks. The doughnut was good; its sugary sweet morsels tasted fine in her mouth. The milk was cold and it chilled her stomach; she huddled into Cissy's pajama top her mother had borrowed for a nightgown, and waited for her mother to wake up.

Cissy and her mother seemed to wake up at the same time; they both sat up and looked at each other, and then they laughed. Cissy said, "Well, Phyllis?"

Her mother laughed again. "What a party."

"How was Al? All right?"

"Al was fine."

"You feel good?"

"I feel good."

Her mother moved the covers and got up. She had her

slip on again. She pulled a shoulder strap up and got into a robe of Cissy's that lay at the end of the bed. She saw the crayon marks then. Marguerite could see her seeing them. Her mother said, "What the devil?" and then looked at her and said, "Marguerite, for heaven's sake, what did you do?"

Cissy got up and looked at the marks, then she looked at Marguerite, too. "Hey, baby, that's not a coloring book, you know?"

Her mother crossed to her, took her by the arms. "Marguerite, look what you did to Aunt Cissy's nice wall. Why did you do it; why were you such a bad girl?"

Bad girl. But she remembered now her mother and the man, she wanted to pick up her red crayon and draw it all over her mother's face. "I was scared," she said. "I was scared." She thought it better to cry, and she did, her dark hair like her mother's falling over her mother's grasping arm.

"Maid might have gone off and left her for a while," Cissy said. "Or just being in a strange place. Doesn't matter; the maid will clean it off."

"But Marguerite doesn't do things like that," her mother said. "She never has."

"Look, Phyl, with everything you've got to worry about, just forget it, okay?"

Her mother took a tissue from the box on the table, wiped at Marguerite's face. "Poor baby. It's a mixed-up time for her."

Cissy and her mother sat over their coffee a long time. They talked, but in quiet voices that Marguerite couldn't hear. Once Cissy laughed loudly and then said, "He didn't!" and laughed again.

It was raining out, the gray air of yesterday having

26

grown heavy with moisture, having turned now to long lines of rain.

"Hell of a day to go out."

Her mother looked at the rain, making a veil that hid them from the world outside. "I've got to pack, though. Find boxes to put sheets and things in."

"Lucky the furniture and stuff's not yours."

"I could never afford to ship it to Grand View if it were."

"Well, look, I'll borrow the band leader's car. We'll find some boxes some place and I'll come help you pack. Then tomorrow I'll take you to the bus."

"God, every time I think about it I get sick."

"Maybe it won't be so bad."

"The hell it won't. Dry, dull town. Dry, dull parents. Dry, dull house. God. I'll go crazy."

"But you've got a kid, another one coming. Doesn't that make a difference? You'll be with them; won't that part be all right?"

"Oh, Cissy, do you think that just because I'm a mother I'm dead? I still like to dance, and laugh, and fool around. Not every night, certainly not every night, but once in a while. Why do you think I went with that man last night? Because I don't know when I'll be with a man again. Or when I'll dance, or drink champagne, or look pretty in a long glittery dress."

"You can always visit me."

"I'll do that. I really will."

Cissy had lunch sent up: chicken sandwiches and potato salad, little round green olives stuffed with almonds. Then they dressed and went down to the band leader's car. It was small and old.

"But it runs," said Cissy, and they piled in and drove around in the rain, stopping at stores, crowding large

27

brown boxes in the back of the car.

Marguerite didn't like the packing. She didn't like seeing cupboards open and sheets and towels laid in the gaping holes of the boxes. She sat in the middle of the round braided rug on the living-room floor and watched Cissy and her mother work. They moved quickly; it was not long before all the boxes were full.

"What a dump this place really is," her mother said. She had sunk onto the sofa, smoking a cigarette. She drew in the smoke and streamed it out with her words. She was not crying, and then she was crying, the tears as they came out of her eyes, falling down her face, making little runnels in the faint peach powder.

Cissy came over to her, sat beside her, and took her hand. Cissy was crying, too, saying, "Oh, Phyl, what a break, what a lousy break," and crying. Marguerite's sudden wail rose above the sound they made crying. She got up from the rug and went to her mother and Cissy and stood between them, gathered into their arms.

"Steve didn't like us to cry," her mother said. "Marguerite and I hardly ever let him see us cry."

"To hell with Steve," Cissy said, and she got up and opened her purse, pulling out a long silver flask. "Get some glasses and some ice," she said. She fixed the drinks, making them a rich dark brown. "Time for one last drink. Then I've got to hustle back to the hotel, get dressed for the first show."

"I don't know what I'd do without you, Cissy," her mother said.

"Don't have to know."

Cissy left in a whirl of flying mink tails, the dark fur edging the scarf of her deep-red coat. Her mother sat still for a long time after Cissy had gone, sipping at the drink

that Cissy had refilled for her. Marguerite grew sleepy
with the waiting, she forgot that she had not had supper.
She curled up on the sofa and was wrapped in the steady
drip of the rain and in her mother's silence.

CHAPTER THREE

The doctor was watching her talk, his eyes were blue and steady. She did not look at his eyes very often, instead she looked at the large diamond ring on her left hand, sometimes moving her hand so that the light caught it.

She had been telling him about moving to Grand View, after her father died, how happy they had all been; she had not missed having a father, why would she miss someone she had not known? Anyway, there had been her grandfather; he had been a father to her. Her mother had been happy. They had settled into the tall green house on Cottonwood Street, her mother had found a little job, not so much for the money, but to feel independent. She and her brother had not been neglected. Their grandmother had cared for them, and they had two mothers, really.

The doctor shifted in his chair. He did not need to look at his watch, because of a digital clock on the bookcase next to the chair that he could see from where he sat. He was moving to end the hour. He took a small book

31

from his inside pocket and opened it, leafing through it. "Is this time next week all right for you, Mrs. Tanner?"

"Then you do think something's wrong? Just from what I've told you? But what—what is it. Do you know? What do you think?"

"I think we'll keep on for a while, see where it gets us." He stood up. He was tall; she had liked that when she first saw him. She wondered if she should put out her hand; she felt oddly hesitant about touching him. There seemed to be something between them that might almost be a barrier to the intimacy they were expected to share.

"Next week's fine, Dr. Forrester. Fine." She picked up her purse; it was the expensive ostrich one she had bought just last week. It had been wickedly priced, but then she had gotten the shoes on sale, and money was just money. She didn't have to worry about that anymore.

She was meeting Grace Whitman for lunch at the club. She drove there in her bright new station wagon; she still regretted the wagon, George had a Corvette. She didn't want a Corvette, but she did want a racy little car she could drive around in, her hair blowing back from her face, her clothes being lightly lifted by the swift air the car created.

"Anyone who drives children around needs a wagon," George had said, and it was true that Alan and Sue did travel in herds, she rarely had only her own two children in the car, and then the groceries, and the sports gear. Well, she would work on George—it wasn't unheard of to have more than two cars, to have the wagon when she needed it and her own little car when she wanted it.

Driving through the town, she felt that it all belonged to her. The lawns that grew with such care and such precision around the houses, each blade of grass adding to

32

the perfect whole. The brilliance of the crepe myrtle, watermelon pink and white and sea-shell pink, flaunting its delicate flowers even in the face of the July sun. The houses—so many houses—rich and pleasant. Now she had been inside many of them, she could go past them and know that in one living room was a blue Oriental rug, in another a span of burgundy carpet.

The club belonged to her, too. She loved to drive through the brick pillars at the entrance, to sweep down the broad roadway to the parking lot on the far side of the clubhouse, to leave her car and walk carelessly across the asphalt to the portico. She always stood in the foyer for just a minute, just to see what flowers were arranged on the table behind the sofa, just to see who was waiting. She could remember when she had sat on that sofa, waiting for Grace. She hadn't been a member at first; she had only very much wanted to be a member, and she had dressed for those early luncheons a dozen times, until her bed was piled high with pants and jackets and skirts and dresses and blouses, their colors tumbled in a mad kind of maze.

Now she wore what she wanted. She had been named one of the Ten Best-Dressed by a local charity organization. She knew some people laughed about that, but she didn't care, they laughed in defense because they didn't have her clothes, or, if they did, couldn't wear them the way she did. It had been silly that morning to worry about what the psychiatrist would think about her clothes. He was, after all, a man. And today she looked good. She looked very, very good.

Grace looked good, too. She was sitting in the paneled bar with the wall of windows overlooking the golf course. Grace had a drink in front of her, leaning back in her chair with her head turned, talking to a woman at the next table. Grace knew everyone. Her mother and grand-mother before her had known everyone—it was like a family trait, handed down to be preserved and cared for.

Marguerite hesitated at the table, then sat down, and beckoned to a waiter. Grace had made a kind of wave with her hand; now she was winding up her conversation with the woman, ending it with her low laugh that always made you die to know what was so funny.

"A vodka martini," Marguerite said to the waiter. And to Grace, "Am I late? I think my watch is slow." She almost said, "I just left my psychiatrist." It might be fun to talk about it with Grace, to take it all out and push it around and make all kinds of things out of this funny feeling she had that had sent her to Dr. Forrester. Then she remembered that Grace was practically a Christian Scientist, she believed in nothing but herself, she directed her own life. She was, she often said, beholden to no one.

"Late, early, what difference does it make? Except that I do have to be gone by three. I have a—well—you could say I have an appointment.

The low laugh hung beneath the words; it gave them a meaning. Marguerite looked up from the cigarette she was lighting. "An appointment? That could be interesting."

"Well, I hope it will be. I'll be terribly disappointed if it isn't."

"Who with?" In the early days with Grace, those wonderful, terrible early days, she would have been indi-rect, almost afraid to know that Grace wanted her curiosity, wanted her shock.

"The new symphony conductor."

"But it's only July. Is he here yet?"

"Not for good. He and his wife are moving down in August. But he's here to start looking for a house, that kind of thing. The Stovers had a dinner for him. Of course, there'll be a big crush of a reception for him when the season starts. This was just for a few people, a few faces out of the crowd kind of thing."

She and George would be invited to the big crush of a reception. George made a healthy donation every year; they wouldn't leave him off the invitation list. But it was to the smaller parties, the more special evenings, that she wanted to be asked. She watched Grace, crunching on the celery stick from her bloody Mary. After all, she had only known Grace for what?—not quite two years. She had moved. They belonged to the country club now, they were a part of Grace's crowd, Grace was her friend. If Grace had had the dinner party, they would have been included.

"Tell me about it." She signaled to the waiter, made a sign over their empty glasses.

Grace's story would slide down her, as the delicious vodka would slide down her throat. There would be the fine curtain between them and everyone else in the club; people might stop at the table, might even stay and talk for a while, but the curtain would not be removed, it would enclose her and Grace in the way that made her feel present, feel there.

"He's about forty. He's French. Well, he tries to be French. I think his mother was, or something. And he has a vulnerable ego. Which is good. Men with vulnerable egos try harder."

"So how are you working it?"

"My dear, I don't have to work it to meet anyone. They work it to meet me." Grace's voice was sharp; for an instant of time, Marguerite had forgotten how proud Grace was of her looks, her conviction that every man

35

who saw her wanted her.

"Of course they do. So where are you meeting him?"

"At his hotel. Which is rather dreary, I must admit. He's paying his own expenses this trip, and he told me, with fake French thrift, that he's staying at the Marlboro. That relic. So I'll sneak up the fire escape or something."

"You know damn well you'll walk in like you own the place."

"I might even own it. Who knows what Jerry does with his money?"

"Speaking of Jerry, how was Mexico?"

"Mexico is Mexico is Mexico. Jerry was tied up with business most of the time. Which could have been boring."

"But wasn't?"

"But wasn't. There was this nice lawyer, the man handling the business for Jerry. He took us out the first night we were there. He wasn't nearly as busy as Jerry was."

"So that's two. In about two weeks."

"And you? What have you been doing?"

Marguerite suddenly didn't want to tell her. The feeling was there again. She felt now that perhaps it was always there, and that the only time she didn't know it was there was when she seemed not to be there, either. She wanted to think about that. She did not want to sit here at this ridiculous New England maple table and have still another drink and tell Grace about Todd McDaniels.

"Order us a drink," she said. "Okay, so what have I been doing? Well, last week I remembered that I really had never finished working all my cards for the United Fund. So, of course, the drive was really over, but I called Shirley—she'd given me the damn things to begin with, and she said, well, if I could get more money, they'd take it."

"What on earth did you want to do that for?"

"One of the names I hadn't worked was Todd McDaniels."

"Todd McDaniels. Okay."

"I thought about you down in Mexico, and there was absolutely nothing doing here, and I said to myself, Marguerite, you need to do something that will really take some doing."

"So?"

"So I called his office and made an appointment."

"He's been hot for you for ages."

"I know that. You know that. And I was damned curious to find out if he knew that."

"And he did?"

They finished their drinks, had lunch, all the while talking in quiet voices, their faces serious, their heads close. Todd had been easy; the kiss she'd given him, for, she'd said, such a nice check. There had been a couch in his office, which they had used; she hadn't even undressed, had just dropped her panty hose on the floor, and lifted her skirt and that had been that. It was far more real, talking to Grace about it, than it had been at the time.

"There's Ruth McDaniels now," Grace said. Marguerite followed her look—yes, there was Ruth in a neat, round-collared, blue linen dress, one hand quietly in her lap, the other lifting a spoon to her mouth.

"She looks like a little girl."

"She looks like an old lady. Either way is no good for Todd."

"Oh, I'd definitely say he was ready."

"I'm still ahead of you," Grace said. She picked up a

piece of creamed shrimp on her fork, lifted it to her mouth that seemed now very wide, very red, very open.

"I think you always will be," Marguerite said. "I think it's easier for you."

"Easier? How?

"I don't know. Just easier. It doesn't take so much out of you."

"You mean I'm just a natural born whore. No, your problem is you take everything too seriously. You should be able to laugh. Can't you see something funny about you and Todd fucking on that sofa in his office while that Miss-What's-Her-Name, the secretary—she's been with them forever—while she typed letters on the other side of the door?"

"It seems funny when you tell it, anyway."

"Look, I'll give you my next prospect, how about that? And I'll make it someone really good.'

They drank coffee, strong, black, in small cups. I should be drinking sense, not coffee, she told herself. How did I ever get into this? But she knew how she had gotten into it. And that she did not want out. For the first time in her life, she was in a place where she didn't want out. Her mother had promised her, all her growing up, that there was such a place.

"Just wait 'til you get to the university," her mother told her. "It'll be nothing like this damn place. Poky, poky. I don't know how I've lived here as long as I have." Her mother had put all of her energy, for years, into preparing Marguerite for college. "You join lots of clubs now," she said when Marguerite started high school. "And I want you to try out for cheerleader. You're pretty and peppy enough. You've got to get people to notice you."

She had had to overcome the fact that her grandfather

was the principal of the high school.

"You just got elected because of your granddaddy," Sally Bowen told her the day she was voted secretary of the student body. "You think you're so smart and so pretty. Well, you're not. You're nobody. Your mother's the hostess at that restaurant, and everyone knows that nobody who is anybody would do that."

Her grandparents felt the same way. They still fought Phyllis, going over the same old ground, saying the same old things. "You don't need to work in that place. You can get a job in the school board office, or some place else that's decent."

"There's nothing indecent about the Mirror Restaurant. It's a nice place, the only nice place in this town to eat. I'm not going to be stuck in some office, breaking my nails typing and getting fat hips from sitting all day. No, thanks. I like to work where it's fun."

"Fun. You looked for fun before; look where that got you."

The conversations ended in exactly the same way each time, with Phyllis stalking up the stairs and slamming into her room, where she sat staring out the window and chain-smoking cigarettes. When Marguerite was older, her mother would pause to collect her and shut her, too, into the hot smoky intimacy of the room.

"God, Marguerite, I'll get you out of this town if it takes every last thing I've got. Bill's different; boys are always luckier, he can get out on his own and make it. I'm not worried about him. But you—you're going to do better than I did; you're not going to end up in a damn dead town like this."

By the time Marguerite was a senior in high school, Phyllis had settled on the University of Texas. "It's big, my

God, it's big. But you'll meet lots of boys there, boys who are going to be somebody. I don't want you going to some East Texas cow college where all you meet is boys going back to the ranch."

Then Phyllis got it into her head that Marguerite had to be in a sorority.

"A sorority!" Marguerite heard her grandmother say. "Phyllis, you've got a head stuffed with cotton! How do you expect that child to get into a sorority? And what difference does that make, anyway? Let her join the Baptist Student Union; that's all she needs. Plenty of nice young people that think the way she does."

But it became an obsession. Dropping into the Mirror Restaurant one afternoon in early May, Marguerite found her mother sitting at a table with a large man, drinking coffee. Her mother was laughing. She wore a silk print dress with a high choker of large pearls around her neck; her face, still unlined, was smoothly pink under her fresh makeup, and her eyes looked young.

"Hey, Bob, this is Marguerite, my kid I've been telling you about. Marguerite, say hello to Mr. Watson, he's an old friend."

There was always an old friend. Over the years of coming by the restaurant after school to see her mother, Marguerite had met most of them. She didn't remember any of them; they had all been very much alike, buying her Cokes and ice cream, sometimes giving her a quarter or a fifty-cent piece "for her bank." Marguerite had never even wondered when a man she had seen for some months was no longer there. They were all travelers, her mother said, and sometimes changed their territory, or got another job. It was some time before Marguerite realized that talking to these old friends was what her mother called fun. Sitting in the Mirror Restaurant all dressed up, drinking coffee with men who were rarely good-looking, often stout from too much on-the-road greasy cooking—the men somehow did not match her mother, who still wore, when she was excited, a look that said something wonderful was about to happen.

Her mother wore that look today. "Marguerite, Mr. Watson's got two girls at the university, what do you think of that?"

"And a boy. She might be more interested in that boy, Phyllis."

"Mr. Watson's been telling me about the sorority that his girls are in. What fun they have."

"They say they have fun. Listening to two girls giggle and carry on is about more than I can take. Don't see how they can stand a whole house full. But girls, shoot, what else is college for, for them?"

"Why don't you get a Coke and sit down a minute, hon?"

It was the usual thing; today Marguerite felt strange. As she sipped her coke, she listened to her mother talk about her, tell Mr. Watson all the things she was in, how good a baton twirler she was, how they could hardly get into the house for falling over the boys that came to see her. She could see Mr. Watson watching her, looking from her mother to her, nodding his head, seeming pleased.

"She's a great kid, anyone can see that. Of course, she belongs to you." Mr. Watson's hand disappeared briefly under the table; Phyllis' smile widened, she seemed to have received some special gift that she had long been waiting for.

"I've got to go, Mom. I need to put in the hem of the dress I'm wearing to the dance tomorrow."

Both Mr. Watson and her mother watched while she straightened her pile of books and lifted them; it seemed as though each act of hers was interesting, special, never having been seen before. She walked through the afternoon quiet of the restaurant, the tables with their red cloths made a field of color that she moved through. She felt a small kind of chill as she walked and heard the indistinct voices of her mother and Mr. Watson pick up behind her.

"What do you think, Bob, can you do it?"

"Get her in my kids' sorority? Pretty sure I can. My wife's some high mucky-muck. Between her and the girls, it ought to be all right."

"Your wife might think it's funny, your being so interested in some girl from a little old town in the middle of nowhere."

"She won't think it's funny."

"But what'll you tell her about me?"

"I don't have to tell her anything about you."

"Just like that, huh?"

"Just like that."

And then the voices stopped, and Marguerite knew they were waiting for her to be gone, to leave them sitting over cooling coffee, their heads close, close, their legs now close, now touching—what was left to touch?

That night Marguerite, studying on the stair-landing windowseat outside her mother's room, heard Phyllis relaying the conversation to Cissy in Houston. "They've got one of those perfect marriages, Cissy." And then a laugh, a laugh Marguerite hadn't heard before. "The kind those friends of yours have, you know? They marry perfect ladies and fuck whores."

As she caught the drift, as the meaning of what her

42

mother was telling Cissy came to her, her skin began to crawl with the feeling it had when a dust storm blew out of the Panhandle, bringing the soft top layer of dirt from miles away to enter her nostrils, her earlobes, invade her mouth and sift softly over her bare arms and legs. She felt swathed in the dust of what she was hearing—when her mother said "whores" with no emphasis, no distance, Marguerite felt that the dust had blown into her soul.

"Mr. Watson is going to talk to his wife about getting you into a sorority," Phyllis told her later, coming into her room. "I was telling Cissy about it on the phone tonight. She's heard of Mrs. Watson, says she's really something pretty big in Houston."

"I thought he was rich. Having kids at the university. And looking so much—well, better, than most of the men coming through here." She wouldn't look at her mother.

"He is better. He's in oil, not some lousy office supply salesman or candy peddler. He says there's going to be the biggest oil boom around here. My God, there might be some hope for this town yet."

"But I still don't see why his wife would want to help me." She turned to look at Phyllis as she spoke the words, turned to catch Phyllis on the hard hook of her eyes, to pull her in and force her to tell the truth. Phyllis looked back, eyes wide, excitement rising in them. She lit a cigarette, blowing the smoke in a thin fine screen, like the scattering of a reflection in water.

"Well, because he's a friend of mine. Don't worry about it. Just thank your lucky stars your mother can still make good friends." She watched her mother cross to the mirror, put her fingertips at the edges of her eyes and stretch the skin taut. "I may not be much at the Circle meetings, but what good did that bunch ever do us, anyway? Listen, all I hope for you is that you meet someone just like Bob Watson. Money. You marry money, you hear? People say money can't buy happiness. Well, I wouldn't know about that, because I've never had the chance to find out. But one thing I can tell you. There's no situation that having money doesn't make better. I mean, it's a hell of a lot better to be sick in a private room with special nurses than lying out on the ward where you could die before they come see about you. Don't you ever forget it. Money. What I could have done if I had just a little money."

Marguerite could watch frustration rising in her mother like a jar of fermenting preserves, ready to explode. Phyllis was always on a tight rein. She lived with a tension that they were fully aware of only when it was gone. The house, with her in it, was charged. A room that she entered seemed ready to fly apart; within minutes, magazines lay open on chairs, a cigarette was burning in an ashtray, a glass of Coke sat ringing a table. She was never still, and she dressed in clothes with floating panels, loose ruffles, skirts that seemed to sway even when she was standing behind the desk at the restaurant. She walked so rapidly that few people could keep up with her; she would move ahead, see her companion behind her, stop, twist and turn, fiddle with her purse, her bracelets, then move on again. She was given to sudden outbursts of speech. Reading the paper, she would come across some item that enraged her, "My God, I can't believe it! Nowhere but here! Some woman had a goddamn shower for her niece and every woman there brought a hint on how to please a husband. I doubt if there's one woman in this town who knows how to please a husband."

It took very little to upset her: a run in a stocking was a

tragedy, a broken nail fatal. When she left for work, tapping down the sidewalk on her high-heeled sandals, a kind of rush of activity followed her out the door. And then the hush of her absence settled over the house; it was almost as though the furniture crept out of the corners to stand stolid and firm again, as though the material of the curtains, the heavy fiber of the rugs, grew once more inanimate.

CHAPTER FOUR

Phyllis' visits to Cissy in Houston were monumental events. She would pick the date, circling it on her wall calendar with a large smear of red nail polish. Her clothes would tumble from the closet, lay over chairs, fall over her dressing table.

"Not a goddamn thing to wear! Cissy'll be ashamed to be seen with me. God, country come to town!" Marguerite would watch her pack, would watch the flowered prints and the sleek crepes and the thin chiffons take their place in the suitcase, making of it a rainbow of the excitement to come. "The only thing bad about going is having to come back. I should just stay, that's what Cissy says, I should just stay. You kids'd be all right with Grandma, wouldn't you? I mean you're getting big now, it's not like you were babies . . . " She didn't mean it, of course, she didn't mean it. Seeing Marguerite's face, she would stop dropping clothes into the suitcase and swirl over and grab Marguerite and kiss her and say, "Look,

47

we're in this together. I'm coming back—I've got to come back—just to get you out of here."

She would return from these trips tired, satiated. "God, we didn't stop. Cissy's bought an interest in a dress shop, can you believe it? She says she can't sing forever. But she looks good, she looks wonderful." The hope of her visit would cling to her for days; she would spend more time at the mirror, would wear a new blouse she had brought back or a new pair of shoes.

"You spend more money on clothes," her mother would complain. "It's a sin, Phyllis, to put so much on your back."

"Got to look good, Ma. Who knows? I might meet the King of England some day."

"Won't meet anyone much in that café, I can tell you."

But Phyllis did meet Mr. Watson. And the hope rose in her again. She talked to Marguerite about it, not able to keep quiet, having to fire Marguerite with her own dreams.

"You'll see what a difference it'll make. Being in a sorority, I mean. They have parties with the fraternities all the time. And that's where the rich boys are. Now, you promise me, Marguerite, you're not going to fool around with some no-count boy who doesn't have a dime."

"But, Mother, I may not even get in."

"You'll get in." Phyllis took out her compact, puffed the powder across her fine cheekbones, lightly over the tight skin under her eyes. "Bob Watson promised."

He was back in town the next week, bringing news that stunned even Phyllis.

"His wife wants to meet you. She wants him to bring you back with him for the weekend. Can you beat that!"

There were two girls, he had said, and a son. Where

would they be? What would she do? It would be worse than it had been the first time she'd tried out for cheerleader, running out to stand before the kids crowded into the bleachers, all alone going through a long slow locomotive and then springing high into the air, her skirt lifting about her legs, her image reflected in the eyes that watched.

"I don't know Mrs. Watson. I don't want to go see her."

"Marguerite, you're going, and that's that. You'll be perfectly all right. You're a beautiful girl—you've got good manners, as good as anybody's. You're cute, you're peppy, what is there to worry about?"

Phyllis called Cissy that night, pulling the telephone from the stair landing into her room, motioning Marguerite to sit on the chaise she had bought at the Goodwill and covered in plum velvet. "Now, Cissy, listen, this is important. Marguerite's going to visit these people, the Watsons. They're rich, and they live in one of those neighborhoods, River Oaks, he said. Now, look, I want you to find out what those girls wear. And then I want you to go to Joske's or Sakowitz' and buy Marguerite enough to get her through the weekend. You just get it and put it on the bus, now hear? You tell me how much it is, and I'll send you the money."

Marguerite heard a long discussion of sizes and colors; at one point her mother turned to her and said, "Blue or green?" When Marguerite didn't answer, she shook a cigarette from a pack and lit it and turned back to her conversation.

"Isn't that going to cost a lot of money?" Marguerite said when her mother had hung up.

"You can't go visiting in River Oaks in stuff your grandma made for you."

49

"But isn't it going to cost a lot of money?"

"Get cost out of your head. There's always a way to pay for something, if you want it bad enough."

"I'll still just be me. I mean, I'll still just be a girl from Grand View that Mrs. Watson never even heard of."

"People never will hear of you, if you don't give them a chance. She's heard of you now. And Friday night she's going to meet you. And she's going to like you, you hear that? She's going to like you."

Marguerite already did not like Mrs. Watson. She did not like the kids in her classes, when it was time for an election. Even when she won. Even when people would come and say, "I voted for you. I'm glad you won." She did not like it that other people could so control her, could decide whether she would or would not have what she wanted. But Mrs. Watson would like her. Her mother had said so; her mother could not be wrong.

On Friday afternoon, Mr. Watson came for her in his blue Cadillac. It was a convertible. It crouched huge and topless at the curb, while her grandmother peered from behind the curtains and watched him come up the walk.

"Silliest thing I ever heard of, sending a child off to visit people you don't even know. Don't know a thing about them, might be a house full of drunks or heaven knows what. Now, Marguerite, that Cissy doesn't have much sense, but she's got some. And if these people, these Watsons, if they turn out bad, you call Cissy, you hear? You call her to come get you."

Phyllis stopped on her way out to the hall. "Ma, for God's sake, shut up. Marguerite's going to have a wonderful time, a wonderful time. It's a beginning for her, can't you see that?"

"A beginning. All right, a beginning. A beginning of

50

what? Marguerite's going to college to learn to be a teacher, that's what a beginning is. This traipsing off to Houston, staying in a fancy house, getting ideas about money—that's no beginning."

Phyllis opened the front door, brought Bob Watson in. "This is my mother, Mrs. Morgan. And Marguerite. You know Marguerite."

"Mrs. Morgan, we surely do appreciate your lending us this little girl for the weekend. My wife's going to take good care of her. She'll have a fine time, and I'll have her back here Sunday evening, about suppertime."

"I'll save you some chicken, then," Mrs. Morgan said, and stumped off to the kitchen, the long strings of her apron striping the back of her dress.

Phyllis followed them out to the car, waited while Mr. Watson put Marguerite's suitcase in the trunk, hugged Marguerite, took Bob's hand, patted the side of the car.

"Well, you be sweet, hon. Don't give Mrs. Watson any trouble. And have a good time." Her voice, strong in the beginning, trailed off. She stared at Marguerite, sitting beside Mr. Watson in one of the new skirts and blouses that had arrived in the big Sakowitz box from Houston. She suddenly leaned into the car, pulled Marguerite's head close to her mouth. "You look as pretty as anybody. As anybody. You remember that, you hear?"

Sitting beside Mr. Watson in the car was different from sipping a Coke at a table while he and her mother talked. She felt responsible for the afternoon, for how it would go. She had not talked to many men in her life; her grandfather, remote, tired from his feeble dance at the altar of education, spoke little. The air between her and Mr. Watson semed to be some kind of stream that must be crossed; she waited, not knowing how to take the first stroke.

"How does all this seem to you, Marguerite?"

She looked at Mr. Watson, saw how his strong neck thrust out of his open-collared plaid shirt, carrying the head that though it looked ordinary enough must somehow be special because it knew how to make so much money.

"I don't know what you mean."

"Well, this weekend. Your coming to our house."

"Mother said Mrs. Watson wants me to come."

"But what do you think about it?"

"I don't guess I think anything about it."

"Do you know what it's all for?"

She heard something in Mr. Watson's voice that she did not quite understand. At first she thought it was anger; she then thought it was fatigue.

"So I can get in a sorority. When I go to the university."

"Do you think that's very important?"

"Mother says it is."

She did not really know what a sorority was. Girls living in a tall-pillared house, making fudge and pinning corsages on and singing around a piano. She had heard the pride in her grandfather's voice when he told someone the Mason lodge he belonged to. She supposed that when she was in a sorority, she would talk about it with that same kind of pride. It would mean, after all, that the girls liked her enough to want her to be part of them. She would not really have to wonder about herself, she could say a magic phrase of membership and belonging, and know.

"Yeah, my girls take it very seriously. And their mother. Well, it's all right. It's fun; girls like that kind of thing. I just thought—how you must feel. You know you're going to be looked over. I just wondered about that. How that makes you feel."

She was angry at first. He wasn't being polite, he wasn't pretending that this was an ordinary visit, for ordinary reasons. He had always seemed a nice man; it surprised her that he would now be blunt. But it was his way of crossing the stream between them, his way of trying to look at the terrain on her side.

"I don't like it much. But most people, most people like me, get used to being looked over. I guess it'll be a while before I get to where I can do the looking."

"Think you'll make it?"

She turned to look at him. There was something he knew, something about money and how to get it, that she must know, too. There was something incorporated into Bob Watson that she must learn to recognize, so that when she saw it in other men, she would know it and use it. "Oh, I'll make it. I'll make it all right."

"Your mother's a fine woman, Marguerite. She thinks she's had a hard life—well, that's right, she has. But you can't make it up to her, do you see that?"

"I'm not making anything up to mother. I don't know why we're talking about all this. And I hope you're not going to tell Mrs. Watson about it. Somehow, I don't know, you're making it seem all wrong. When all I want is just to do what other girls do."

"As long as you know why you're doing it," he said, and leaned forward to turn on the radio.

The music carried them all the way into Houston, then across it to the broad streets and deep lawns of River Oaks. They passed house after house, each large, elaborate, expensive. The very grass grew differently, drawing up neatly at the edge of the sidewalks, well-trained, too well-behaved to straggle across the line. The houses seemed to gather around her, to become alive and threatening. There were people who knew how to live in these houses, who emerged yawning in the early mornings to pick papers up off the lawn, who took showers and ate their meals and dressed for parties in these houses. These people did exactly the same things as any other people anywhere else; it was the fact that they did them in these houses that made them members of a far country.

The Cadillac swerved into a wide brick driveway, followed its curve around to the back of a tall gray house, that, flat-fronted and narrow-windowed, presented a stiff face to the dark green of the planting around it.

"What kind of house is it?"

"What kind? French townhouse. Copied from one in Paris. Had to pay an architect a fortune just for a copy."

The house was huge. There was a slate terrace across the back; they reached it through a covered walkway from the garage. The terrace ended at a slight slope. At the foot of the slope was a swimming pool, the bright-blue water split down the middle with a cork-buoyed rope. Beyond the pool was a tennis court, where four people were slamming a ball back and forth in the dimming light. Watching the players, Marguerite stumbled against a wrought-iron chaise lounge. There was a woman lying on it; she was fair, somewhat plump. Her small round body mounded against the print cushions, as she pushed herself forward, her navy skirt lifted above her knees, showing the soft padded bones.

"This is Marguerite Robertson. Girl I told you about."

The woman got up awkwardly, sliding down the length of the chaise until she could stand. She stood and looked at Marguerite; she was interested, she was curious, what

54

was this her husband had brought home to her? Marguerite remembered Mr. Watson's questions in the car. She was sorry that he was standing there, watching this.

"How do you do, Mrs. Watson?" she said. "It's very nice of you to have me here."

Mrs. Watson laughed. It came to Marguerite that she was the only person who was really involved in all of this, she was the only one who really cared what happened. It gave Mrs. Watson, and even Mr. Watson, a power over her. Mrs. Watson knew why Marguerite was there; Mrs. Watson knew that she could give Marguerite what she wanted. Or she could just as easily refuse it.

"I'll leave," Marguerite thought. "I'll call Cissy. Nothing is worth this." But Phyllis would know; Phyllis would have to know. Right now, as Marguerite stood on this patio, the wealth of the house around her, Phyllis was handing out menus and flirting with the salesmen passing through. Phyllis was waiting, waiting for Marguerite to come home on Sunday with a sorority pin firmly shining in her future.

"I'll show you your room," Mrs. Watson said. A young Mexican suddenly stood beside Marguerite, her suitcase in one hand and Mr. Watson's in the other. "Juan, bring Miss Robertson's suitcase."

They filed slowly through the house, vistas of rugs and sofas and paintings and silver and tables and lamps stretching out on every side. "This is ridiculous," Marguerite thought. "I don't belong here, I'll be miserable, how will I ever know what to say." But there was a feeling about the house that she liked. She could see how when Mrs. Watson left the house, she could carry that feeling with her. All of her rugs and sofas and paintings and silver and tables and lamps would go with her when she went out. They would form a soft aura around her, an aura that was misty and rich and very quiet, but at the same time very strong. No one would get to Mrs. Watson through that aura. Marguerite suddenly saw how little Phyllis really knew.

She met the girls at dinner. Sara and Sue—twins—blond, lithe, pretty. They sat across from her and watched her, talking to their mother, teasing their father, but watching, watching.

"Dad says you're a cheerleader," Sara said. "Maybe you'll do a few cheers for us after dinner."

For the rest of her life, Marguerite would never know if Sara were being deliberately cruel, or if she were just stupid. It was a distinction she was never to make.

"I think that would be fun," Sue said. "Because of course it's important to the sorority that members win a lot of awards. Being a good cheerleader would help a lot."

They were not even going to pretend that she was not here on trial. That might make it easier. She waited for the anger to rise, waited for her tongue to answer them, to tell them that she didn't give two damns about their sorority, that they could take it and their money and their house and the whole crappy bit and cram it.

"I'd love to," she said. "I'll just run up and put some shorts on."

The Watsons sat on the patio as she walked down the slope to a grassy place near the pool. The outdoor lights were on, the glow from their lanterns met the still-pink glow in the sky; between the place where the two lights met was a slow band of gray. Marguerite saw only the four still figures, grouped around one of the glass-topped tables. They were drinking coffee; she could hear the faint click of cup against saucer.

She shut her eyes and thought of the September heat,

when the first game was played. It was hot like that now, strong heat that brought her to life, that made her think of the full stadium and the boys on the players' bench yelling, "Hey, Marguerite! Show us some leg! Get into it, kid!" She could feel the eyes of the crowd, welded now into one huge eye that was focused on her. The other cheerleaders dropped slowly away; her partner stood aside and watched her. She knelt, beginning the long slow locomotive that allowed her to thrust her breasts forward, to arch her back, to finally leap high into the air, her body a bright torch. She forgot the Watsons then. There was only the loving, sweat-bringing heat, like the heated sweat when she sat on the back seat of a date's car and they groped themselves to liquid passion. There was only her body, the body which belonged totally to her, which obeyed her, which was her own secret, her own strength.

"That was pretty good," Sara said, when Marguerite climbed back to the patio.

"You really do have a lovely rhythm," Mrs. Watson said. "I've been looking at these other things."

Her hands were turning the pages of something lying on the table. It was Phyllis' scrapbook. How could it be Phyllis' scrapbook? But, of course, that was exactly what Phyllis would do. She would leave nothing to chance, to Bob Watson's faulty memory. Every twirling contest, every prize, every "A" in conduct, every report card.

"My mother shouldn't bore you with that," Marguerite said.

"I should like to meet your mother," Mrs. Watson said. "I think she's a very smart woman."

"You know, that's really what got you in," Mr. Watson said on Sunday, driving her back to Grand View. "My wife recognized a sister under the skin. Not in you . But in your mother. My wife knows how to value everything that she has. That's why she doesn't keep a tighter rein on me. I deliver to her exactly what she wants me to. She liked it that your mother knows exactly how to value you—what's important, what isn't."

"I might not live up to all that," Marguerite said. "I might just go into a complete funk."

"Not for a while," Mr. Watson said. "Not for a while."

And so she had gone to the University of Texas with a sure welcome to one of the best sororities on campus. Her trunk had been full of the clothes she and her mother and Cissy had bought on several weekends in Houston, her head had been full of her mother's urgings. "Look for a rich boy, Marguerite. Get into everything, you hear? Now, make me proud of you!"

CHAPTER FIVE

She met rich boys, of course. The fraternities were full of them; she stumbled over them on her way out of the sorority house, they clogged her phone line with calls, she dated them in a rush of football game and beer parties and dances and Sunday drinking parties—by the time she had been there three months, she realized that most of them were looking for rich girls.

And then there was George. She had met him her second semester at the university. He was a fraternity brother of a boy she dated a while. She had been at the fraternity house on a late-spring afternoon, playing a lazy game of badminton, sinking finally on the spring-damp grass to drink beer in paper cups. She had watched a tall boy with almost white blond hair come down the front steps; the sun slanting through the trees at the corner of the lot seemed to funnel all of its light on him, so that he stood sharply out against a light-hazed background.

"Who is that?" she asked.

Her date rolled over and looked up, holding his hand against the sharp falling light. "George Tanner. Junior. You've met him."

"I'd remember," she almost said. "No, I haven't," she said.

"Hey, George, pretty girl wants to meet you," her date called.

And she had felt awkward then, had felt that George was coming over to see if she were in fact pretty enough to meet him. But he had not been awkward, he had leaned a large portfolio he was carrying against a tree and had sat down, taken a cup of beer, and talked to her. When she thought about it later she remembered that they had started in what might be considered the middle of the conversation—she had found out none of the important things about him.

"What's in there?" she had asked, pointing to the portfolio.

"Drawings. I'm an architect. Well, I will be, come next June."

"Could I see them?"

"Show her your etchings, George," her date said.

"Do you really want to see them, or are you just flirting?" George asked.

"I really do want to see them," she said, but she blushed anyway, and when they went inside and found a big table and George had opened the portfolio and spread the sheets of neatly lined drawings over the top, she prayed that she would think of something to say.

"I've never seen anything like them," she said at last.

George laughed. "I hope not. I haven't put in all this time learning to be a copyist."

Marguerite thought of the Watsons' house in River

Oaks, of the houses around it. "Some people like copies, don't they? Some of those big houses in Houston, in River Oaks . . ."

"Those. Dead. That's not architecture. That's just some poor fool giving a rich client what he wants. All you have to be able to do to design that kind of junk is draw a straight line."

"But it pays well, doesn't it?"

"This does, too. It's good, it'll sell."

The lines before her eyes looked better, then. She could see how all that glass would be pretty—if you lived in a house like that, you could put a lot of plants outside, and inside, it would be like living in a garden all the time. She leaned over the table to look at a drawing. Her dark hair fell forward and she lifted a hand to brush it back.

"You're the prettiest girl I ever saw in my life," George said.

For a moment she felt a small pain; she had wanted to tell him about the garden, about how looking at his designs made her see things she hadn't seen before. Pretty girls didn't have to say things like that; pretty girls did not have to have long earnest conversations with boys. Pretty girls had only to lift a hand, to show the sweet curving inside of an arm, to walk with a quick high step.

"Thank you for saying so," she said, and she smiled the smile that she had seen in a thousand mirrors.

"Thank you for being so," he said.

After that they were inseparable. She found out the important things, and conveyed them to Phyllis exultantly. "George's father is a judge in Waco," she wrote. "The Tanners were in town last week for some kind of legal meeting and they took us to dinner. They are very nice, and I think they liked me."

61

Judge Tanner, tall, like George—George's white-blond hair turned white on his father. Mrs. Tanner, little, soft, a print silk with a fussy bow, small blue eyes that peeked out from her pink face, soft gray hair waved over it. "What sorority are you in, dear?" she asked, and nodded and talked about her own sorority and how she still belonged to the alumna chapter in Waco, and how wherever Marguerite went, being a member of that sorority would mark her as a special sort of person, how very good it was that she had that to fall back on. "I have forgotten every bit of Latin I ever took," she said, and she watched Marguerite while she said it. "But my Greek contacts have lasted me all my life."

George and Judge Tanner laughed. Marguerite realized it was a family joke, that Mrs. Tanner probably said this same thing whenever the subject came up.

"Mother doesn't believe in education for women," George said.

"I've never said that. But the really important things about being a woman, you can't learn in books."

"Women don't always want to sit around all their lives," George said. "Some women want to work, to do things on their own."

"I'm sure Marguerite doesn't have any such silly ideas," Mrs. Tanner insisted. "Who could have a nicer life than I've had? Spoiled by your father, doted on by you and your brother, waited on hand and foot by servants—I am a lucky, lucky woman."

"Your mother's so sweet," Marguerite said to George, driving back to the campus.

"Why shouldn't she be sweet? She's had her way all her life. It's very easy to be pleasant when you get your own way all the time."

62

"Don't you like your mother?"

"You heard her. I dote on her."

"But what do you want?"

"From who? From Mother?"

She didn't mean that. She didn't care what he wanted from his mother. She only wanted to know what he wanted, or needed, from her. Because he was the son of a judge, he was going to be an architect, his mother wore silk prints that cost two hundred dollars if they cost a penny, and anyway, he thought she was the prettiest girl in the world.

"From anyone."

"Believe it or not, I don't want anything, from anyone. I know exactly where I am going, exactly what I am going to do—I'll make it."

I know exactly where I'm going, too, she thought. Exactly what I am going to do. And I'll make it.

She curled into his arm. "I'm glad you don't have a car with bucket seats. I like to sit like this."

His hand dropped gently across her shoulder, then fell forward, casually covering her breast.

"No, George."

"No, George?" He looked at her, a faint smile making her want to cry.

"I don't believe in petting."

The way he looked at her made her blush. It made her want to defend herself, to explain to him all the afternoons of listening to Phyllis, watching Phyllis sit in a lace-laden slip, slim, full-breasted.

"Listen, Marguerite, there's no big mystery about it. From the time a boy hits puberty all he wants is to be in some girl's pants. And believe me, it doesn't matter a hell of a lot to him whose pants it is. So you remember that.

Remember when some boy is sweating over you and begging you and telling you he can't live without it—well, he's not going to go without it. If you don't put out, someone else will. Sometimes a real louse will use that to pressure you. 'If you don't go along, that'll be it.' Come right out and tell you. But don't listen. Don't listen to one argument those sons-of-bitches give you. Because that's all you've got going for you. That you are pretty. That you are so damned pretty every man who looks at you is going to want to get to you. And you can use that, Marguerite. You can use that to buy what you want. So you don't use it up, you hear? Don't you spend it a little at a time, a little petting here, a little heavy necking now. Sex is sex—it's not going to change if you wait a few years."

"Are these religious principles of yours?" George asked.

"I don't care anything about that."

"Okay. So you don't believe in petting. Why not?"

"I'll bet your mother doesn't believe in petting."

George took his hand away. For a moment the warm feel of it stayed at her breast. She wished Phyllis were not so right; life would be much simpler if she could leave her mother, and George's, out of it.

"You're smart, Marguerite. Pretty and smart. You're very right about my mother. She doesn't believe in petting."

He kissed her goodnight, a chaste kiss at the sorority house door. He didn't call for three days. She lay on her bed at night and cursed Phyllis. Once she took off all her clothes and stood and looked in the mirror at her long body with breasts so round they lifted out on either side and above her high ribs, hips in a gentle slope, long, long legs.

He called the fourth night. They began going out again, and he held her, he kissed her, his hands stayed away from her breasts, and she thought that she had won.

Toward the end of May, Phyllis called, her voice excited, all the tension of her life pouring down the telephone wire. "I've decided you've got to stay there for summer school," she said.

"But I was supposed to work this summer."

"Someone else can clerk at the dimestore. My God, Marguerite, haven't you got any sense?"

"But, Mama—"

"If you're not around all summer, George may very well find another girl. And marry her."

"George can't get married, Mama. He's got a year of school left."

"Of course, he can get married. He's got a rich father; he could do all right. You stay in Austin this summer and you get that boy to marry you, you hear me?"

"Mama, I'm only a freshman. I've got years, I like George, but there's time, really, Mama, I'll find someone rich, I'll—"

"You like George. Fine. You don't have all that time. Your sorority dues and your clothes and tuition and all that have set me back plenty. I can't finance this high-style operation for four years. The sooner you do what I sent you down there to do, the sooner I can start repairing my bank account for my old age."

Phyllis would never get old. Marguerite herself would begin withering any day now. Looking in the mirror in the mornings, she tried to keep her face like a mask so that the lines around her eyes and mouth would not form. Phyllis should marry George.

But she stayed at Austin, and she worked on George.

65

She went to the bookstore and bought sex manuals; she found a thousand ways to tantalize George, bring him to the point where he was ready to rape her before she ducked away and lit cigarettes for them both, and pretended that she didn't know what was going on. She wore blouses that fell away from her breasts when she leaned forward; she learned that if she sat with her elbows raised on the table close before her, her hands propping her chin, that the neckline of her dresses would gap open, and that her breasts, pushed high by the low-cut French bras, would be full in George's eyes.

One weekend that summer they went to Waco—the Tanners had a low, long white house, three sides of porches, heavy blue shutters. A Mexican couple lived in the cottage in the back. They were in the kitchen by six-thirty to make the Judge's breakfast, stayed until after nine at night.

They arrived late on Friday afternoon. "There's a party tomorrow, a barbecue," Mrs. Tanner told them. "At the Hylands'. It's Dorothy's birthday."

"Oh, God," George said.

"Mamie Hyland and I have been friends forever," Mrs. Tanner said. "We've always wanted Dorothy and George to marry. They're so naughty, they won't have a thing to do with each other."

"You're being polite," George said. "Dorothy is after me all the time."

"Nice boys don't say girls are chasing them," his mother said.

"But I like to have girls chase me," George said, and smiled his faint smile that always tore at Marguerite like a knife.

"Marguerite doesn't chase you, does she?" asked Mrs.

66

Tanner. She was eating a fresh pear, peeling and cutting it with a small ivory-handled silver knife. A bit of juice ran from her mouth down her chin; it was suddenly as though she were bleeding.

"She doesn't have to," George said.

They went to the barbecue and Dorothy Hyland was pretty, and she did like George and at the end of the party, when most of the guests had gone and only a few were left, standing at the bar getting more drinks, arguing with the bandleader, Marguerite missed George and wandered off to find him. She came to the end of the path that circled the swimming pool and turned behind a small storage shed and found George with Dorothy—they were standing faced away from her, but Marguerite could see what Dorothy Hyland was doing, she had pulled her blouse off and was taking off her bra and then she was naked from the waist up, the moonlight making her breasts look grotesque. The rest of her body was in shadow, but the two huge mounds stood out in the moonlight, very white except for the dark nipples.

"What am I supposed to do now?" George said, and Marguerite could imagine that faint smile.

"I just want you to see what you're missing," Dorothy said. She was tight, and she slurred her words.

"Didn't you meet Marguerite?"

"I still want you to see what you're missing."

George turned, he saw Marguerite, and she was right, that faint smile was on his face.

"Marguerite, come see what I'm missing," he said.

Dorothy turned, too, her drink-blurred eyes trying to see Marguerite. Her gaze cleared, she grabbed her clothes and began to dress, turned from them with her back a column of outrage.

"People in Waco are very hospitable," George said to Marguerite, taking her arm and steering her back to the party. "Dorothy senses that I'm on very short rations usually. She was just being friendly."

"I don't think you were very nice to her," Marguerite said.

"If I had been nice to her, I don't think you would have liked it."

"That's not what I meant."

"Can't help it if Dorothy wants to make a fool of herself. That's entirely up to her."

Marguerite saw Dorothy coming back to the party from around the far end of the pool. "She'll never want to see you again," she said.

"That's a risk I'll cheerfully take."

She woke late the next morning, woke to hear voices seemingly in the room. It was only when she roused and sat up in bed that she realized that George and his mother were sitting on the porch around the corner from her bedroom, and that their voices were coming to her though the clear July air, coming through the window she had opened last night despite the air conditioning, opened for the heavy scent of the magnolia and sweet olive.

"Mrs. Hyland called early this morning, George. She was very upset."

"I'm sorry to hear that."

"She found Dorothy stumbling by the pool last night with her clothes half off. Dorothy was drunk, she said, and Mamie couldn't get over that. She says Dorothy never drinks. Don't laugh, George, that's what she said. There was something about you, I couldn't understand what it was, the whole thing was very confusing and upsetting."

"So why was Mrs. Hyland calling you?"

"I don't know. To ask if you'd said anything. To find out what had happened. How do I know? So what did happen?"

"Dorothy got smashed and started taking her clothes off. That's it."

"What do you mean, that's it?"

"That's it. Nothing happened. I told her to put her clothes back on. That made her mad. End of story."

"But, George, that's preposterous. Why should she take her clothes—?"

Marguerite could hear Mrs. Tanner's voice stop. The way it stopped was louder than the sound had been when she was talking, and then after that sudden explosion the silence was very, very silent, the stillness very, very still.

"Ted Hyland is a rich man, George."

"If I were homosexual, that might matter."

"George!"

"Sure. If I were looking for a man to mate with, Ted Hyland's money might mean something. Stop waving the Hyland money in front of me, Mother. I'm not marrying Dorothy and that's the end of it."

"Are you going to marry this Marguerite?"

"I'll get up and close the window now," Marguerite thought, "just any second I'll slip from the bed and pull it closed, they won't hear it, it's around the corner from them." But she heard the sleetlike fall of Mrs. Tanner's voice, making a small rain of chill in the air around her, and she pulled the sheet around her and listened.

"She isn't 'this Marguerite.' She's a very beautiful girl, a very nice girl, a hell of a lot nicer than Dorothy Hyland."

"Her family is nothing. I suppose you know that."

"Again, Mother, I'm not marrying her family."

"I talked to some people who live on a ranch near Grand View. Her mother's a hostess in a restaurant, George. A hostess in a restaurant. Do you want a restaurant hostess for a mother-in-law?"

"At least she would be pleasant. That's her trade, right, being pleasant to people?"

"Of course, you can tell what kind of girl Marguerite is the minute you lay eyes on her," the long iced voice went on.

"What kind is that, Mother?" George sounded quite disinterested. He sounded as though he had asked the question out of politeness. Marguerite thought of his hand on her breast, of her pushing it away. She wanted to break off the bottle of perfume standing on the dresser and gouge Mrs. Tanner's eyes out.

"I'm sure you know better than I do, George."

Silence held in the room, silence held out on the porch. "She didn't say that, she didn't say that," Marguerite whispered into the silence. But the words were a freeze around the room, everywhere she looked she could see them curling their wild tendrils in the air; some of the tendrils caught at her, she felt pulled into the dirt of Mrs. Tanner's mind.

"More coffee, Mother?" George's voice was cool, breaking through the hot edge of the silence. Marguerite knew he was smiling.

There was a knock at the door, then the soft Mexican face appeared, the soft Mexican voice asked what she wanted for breakfast. She got up, closed the window, and showered and dressed, and then she remembered Phyllis' training and she made up her bed and then left the room and went on through the living room to the door leading out to the porch where George and Mrs. Tanner were. She

70

felt a rise of exhilaration. It was better this way. She was not the kind of girl Mrs. Tanner wanted for George, and she would only waste her time trying to be. It was out in the open now, that was good. She would work on George, only George, she would get him to marry her and Mrs. Tanner could go to hell.

But the exhilaration put her off balance, when she rounded the corner and came upon them, sitting in blue wrought-iron chairs at an iron and glass table and George looked up and said, "What in the hell are you doing here?" She felt slapped.

"I came for breakfast."

"You're supposed to have that in bed. Didn't Madalena tell you?"

"She did. But I wanted to eat with you."

"Now, George, maybe Marguerite doesn't like to have breakfast in bed. Some people aren't used to it." Mrs. Tanner's eyes, as they looked at her, carried the image of Dorothy's nakedness on the pupils. She felt that Mrs. Tanner was projecting that image onto her, and that in some way she was being blamed for Dorothy's stupidity.

Madalena brought the tray and set it on the table. Marguerite felt the crispness of her piqué sundress against her skin, the soft wafting air from the ceiling fan above them. She smelled the hot smell of the sausage, the dry smell of toast. She wished suddenly for Phyllis, but she knew that time was the only thing she had, time here in Waco with George. She must use that time, she must make George want her so much that his mother's eyes, mirroring always Dorothy, would not matter.

Mrs. Tanner drank the rest of her coffee in one quick gulp, and rose, the pink linen skirt falling smoothly over her nyloned legs. "There's a D.A.R. luncheon today,

George. I have to go early, I have to register everyone. Dorothy and her mother will be there. I wish I could take you, Marguerite, but of course you're not a member, are you?"

"Marguerite's ancestors have fought in better wars than that one, Mother," George said. He picked up Marguerite's hand and placed a kiss in the center of the palm and closed her fingers over it. The touch of her fingers was like the touch of George's lips, she kept them closed until she saw Mrs. Tanner's eyes on her hand, and then she opened it and put sugar in her coffee and wished that the swirling would suck Mrs. Tanner up and away from them and keep her spinning harmlessly above them, her pink bulk fanning through the heavy summer air.

She heard the sound of Mrs. Tanner's leaving, heard the click of George's cigarette lighter, smelled the morning-bitter smell of cigarette smoke. I'll be eating this breakfast for the rest of my life, she thought, and looked up to see George watching her, watching her almost as she had seen him studying pictures of old buildings in the art books he pored over in the university library.

"We'll get Madalena to pack us a picnic lunch," he said. "I know of a nice place we can go."

Ridiculously, she thought of Sam Short, back in Grand View. She had dated Sam in high school, had been worshiped by Sam, by his parents, by his whole family. The day after she broke up with him his mother had come to see her, carrying a bouquet of daisies that she pressed on Marguerite before she sat on the stiff blue couch in the front room and cried and said Sam's heart was broken, and wouldn't Marguerite think again, just write to Sam from college, maybe a postcard, or a phone call now and again. Sam could call her. Didn't Marguerite know Sam's heart was broken?

Of course, she did know that. The whole time they dated, Sam had been in wonder at his good luck. He had handled her gently, when she let him kiss her, he had kissed her in wonder. He had never tried to pet her. He held her in such awe that she grew bored long before she finally told him goodby. She waited to do that until summer was over and she was ready to go off to school. It was kinder, she thought, to give Sam those last three months. George, she thought, did not hold her in awe.

They drove out beyond the town, coming finally to a sprawling reach of wire-fenced land.

"Dad's ranch," George said. "Something to do when he takes his head out of the law books."

They took a track that led from the main ranch road to a grove of trees. Trees that stood green, freshly green, above the dusty grass beneath them. George was competent; he spread out a blanket, placed the basket in the exact center, opened the red wine with a corkscrew he took from the glove compartment of the car.

"I've barely finished breakfast. I couldn't eat a thing now," she said.

George, already stretched out, patted the blanket next to him. "We'll wait. Come sit down. I've got something for you."

She went slowly, almost afraid. A dim whisper of boys' mockery, of low-voiced "I've got something for you," as a hand passed low in the crotch of pants. But, George was lying there, his hands crossed above his head—silly to have this small chase of fear.

She spread the skirt of her sundress out carefully, bent her legs beneath her. "It must be awfully small," she said. "I don't see a thing."

He sat up then, beginning to smile. "In one way it is small—in another, it's pretty big. Now close your eyes and put out your hand. No, the other one."

She felt his fingers light on her left hand, felt the slide of her high school ring as it left her finger, felt another cool piece of metal ring her finger.

"Now, look," George said.

Her eyes focused on the diamond, high-set, catching back the sunlight that it tossed forth in a rain of colored light. "Oh, George! George, it's beautiful! But you haven't—you never . . ."

As he pulled her to him, he whispered against her neck, "I'll say it now. Will you marry me?"

The world fell into place then. She could write to Phyllis. Phyllis would be happy. And she was happy. She would marry George Tanner, who loved her, whom she loved. They would be happy.

"Will you do something?"

"What is it?"

"Will you undress for me?"

"Even if we're engaged, George, I want to wait. I don't want—" Visions of the ring returned, visions of her black hair flying from George's belt.

"I won't touch you. I promise. I just—look, it's not going to be easy, telling Mother about this."

"I know. She doesn't like me."

"Don't say it that way. She doesn't like anyone who isn't Dorothy Hyland."

"What's so special about Dorothy Hyland?"

"Nothing. But she's under her mother's thumb. If I married her, between Mamie Hyland and my mother, our lives would be settled, forever. They'd probably even help her decide what color toilet paper to buy. That's not for me."

"And I am?"

"You are. And I want to see you. I want an image to carry with me, so when Mother starts in on me, with all the hurrah and commotion, I can think what's waiting for me. And hold fast."

It seemed suddenly so reasonable. And exciting. It matched her dreams of herself, as she stood naked before closet mirrors and watched the long smooth lift of her body, the lines that converged and grew round and large and soft at her breasts. She stood up and reached around and unzipped the back of her sundress, letting it fall to her feet. She had on a cotton slip, a little girl's slip, and she pulled that off and let it fall, too. She wouldn't look at George's face until she was finished, she wanted to see him the first moment when he looked at her.

She said, "Close your eyes a minute. I'll tell you when."

And then she stripped off the bra and pants and tossed her hair back and said, "Now," and George opened his eyes and she waited for the admiration, the lust, to come into his face.

Instead he said, "Jesus," and a look she didn't understand was on his face. "Turn around," he said, and she did that, feeling silly all at once in her diamond ring and her sandals, she should have taken her shoes off. She felt the diamond hard on her finger.

"In a minute," she thought, "I'll look at it again and get excited all over that I'm going to marry George," but at that time and in that place, all she really thought about was whether that tiny figure on a tiny horse way across the pasture had binoculars, and, if so, whether he were admiring what was waiting for George, too.

CHAPTER SIX

They were going to a dinner dance at the country club. When Marguerite came out to join the others, a strapless white organdy dress swirling in a lace-edged waterfall to mid-calf, thin heeled white sandals on her feet, she knew that George had told his parents, and that his mother was not pleased.

"What a pretty dress," she said, and she smoothed the skirt of her own sedate silk print, smoothed the skirt to below her knees, sat back, and looked fixedly at Marguerite's throat.

"I think maybe I'm too dressed up. George said it was semiformal, I thought—"

"Well, we can never depend on what men say, can we?" Mrs. Tanner said, and she seemed suddenly cheered.

"I'll just go change, I have a white linen—"

"Change! Pretty as a picture, don't change a thing." Judge Tanner came up behind her, put his arms around her waist and pulled her around to face him. "Finally going to get myself a daughter! And damned if George didn't bring me the pick of the litter! The Tanner luck, that's what it is. Helped me marry Maribeth, helped George get you. Angel's bringing some champagne, we're going to toast this engagement, make it official."

Mrs. Tanner became very involved in the whole business of the champagne. She kept up a line of comment to Angel as he brought in the cooler and gently popped the cork, and poured the first sip for Judge Tanner and then filled the other glasses. "My goodness, Angel, you did go all out. That is very fine champagne, it really is," she said, squinting at the label as the bottle tilted over her glass.

"Well, for God's sake, man's oldest son just gets engaged once, right? Best champagne in the house, that's what's called for."

"Yes, I suppose a man does get engaged only once," Mrs. Tanner said, and she drained her glass and motioned to the Judge to pour her more.

The champagne was like bubbles of time in Marguerite's nose. It seemed to be not really connected with the Tanners and George and being engaged; it seemed to be more in touch with Aunt Cissy, and her mother. She could imagine them sitting on the green velvet chaise in Cissy's bedroom in her Houston apartment, pouring golden bubbles of joy and excitement, and good fortune, and yes, purpose, into thin-stemmed glasses, and laughing with the bubbles as they broke in their warm red mouths and slid gently down their long white throats.

"It'll be one hell of a celebration next June," Judge Tanner said. "Graduation one day and wedding the next—that the way it's going to be?"

"Not quite," George said. Marguerite wondered if she were the only one who noticed his smile—his parents, seeing it from his babyhood, apparently saw it not at all. But she was prepared, she knew something was coming, and when he said, "We're getting married in August—soon as summer school is out," she found herself smiling and nodding as though she had known it all along.

"August! What's the rush, why are you in such a hurry—" Marguerite saw the eyes go to her stomach—consciously, she sucked in, and the white organdy fell against the hollow with a small sigh.

"If you can look at Marguerite and ask me why I'm in a rush, you haven't got eyes, Mother."

"But, George, be sensible. What will you live on, you should give yourselves time—"

Marguerite left the conversation. She knew everything Mrs. Tanner would say, everything that George would say back. She knew that in the end the Tanners would give George the money they had been giving him, and she knew that she would drop out of school and go to work. Phyllis had invested enough in her already. The investment had paid off, there was no reason for Phyllis to continue supporting her. While George and his mother argued, Marguerite was planning the wedding. It would be in Austin, because that was where their friends were. And because she did not want a wedding reception in the private room of the restaurant where her mother worked.

Four weeks later, they were married in a chapel on the University of Texas campus. They went to New Orleans for their honeymoon. It was hot and sticky and the lights and noise of Bourbon Street came through the shutters that slanted across their bedroom doors, but it didn't seem to matter, because they never slept for more than a few hours. The whole time, when she remembered it later, was a montage of heavy food, chilled wines, jazz, jazz, jazz, hidden courtyards, and over it all, a large image of a naked woman with her legs spread wide open and a look of surprise on her face.

CHAPTER SEVEN

Grace's voice jerked at her. "My God, you look shocked. Haven't you ever heard that word before?" There was amusement in that voice, amusement and—challenge?

"I'm never shocked." Marguerite said. "I don't have the nerve to be."

And then they both laughed, but though they left the remains of their lunch, the mayonnaise-smeared lettuce, the lipsticked napkins, the litter of the story Grace had been telling her stayed and joined what she was beginning to think was a trash pile she and Dr. Forrester would sift through for weeks, months, years, searching for something worth saving.

After lunch, they stood for a minute in the parking lot, their eyes, their faces, shielded by the large sunglasses that covered their eyebrows, came down past their cheekbones. Lois Tremayne and Betsy Harahan walked toward them from the tennis courts, their short white dresses stained with wet, their hair wet and clinging to their necks. Lois' thighs bounced as she walked. She was plump. Although she played tennis every day, she was still plump, the fat rolled itself around each bend and joint of her. Marguerite's hands smoothed down her own slimness; even the three martinis and creamed shrimp would not put an ounce on her. It was a gift she had, it was, she thought, the reason Lois did not like her.

She turned to go, thinking that she would not stay to go through the kind of civil greeting Lois and Betsy would give her before they turned to Grace and talked about all the things they knew and she still didn't know, the things that came from growing up together and going to college together and marrying together and joining clubs together and in fact living in each other's pockets from babyhood on. She was tired of smiling nicely and trying to remember who all the people they talked about were. When she was with people like Lois and Betsy, she remembered how small a part of Grace's life she still belonged to. The martinis and shrimp turned in her stomach. It was very hot; the silk dress was beginning to stick to her and she could feel sweat pouring down the inside of her arms.

"I'll call you tomorrow," she said, and moved to her car through the heat that seemed to fight her. She could feel the air wrap itself around her, cloak her with its heat, beat down at her coolness and her thin layer of makeup and powder. It would bring her to her knees; she could not support herself against it.

But the car air-conditioning was powerful, it roared and then settled down into a cold hum that poured over her; the sweat dried on her arms, her face felt cool again. She thought of Grace leaving Lois and Betsy and going to meet the conductor. That was something she knew that they did not know, for all their going to kindergarten together and learning ballroom dancing together from the same crazy teacher she'd heard about ten dozen times, they did not know all there was to know about Grace Whitman. That was something for her, and her alone.

She did not like where their house was. When they had bought the lot, seven years ago, she had loved it. It was in a new area, and the lots were large and wooded. She and George and the children would drive around on weekends and look at the place, and she had pushed George, she knew she had pushed George, to borrow more money than he had really wanted to, and buy it for them. "If I can only have this lot, I'll never ask you for another thing. I mean it, George. It's all I want."

And so they had bought the lot, and built the house, far sooner than they thought they would. She didn't like to think about how they'd done it.

Now she had found a better lot, it was near the Whitmans, and cost $65,000. But it was an investment, they'd be able to sell it for thousands more, even if they never built so much as an outhouse on it. George was balking; he always balked—but she always got her way.

There were messages from Lora Mae on the phone table. Of course, Lora Mae had left, tooling down the long pea-gravel drive in her old red Ford, cigarette smoke trailing behind her, mingling with the blue exhaust. Marguerite had been trying to get George to let her hire a cook, too—someone to come in when Lora Mae had gone. It would be nice to play tennis late, nice not to have to fit cooking dinner into any part of her day. But George couldn't see it. "The kids are at camp, and we eat out a couple of nights a week anyway. In the winter, you need to be home when the kids are home from school. If you're at home, you might as well cook. Next thing you'll be wanting me to hire someone for bedroom duty," he said. Looking at her from wide blue eyes that always looked so transparent until you tried to look past them, and couldn't. So there were still times when she didn't get her way. For now.

"Mrs. McDaniels called. To remind you of the Museum Auxiliary Bazaar. She wants you to bake something." Marguerite could picture Lora Mae writing that, the omnipresent cigarette smoke pointing up over her head like horns, that deep magenta mouth clamped over a burst of derisive laughter that would, Marguerite knew, be let loose later for the entertainment of Lora Mae's family.

"*My* madam bake something? *No* way. Old Lora Mae gonna produce her famous pound cake—right out of that ole box with Massa George's best twelve-year-old bourbon instead of water. Why, we are *famous* for that pound cake."

Bother Lora Mae! She might just bake something. She felt funny about Ruth. It had been awful seeing her at the club, because now she knew how Todd fucked, and she'd never be able to see Ruth without wondering if she wore a blue round-collared nightgown to bed. And what happened when she pulled it up. That was part of the litter. Everything she'd just thought. She reached quickly for the second message, read it. "Mr. Lou Armitage called. About some plants. Will call back."

Lou Armitage! That man she'd met at the Bakers' last week. She hadn't liked him. He had been laughing at her the whole time he was talking to her, not the kind of jollying, pleasant laughter that she was used to from men, but a knowing kind that made her feel very silly. She did not like to feel silly, and she did not like Mr. Armitage. He

84

had left the party at the same time they did. She watched a chauffeur bring round a Silver Cloud Rolls, and she had clutched George's arm and said for heaven's sake, who is that for? and he had said, "Well, Armitage is getting into it," and she had watched the chunky body in its tightly tailored suit climb into the Rolls and she had thought, well, no man has everything. Now he had called about plants, which must be a mistake, because surely they had not talked about plants. She didn't know what they had talked about; Lou Armitage's eyes had been on her cleavage, which that night had been extensive, and she had been so busy watching him watching her that she had talked automatically. There had been something about the way he looked at her breasts, not really admiring them, but almost as though he were comparing them to the many others he had seen, giving her a small question mark of a rating, which he would change later as the need might arise. She hoped that he did not call her back. She liked men to look at her breasts, but she did not like to be compared to anyone else. Even flattering comparisons were insulting.

She went to the kitchen, fixed a glass of iced tea, and carried it to her bedroom, the room that Shaw Interiors had just finished last month, and that she was finding she hated. Because everyone who came to see it said, "Oh, Shaw did it!" and while her old decor had not been as smashingly elegant, or whatever in hell the effect was that Shaw had done, it had been what she herself liked, and no one had ever thought anyone else had done it.

So she didn't even take off her shoes when she sat down on the chaise and lifted her legs the length of it. She let the heels dig into the yellow silk, and she thought, if they tear a hole in it, what the hell. She drank her iced tea and thought of Grace and of Todd, and she thought that once, just once, she would like to feel something when sex was happening instead of when she was talking about it. Maybe if she had talked about it in the beginning with George—that was funny. Now that was really funny. George communicated with his penis, not his tongue. And it was one way. Even when they'd just been married a few months, even then—

She remembered the first time she found out about the one way, the one way that was set by George. It was November, she'd been working at the trucking company for two months, the newness of everything was wearing off a little, maybe. She'd been in the kitchen, she could see it, the brown water stain that looked like a map of Russia on the kitchen ceiling. She'd cleaned the kitchen, and then she had gone to the back door and looked out, and then had stood idly tracing a heart on the frosted glass, filling it in with George + Marguerite. It would smear the newly cleaned pane; she took a paper towel and carefully wiped it dry. She had cleaned the refrigerator and the oven, and it was still only nine o'clock. Walking to the doorway that separated the kitchen from the living room, she looked at George, books spread out on the dinette table, head on hands, light glimmering on his blond hair.

She didn't think of complaining. George's work was too important. But it was hard, in a small apartment, to keep so quiet that she couldn't even listen to the radio for fear of disturbing him.

"Want some coffee?"

His head didn't lift from his book, but he nodded and said, "Sure."

She went into the kitchen, measured coffee into the pot, poured in water, plugged it in. There was a small mirror near the sink, she looked in it, saw the small shadows under her eyes, the mouth with lipstick eaten off. She thought of a book she had read once, *A Bride's First Year,* or something equally stupid. The girl in the book spent her time either in frilly nightgowns or frilly aprons; she apparently had nothing to do all day but take care of herself and her home—both were shining and immaculate.

Let her try working all day and coming home to cook and clean. And then at night, George, insistent, the heavy penis pushing at her. Not that she minded. Well, most of the time she didn't mind. It was just that it overwhelmed her, the complete giving over of herself to someone else. She looked at George again. She wanted him then, and she slipped past him, went into the bedroom and opened her dresser drawer. A pile of soft, sheer gowns lay there—the trousseau that she, Phyllis, and Cissy had picked out, she protesting that it cost too much, Phyllis telling her to hush, that a girl married only once, and that she should have a trousseau that would fit the importance of a marriage to George Tanner.

Her hands moved through the lace and ribbons, paused at a white gown with blue ribbons at the waist and small lace straps over the shoulders. It had only one layer of material, when she put it on it was as though she were wrapped in slightly opaque paper, but the pink of her nipples and the small indentation of her navel and her dark pubic hair pressed through the opaqueness so that it was just one step from having nothing on. She pulled on a robe and went back to the kitchen, poured the coffee and fixed a tray. Then she let the robe fall from her and went back to the living room, carrying the tray carefully before her.

She set the tray down, put sugar and cream in George's cup, placed it near his hand. Then she stepped behind him and put her arms around his neck, pulling his head back to her breasts. She leaned forward, and her tongue was warm and moist in his ear.

"Umm, I love you, too," George said, pulling his head away, reaching for the coffee.

She moved in front of him so that he could see her, leaned over him and kissed him. "Come to bed, George, won't you?" She half-turned, waiting for him to get up, to follow her.

"Christ, Marguerite, you know I've got a test tomorrow." He gave her a quick glance, looked back at the notebook in front of him, sipped at his coffee.

"I won't keep you long," she said, and again she could feel a pulse that strongly measured her need.

"I told you, I don't have time for that right now." He sounded cross, as though she were a child that he must make things clear to, or an unwelcome neighbor who had dropped in.

She felt the sudden nakedness of her gown; with a small sound of pain, she ran into the kitchen and pulled the robe around her, catching sight in the mirror of her newly made up face, her freshly brushed hair. She felt hot again, but it was no longer desire that engulfed her. It was pain and embarrassment and perhaps anger, though she would not admit to that. She should have known better; George was fond of saying that nothing came between him and his work, and she now believed that.

She went into the bedroom, closed the door and changed to a yellow gown with a heavy layer of silk under the chiffon overskirt. Fuck George, anyway. But she immediately denied her anger. After all, George was in his

88

last year, he did have to study. And, as he often said to her, how could she know how difficult the upper course work was, when she had had only one year of college? She picked up the murder mystery she'd brought home from work, found her place and began to read.

It was after ten when George came to bed. She had turned out the light and was lying quietly, waiting for sleep. She heard him moving around, taking change from his pockets, the small click of his belt buckle as it hit a chair—she turned over and lay more deeply into the pillow. Six o'clock would come soon enough, she would sleep.

But when George got in bed, his hands were immediately on her, he was turning her over, lifting her skirt, pulling the bodice of the gown away from her breasts. She felt cold; the chill of the November air in the room, she supposed, and she tried to meet his hands, to make it easy for him.

But when he was finished, was still lying on her, she said into his weight, "Why couldn't you have done this when I wanted it?"

He rolled off her, sat up, and reached for his pajamas. "Couldn't. I was busy."

"And I was asleep."

"You're saying you didn't like that?"

"I didn't say that. I just want to know why we always make love when you want to, not when I want to."

"But, baby doll, I'm not the one with the convenient little hole that's always ready. I can't perform just because you snap your fingers. Or flit around in a gown that barely covers you."

"I don't believe it's that simple."

"I don't care what you believe. I can't get it up when I'm

89

trying to learn the history of architecture. Anyway, what's the difference? You wanted it at nine, it's ten-thirty, so what's the big deal over an hour and a half? You still got laid."

"Don't talk like that; it's vulgar," she said. She felt tears, but she wouldn't cry, she wouldn't. Tomorrow she would resurrect those sex manuals. Surely George wasn't right that just because she could always be entered it was up to him to choose the times and places and ways in which they would make love. And lying there, she wished that she had had an affair before marriage.

The phone rang, she thought of letting it ring, telephones could be like penises, they pushed and intruded and kept on and on and on. But whoever was calling knew that she was there, the phone would go on ringing until the lavender dusk fell. So she got up and crossed the room and said, "Hello," and then heard a heavy voice say, "This is Lou Armitage."

She was tired of being afraid of people. Someday she would answer the phone and whoever it was would say their name and she would not be afraid. "I've got those plants you said you wanted," the voice went on. "If you'll tell me when it's convenient, I'll have somebody bring them out to you."

"Mr. Armitage, are you sure you've got the right person? I don't know what plants you're talking about."

"At the Bakers' party? We were standing out on the patio, you remember that?"

A vision of lights tossed back from the surface of the pool, of the colors of her long print dress darkening and lightening in the flickering light of the tiki torch behind her, of a stocky man standing before her and nodding when she looked around her and said the Bakers must

90

have spent the earth on the plants on the patio, it looked like something out of a Tarzan movie.

"I do remember now. I said something about the plants—"

"Yeah. So I've got some for you. Some of those big ones. Damn things weigh a ton."

"You got me some plants?"

"Sure. You said your husband wouldn't buy those big ones, he said they cost too much and would probably freeze anyway. Hell, I had some hanging around, you can have them."

She had a thought that you did not laugh at Lou Armitage, but she did, anyway. "Hanging around? You have some hanging around?"

"In the courtyard of a hotel I own. Tired looking at the damn things. Want to get rid of some of them. So I thought of you."

"But, Mr. Armitage, I can't possibly let you give me those plants—they're too expensive, I don't even know you—" But the excitement was rising; he had noticed her, he remembered her, that made remembering him less nagging—she felt that they now stood on the same level.

"Oh, God, what crap. Look, you're a hell of a beautiful woman, right? Now the way I look at things, beautiful women ought to have every damn thing they want. Keeps them happy. There's nothing better than a happy beautiful woman."

"Are you just absolutely determined to give me those plants?"

"Absolutely."

"It's very nice of you, and if you'll just tell me when is a good time for your people to bring them, I'll make sure I'm home."

"The good time for them is the good time for you. Those guys work for me. Who the hell cares what's a good time for them?"

"I'll be home all day tomorrow."

"Okay. I'll send them out about ten. And look—can I come by for a drink, see how they look?"

I should say no right now. I should tell Mr. Lou Armitage to take his plants and his men who are so flexible and amenable and stuff them.

"Come by at five. I'll be waiting for you."

She told George about it at dinner, making a funny story out of it, finishing by saying, "Thank God we weren't at the zoo and I wasn't admiring elephants."

George smiled at her, then got up and came around the table, and put his hand down the front of her dress, worked it beneath her bra, and squeezed her breast.

"See what having nice round white-boobs does for you," he said.

"George, it isn't like that, don't go making something out of it—"

"Hell, you know who Lou Armitage is?" He had taken his hand out and was using both of them now to unbutton her dress.

"Somebody rich who owns a hotel," she said. She thought of the chocolate pie in the refrigerator, as George pulled her dress off her shoulders and reached around to unfasten her bra, she thought of her white flesh on a plate and George spooning it up.

"Somebody rich who owns a damn sight more than anybody knows about. Somebody rich who has connections in all the right and most of the wrong places. Somebody rich who might give me a very nice commission—hell, we could go around the world on the fee from

92

that shopping center and office complex he's planning out on the north side of town."

"Have you talked to him about it?"

"Armitage isn't that easy to see. You might mention what a brilliant architect I am when he comes for that drink."

Her dress was around her waist now, her bra a streak of white on the floor. She waited for George to kiss her, to fondle her.

"Go get me a piece of that pie, will you," he said. He wandered to a window, looked out on the patio. "Those plants will make the place look good." He sat down and saw her still sitting, looking at him. "What are you waiting for? I want some pie."

She started to pull her dress back up. "Don't," he said.

"Don't?"

"I like to look at naked women," he said. "Now, go get my pie."

The loose dress fell away from her and down around her feet as she got up. She stepped out of it and caught a flash of herself in the mirror, naked except for the bikini panties that stretched around her bottom. In a sudden moment of terror, she didn't know the woman in the mirror; the Marguerite she knew was never naked.

The plants were spectacular; they made the patio rich, luxuriant.

"Boss says to tell you we'll pick 'em up in November, put 'em in a green house 'til spring."

After the men had left, she sat out on the patio and just looked at the plants. She was happy inside. As she recognized the happiness, she thought of Lou Armitage. "Beautiful women should have anything they want." She laughed in the hot July sunshine and thought how very nice it was to be beautiful, to be happy.

She heard the doorbell ring at exactly five o'clock. She had showered and changed at four; she had on white linen slacks and a scarlet pima cotton shirt that she had unbuttoned and buttoned at least ten times, trying to decide how much throat to show—she had finally left only the top button unbuttoned, which was less than she usually did, so that she felt the outfit was off-balance and that made her cross.

She was still cross when Lou Armitage rang the doorbell; she told herself that if it were not for George's comment about the shopping center and office building complex she would have let the doorbell ring on forever. Something told her, though, that no one kept Lou Armitage waiting for long, and this made her even crosser.

"What's the matter? Don't you like the plants?" He walked past her into the foyer, looking around with quick, searchlight looks. "Hell of a house. Your husband did it, right? Good ideas—nice use of glass. He knows I'm here, right? You got some decent Scotch?"

"Where do you want to sit?" she asked.

"It's your house. How should I know?"

"I thought maybe you'd want to see how nice the plants look."

"So you do like them. When you answered the door, you looked like you were about to blow my head off."

"They're gorgeous. They really are. I can't thank you enough."

"No thanks needed. If I hadn't wanted to give 'em to you, I wouldn't have. It's been a long time since I've done anything I didn't want to do."

She stopped pouring the Scotch, looked at him. "Is that true?"

"Is what true?"

"That it's been a long time since you've done anything you didn't want to do?"

"A very long time."

She brought the drinks to where he was standing, handed him the Scotch, sipped at her own bourbon. "I wonder how that feels."

A large hand caught her chin, held it. "Hell, don't give me any of that crap. You do damn near exactly as you please, don't you? I watched you at the Bakers'. You know damn well what you're doing, every minute."

"I sometimes think there's a difference between doing what you want to do and knowing what you're doing."

"Let's talk about baseball," Lou said. He had settled on the long pale green couch. He pushed a stack of pillows aside and beckoned to her. "Sit down. Okay, so who you like in the National League?"

She laughed. "I don't know anything about baseball."

"Okay. And I don't know anything about all this philosophy stuff, people sitting around and moaning about who the hell they are and where they're going and all that crap. I live, okay? I eat good, I sleep good, I live good. And I don't think about any of it."

"Will you talk to George about that new center you're doing?" The suddenness of her words shattered through her. What an idiot, how could she have just blurted that out—

"Hell of a stiff price for one drink," Lou said.

"George is good. He's as good as anyone you could get. Why shouldn't you talk to him?"

"See what I mean? You do exactly what you damn please. Other women, they'd have pussyfooted around. Hinted at it. But not you. Bang, first time around the track,

95

out with it. Will I talk to George?"

"It was probably a tacky thing to say. I'm sorry."

"Don't do that."

"What?"

"Ask me to talk to George and then try to apologize. That's a bunch of crap."

She could think of nothing to say. The lush room seemed suddenly obscene, she saw it now as a carefully planned backdrop for her—that was of course what it was, the colors, the textures, were those that most flattered her, most became her. But Lou Armitage brought something into the room that clashed, and at the same time seemed more fitting than anything else there.

"I'll take you to lunch tomorrow," he said. "We'll drive down to Beechwood."

"I don't understand any of this."

"What's the matter?" he said. He got up and went over to the portable bar and poured another Scotch. "Haven't you ever been chased?"

"But you're not chasing me. You're acting as though— as though somehow I know what you mean by everything you say."

"I haven't said anything very complicated. What's complicated about saying I'll take you to lunch tomorrow?"

"Nothing."

"Okay. So I'll pick you up around eleven. We'll take the old road down. It's prettier."

"Don't I even get a chance to say no?"

"You don't want to say no," he said. He put down the glass, picked up his hat, started for the door. "I'll let myself out. And you can unbutton your shirt now."

CHAPTER EIGHT

"Mr. Armitage said to tell you to call him," she said to George at dinner.

"Thanks."

"Don't thank me. He liked the house. He wouldn't have said for you to call him otherwise."

"Oh, I think he would have." George smiled at her; he was pleased. She felt a denial rising in her; but then it was no use, George had his view of her, of the world, there wasn't much point in trying to change it.

"We're going to—" she stopped.

"What did you say?"

"Grace and I are going to lunch tomorrow."

"And the next day and the next day and the day after that."

But that pleased him, too. He had said to her, after she had met the Whitmans the first time, at the opening of the shopping center George had done for Jerry and his father—"They liked you. I saw Grace watching you. I

97

think you interested her."

At first she had been excited for herself—if Grace Whitman liked her, was "interested," she had a chance. She had a chance. But then the obligation fell heavy on her, the obligation to bring Grace home to George. And she had thought, not for the first time, how crazy it was that George, whose mother gave the most perfect parties in Waco, didn't know a damn thing about why you really met people, talked with them, knew them. And she, whose mother did all that for pay, did.

Their first party had proved that. And she'd never enjoyed giving a party again. Now she called caterers and florists, dared George silently to count the cost—and fucked him and sucked him to make sure he didn't.

That first party—God, what a joke. They were still in Austin, in school, and George had come home one afternoon, the small twist of a smile hallmarking his face.

"I want us to have a party," he had said. The apartment was hot; he took off his shirt and stood in front of the window fan, perspiration drying on his chest.

"When?"

"On the weekend. Saturday."

"It's so hot. This apartment is bad enough with just the two of us in it. It'll be awful with a crowd of people."

"I thought we'd use old Bowers' patio."

"Do you think he'll let us? I mean, when we rented the apartment, he didn't say anything about letting us use his private patio."

"He will if you ask him."

"Oh, George, won't you? He's so big, and when he talks it sounds like his words are coming out through a mouthful of nails. He scares me."

"But you're prettier than I am," George said. He crossed

the room and leaned over to kiss her. She had a sudden foreshortened vision of the blond hairs curling on his chest; for a moment it was like being kissed by a great furry beast and she felt enveloped by him.

"Who do you want to have?"

"People from school—some of the profs. A mixed bunch."

"Some of the professors? Let's not have them."

"But I particularly want to have them." He had pulled away from her, he was looking at her with that little smile, and she knew they would have the professors. Would have the devil himself, if that's what George decided.

"I guess we'll have beer. And what else? It's too hot to fool with a lot of food."

"We'll have a bar. Maybe some beer. But bourbon and Scotch. And vodka."

"But, George, that will cost the earth!"

"Hang cost. I'll pay for it."

She thought of her job, of filing endless reports and letters and forms in a dim office. How many hours would she have to work to pay for this party? Anger forced the words, "You will? With what?"

"I called Dad. He's sending a check."

"Your father is paying for this party? Why would he do that?" A remembered fight, Mrs. Tanner saying through her small tight lips, "We'll give you just what we gave before. Not a penny more." Of course, not a penny more. This way, they were still paying only for George. Marguerite could pay her own way.

"Dad isn't against us. He'd send a hell of a lot more money if Mother weren't such a bitch about it."

"But money for a party—" We need other things, like food. Like rent payments.

"We're having this party," George said. "And I want it to be good. No popcorn and onion dip. Do what you have to do, but fix good food. Okay?"

"Okay." She should be happy, a party, a chance to dress up, to be with people. But she was with people all day. They had only been married five weeks; when she got home, George was enough for her. She went to the low bookcase and took out her wedding-gift cookbooks. Planning a party couldn't be that hard. People did it all the time. Phyllis couldn't help her. As far as she knew, Phyllis had never given a party. Mrs. Tanner—wouldn't Mrs. Tanner love to have her call, beg for help? The hell with Mrs. Tanner. She could do without her. She looked at the lists of party recipes; they were endless. "I'll call Cissy," she thought. "I'll go to a pay phone and I'll call Cissy. I've got to have some help from someone."

And when she called Cissy, leaving the office on her lunch hour, cramming herself into the phone booth at the back of a drugstore, Cissy was pleased.

"There's nothing to it," Cissy said. "Fix food the men will like; if they're happy, it's a good party. Women just piddle with the food, anyway. Recipes—recipes. Look, I'll write out a menu tonight. This is what, Monday? Get it in the mail special delivery tomorrow; you'll get it Wednesday. It'll all be there. You'll show 'em."

I will show them, Marguerite thought, pushing her way through the heavy September heat. Though who she would show what to she could hardly say.

So when the menu arrived, carefully typed with Cissy's broad scrawl adding notes across the top, she sat down and read it, almost committing it to memory. Cissy had included a shopping list; the whole thing was as well-laid-out as a battle plan and, for the first time since George had mentioned the party, she felt almost good about it.

"What are you wearing Saturday?" George asked her. It was Thursday, she had gone shopping for the party food after work and they were sitting late over supper.

"I don't know. A sundress. Even on the patio, it'll still be hot."

"Wear that white one. And put a flower in your hair."

"All right." She felt a question urging itself: What was it about this party? Except for the fact that some of the architecture staff was coming, surely it would be much like any other party? But, of course, it wasn't. It was not a casual beer bust, drinking keg beer from paper cups. It was a real party, even though she did keep telling herself that it was no big deal, just another evening, just people, like herself.

By Saturday evening, she was worn out. She stepped out of the shower exhausted; cooking all day in the small kitchenette, the heat from the stove meeting and intensifying the heat from the open windows had wrung her out. She blotted herself dry with a towel, put a cascade of bath powder on her body. She could hear George moving around in the bedroom; he was humming, he sounded happy. She walked toward the bed, reached for her underthings lying there. George saw her in the dresser mirror and came toward her; she saw his penis, large, hard, and picked up her panties. "Wait a minute," he said. He pushed her back onto the bed, reached a hand down to open her legs.

"George, there's no time. For heaven's sake, George, I've got to get dressed."

"There's time," he said, and came into her, the thrust against her dry flesh painful and rough, the feel of his hands on her shoulders heavy.

He left her almost immediately, left her and went into the bathroom where she could hear water running. She felt the wetness now on her legs, worried that it would seep through to the bedspread. She got up carefully and wrapped a towel around her, waiting for George to be finished and leave the bathroom to her.

There were runnels of wet in the white powder on her thighs, she wet a cloth and sponged it off, powdered herself again, slipped into her bra and panties and dropped the white dress over her head.

"Why did you do that?"

"Can't an old married man make love to his wife?"

"That wasn't making love."

"All right. Can't an old married man have sex with his wife?"

"You had it. I didn't," she said.

"And sometimes I'm hungry and want a snack and sometimes you aren't."

"It's not the same."

"Then make it the same," he said, buttoning up the Mexican wedding shirt.

"I'll go down now," she said. "Someone may come early."

"Your lipstick is smeared. Better fix it."

She turned to the mirror, wiped a tissue across the blotted red line. Her fingers held the smooth cylinder of lipstick. It was cool and firm in her hand, she stroked it on surely. You're a pretty girl in a white dress who is going to have a wonderful evening, she thought. You are a pretty girl in a white dress who is going to have a wonderful evening. You are—

"You're beautiful," George said, and she thought, I will remember only his mouth, only the way it feels on mine.

102

The patio was fine; they had carried Mr. Bowers' kitchen table out and covered it with a print tablecloth. Marguerite had bought cheap hurricane lamps, but with candles glowing in them, with ivy tucked around them, they looked better than cheap; they looked good. The food looked good, too, the thin sandwiches, the smoking meatballs in the chafing dish, the platter of vegetables with the sour-cream sauce.

She felt arms come around her waist and tried to turn, but she was held fast against someone's chest, someone who was breathing heavily into her ear.

"Ah, zee lady in white," a voice said. "Come wiz me to the Casbah." And then she knew it was Ted Beamish, an old friend, a friend of hers as well as of George's.

"If it were anyone but you, I'd say no," she said, and turned to kiss his cheek.

"This is quite a bash," Ted said. "I wore my old beer-drinking clothes. I think I'm out of place."

"We're celebrating our six weeks' anniversary," she said, and moved across the patio to meet incoming guests.

And then the evening was a mist of laughing faces and refilled sandwich trays and smoking cigarettes and compliments, so many compliments that she became embarrassed. "Everyone thinks we're really putting on, having a party like this," she said to George at one point.

"The hell with 'em. They're having a good time, aren't they?" But his eyes weren't on her; they were on someone across the patio. George was watching someone and smiling. She followed his gaze and saw Ted Beamish, leaning against the food table and talking to a man with a heavy white beard.

"That's Dr. Falkner," George said. "I want you to meet him."

They moved across the patio. She felt that she was drifting, the white skirt a small cloud of movement. She was shocked to see that Ted was drunk, really drunk, and that he was holding forth almost incoherently. It was only nine-thirty, how could he be drunk so fast? The drink in his hand was dark; it had no water in it, she thought, and shot a glance at George. George should take care of Ted. Ted certainly shouldn't have any more to drink—and then George moved in, placing her carefully on Dr. Falkner's right, introducing her as though Ted did not even exist.

"This is Marguerite, Dr. Falkner. My bride."

The white beard moved when Dr. Falkner spoke. He was, of course, like the Sunday School Santa Claus of her childhood, and she felt a sudden rush of warmth.

"I was pleased to hear of your marriage, Mrs. Tanner. Nothing like marrying to settle a young man down. Though George didn't really need settling, I suppose. A very fine student, yes, a very fine student. Perhaps not as original as some of the others—but dependable. Yes, dependable."

She saw the dark look cross George's face, heard him say to Ted, "Your drink all right? Come on, we'll go get one."

"Where's George?" Dr. Falkner lifted his head, followed Ted and George as they crossed the patio.

"Gone to get a drink, I think."

"Beamish doesn't need anymore," Dr. Falkner said. "Surprised to see him drink so much. Almost as though he can't stop; doesn't know when he's had enough."

She remembered George fixing drinks, handing full glasses to Ted and taking his empty ones. "He probably doesn't realize—you know, you get to talking—"

"No one else like that. Right? Everyone else all right."

Falkner sounded angry; she hoped this wouldn't some-how affect Ted's grade in his course. George shouldn't be such a generous host. Should have said to Ted, you've had enough.

They came back then, George holding a bottle of Coke in his hand, Ted clinging to another dark-brown drink. George began talking to Falkner, telling him easily about a new office building going up in Waco, speaking of the design details, pointing out certain innovative ideas. Ted looked bleary; at times he jutted forward into the conversation, dropping aimless words, losing his thought, lapsing back into sudden silence.

Something's happening here, she thought. George looked very much the way he had looked upstairs, before the party, just at the moment he had pushed himself into her.

"I've got to see about the food," she said, and left them, hearing as she moved George's full strong voice, the heavier voice of Dr. Falkner, and then, intermittently, like a discordant note, Ted.

"It was a good party," George said. They had cleaned up the patio, all but carrying Mr. Bowers' table back inside. They had collapsed upstairs, picking at the leftover food, having a nightcap.

"It seemed to be." She watched his face. Maybe now he would tell her what had been going on, would explain the strange tickle of bad feeling she'd had.

But when he crossed over to her, unzipped her dress and pulled it over her head, she knew he would say nothing. "Take longer, please," she said, not looking at him.

And when he had taken longer, when he finished, and then fell asleep beside her, she rose and went to sit in the square of moonlight coming through the living-room window. For the first time since she'd known George, she was frightened of him. Which was silly. Which was dumb. Which was real.

Three days later, George met her at the door with roses. "It's a celebration," he said. "We're eating out."

"What are we celebrating?"

"You're looking at Falkner's assistant for the year."

"I don't know what that means."

"It only means that I've got the most prestigious position in the whole damn department. It only means that Dr. Falkner's recommendation will go on my job résumé—and he's a hell of a big name in this profession."

"But that's wonderful! I didn't even know you wanted it. That's funny, something that important, and I didn't know you wanted it."

"I didn't tell you on purpose. I was afraid you'd be nervous around Falkner at the party—that he'd think I was trying to set him up."

"Was that what the party was for?"

"You think a man like Falkner would give me an honor like that because he had a good time at a party?"

"I guess not."

"You damn well better guess not. This thing means I've got talent, ability—that he likes my work."

She remembered Falkner's bearded voice: "Maybe not as original as some of the others." Maybe he liked dependability better than originality.

"I'm very happy for you," she said.

"Be happy for us. For what this means to us."

"I'm very happy for us," she said, and wondered why she still felt it only for George.

They went to a Chinese restaurant they'd discovered

early in the summer. They'd told a few people about it; now, most nights there'd be architecture students and their dates there. Tonight there was a scattering of kids from school. Some of them came over and congratulated George.

"There's Dan Rush sitting over there," Marguerite said. "I wonder why he hasn't come over."

"Not everyone's glad I got this job."

"Did Dan want it?"

"Dan's only a junior. He's not eligible."

But then Dan did come over, bringing his cup of tea with him, turning one of the chairs around and sitting astride it.

"How's it feel to be the white-haired boy of the department?"

"It feels pretty good."

"Bothered by the necks under your feet?"

"Don't feel any."

"Not even Beamish's neck?"

"Ted's a pretty big boy. Seems to me if I'd walked over him I'd know about it."

"What's he talking about, George?"

"Silly talk. Idiot talk."

"Of course, you weren't to blame that Beamish got drunk at your party. Of course, it wasn't your fault that he made a fool of himself in front of Falkner—who just happens to hate drunks, to hate excess in anything."

"I can't stop a man from drinking."

"Sure. It's simple. You just whisper in his ear, 'Ted, old chum, don't drink too much. You're the top candidate to be Falkner's assistant, but if you get drunk, he'll drop you like a shot.' Why couldn't you say that, George? Why couldn't you?"

"Not my place to say that."

"Couldn't be because with Beamish out of the way, you're in? Couldn't be that, now could it?"

"You're as crazy as your friend Beamish. I'm not responsible for how anyone else lives."

"Sorry, Marguerite. It was a good party—for most of us. You went to a lot of trouble. You couldn't know you were helping old Machiavelli out."

"Have some tea, Dan. And a cookie?" George is enjoying this, she thought.

"Thanks, no. It's probably poisoned. I just wanted you to know, George. Not everyone's so damn happy you got it."

"Sorry about that," George said. His eyes were light; strange that she had never noticed before how light his eyes were. They were reflecting the beam from the Chinese lantern overhead, they were not only light, but almost opaque in the softly filtered light. For a moment she thought of eyeless statues and a chill crept along her spine.

"Did you really do that?" she asked when Dan had left.

"Do what?"

"Get Ted Beamish drunk so he'd lose out."

"I don't like disloyalty, Marguerite."

"I'm not being disloyal, I'm just trying to find out—"

"Either I got the position because I'm the best or I didn't. Loyalty would require that you believe I got it because I'm the best."

"All right. I believe it. You did."

"People at the top are always sniped at. You ought to know that. Haven't there always been girls, plainer girls, fatter girls, who took potshots at you?"

"I guess so. Yes, all right, yes."

"That's what I mean. But if you're high enough, the sniping bounces off. It can't hurt you. Okay?"

"Okay."

Grace felt that way, too. "Hell, Marguerite, why give a shit what anyone thinks? No one likes rich pretty women—no women, anyway. So they bitch and gripe, and you and I keep right on doing things they'd give their souls to do just once." And she'd looked at Marguerite with those big eyes, eyes that now had the look Grace could pull out like a blade from a sheath. It wasn't meant for Marguerite, it was used on other women, and it terrified them. Well, it was easy to be afraid of Grace. She had been, when she'd first met her. If George hadn't said, "I think you interested her," she'd never have had the nerve to push the friendship. But she had pushed. The next time she saw Grace in George's office, she had been able to relax and talk; when George told her he was going to do the Whitmans' house, she had been able to see that as the opening for her that it was. And when Grace called at the house one day to drop off some ideas she had sketched out, Marguerite had asked her in for a drink, and they had chattered and laughed and made a date for dinner, and then, of course, it had all started.

CHAPTER NINE

Imagine, that first afternoon, she had just finished moving the low pine chest into the living room when the doorbell rang. And she had been slow going to the door, thinking it a neighbor coming to call, the cleaner running late—she'd pushed her hair out of her eyes and gone to the door and found Grace Whitman on her doorstep.

"Hi. I'm Grace Whitman, or do you remember, we met at that style show. You were Lorenzo's pet, I think, and the rest of us hated you for it."

Though she had dreamed of just such a thing happening, of Grace or someone like her coming to see her, she couldn't think now what to do, to say, that would take Grace from the doorstep into the living room, that would take the conversation from politenesses murmured to the kind of talk she so wanted to have.

But Grace was perfectly capable of sweeping past her, of going to the door of the living room, of seeing the chest standing in the middle of the room, and of going over to it, circling it like a panther or some other dangerous and beautiful beast, then saying, "What a love of a piece. Where are you going to put it?"

"I'd thought between the windows," Marguerite said, her voice for a moment echoing tinnily in a throat that was suddenly too large for the small sound issuing from it. And then she got hold of herself —this was her house, it was a fine house, though they did owe too much money on it, it was her pine chest, and who was Grace Whitman, anyway?

"Maybe," Grace said, squinting her eyes through the huge round glasses and making a kind of frame with her hands. "You might just be right. Let's try it."

And incredibly they did, Grace helping her lift the chest, helping her set it carefully between the two windows, where it immediately settled in as though made there.

"It really is darling. Where did you buy it, or do you give away your secrets?"

They had in fact bought the chest from a newspaper ad. It was selling for ten dollars, and had layers of chipped paint on it, but they needed more drawer space in the apartment, so they'd bought it, from a doctor's wife, who said she thought it was cherry under all that paint. The blue and green, and even red, layers masked the identity of the piece as effectively as if it were masonite from Montgomery Ward's. They had dissolved the paint with stripping solution and had worked at it with steel wool, and finally had come the time when the wood emerged, not cherry after all, but pine. She had been disappointed at first, until George pointed out the pegs that held the piece together, and removed the carved scrolls that had been nailed to the front as a kind of afterthought. And when they had rubbed it down with wax, it took on the soft golden look that she loved. She had said excitedly that this

112

was their first antique, and that no matter what else she bought later, this piece would always be special.

"It was a private sale," she said now, the words giving rise to a large estate sale with many priceless objects going under the auctioneer's hammer.

"Those can be good," Grace said. "Though I've been to some that were so depressing I could hardly stand it. All the junk and trash of years of living piled out for everyone to see—God! When I die, Jerry can just set a match to the whole thing. I don't want anyone pawing over my leavings."

"The coffee's hot," Marguerite said. "Would you like some?"

"Sweetie, could it be possible for me to have a drink instead? I mean I love coffee in the morning, but it's going on five—a little gin? And a tad of vermouth?"

Thank God for George, who kept the bar well-stocked even if they couldn't afford it. She fixed two drinks, making her own a little weak—she felt an exhilaration that defied alcohol, with Grace there, sitting in her living room, propping her feet up on the huge stuffed ottoman. She didn't need alcohol, she didn't need anything, just a little time, and she would make this visit of Grace's turn into something.

"Well, you do make a decent martini, thank God, so many people don't. Why is that, do you think? It seems simple enough. Well. Why I'm here. I got so involved I almost forgot. But I brought some pictures for George to look at." She dug in the large purse at her side, came up with a manila envelope. "In here. And I hope he doesn't have a fit. I mean I'm not trying to undermine his integrity and all that. Jerry told me George wouldn't want to see my pictures, that George would draw us what he thought we ought to have. And, of course, I agree with that up to a point, but it is our house, isn't it? And we're going to live there. So why would George object to just a few ideas I have — some I got from other people — but some sketches of my own. Well, anyway, sweetie, you give these to George and tell him I hope he likes them."

"I'm sure he will," Marguerite said, and carefully put the envelope on the table next to her chair. "George says he's only happy when the people he's designing for are happy." Which was a close approximation of what George said, which was that he was happy when the boneheads who hired him let him decide what would make them happy, but in the case of the Whitmans, he would have to unbend a little. It was too important that the Whitmans like what he did, how many doors would that open?

And then they talked about other things, about modeling, about children — briefly, because Grace said lightly that children should be seen seldom and heard of never — Marguerite thought she was joking, but then she thought that perhaps she was not, and she prayed that Alan and Sue would not choose this time to come in, bedraggled and cross, to pester her.

"I can't believe that you've lived here as long as you have and I've never run into you before that style show," Grace was saying.

"I don't know. We were busy. George was busy. And I — well, I didn't know anyone when I moved here. I joined the alumnae group of my sorority. But the other members were either a lot older, or fresh out of college."

"Oh, well — that's not a hell of a lot of fun anyway, is it? I mean all they do that I can see is have bazaars and dreary meetings and make sandwiches for the actives during rush. I wouldn't think that would appeal to you. I may be wrong."

Marguerite heard the challenge. In the space of time before she answered Grace she could see the whole day before her. How ordinary a day it had been when she had gotten up and made coffee and fixed French toast and loaded the washing machine and vacuumed the rugs. How ordinary a day it had been when she had seen George off and sent the children to school. Nothing to indicate that today was a day when the world would change. When her world would change. Because it would. She knew that now. Grace was interested in her, miraculously interested in her.

She got up and reached for Grace's empty glass. "You're right," she said. "I was bored stiff." She went to the bar in the corner of the room and fixed two more drinks. She made hers as strong as Grace's this time; she still didn't need the alcohol, she was flying high above where any alcohol could reach—but she wanted the happy vagueness she felt when she was just at the border of being tight. She wanted the rest of the world to be held apart by the small wall of alcohol she would draw around them.

"We'll have to do something about that," Grace said. She swallowed some of her drink, then chewed on the olive. "Come to dinner tomorrow night. I've got some people coming—fun people, people you'll like."

"Sounds great. We'd love to." She remembered then that George had said something about taking the new draftsman and his wife out to dinner—well, they would just postpone that. The draftsman could wait. And so could his wife. Dumpy little thing, the first time she'd seen Marguerite she'd called her "m'am" and earned Marguerite's instant dislike. George wouldn't give her any trouble about changing the plans. When people like the

Whitmans asked you over, you dropped everything else and went. And some day that would work for her in the same way. It would be a prize to be asked to the Tanners' house, a prize that people worked for and hoped for, just as she worked and hoped for an invitation to be with Grace. Or if not Grace, someone just like her. Someone who could call sorority alumnae meetings dull, and who could skip boring mornings baking cookies for a sale, or digging up white elephants for rummage.

"God, look at the time. I've got to meet Jerry at the club. He has some dreary businessman with him, we're going to have an early dinner so Mr. Whosit can go to bed by nine-thirty. Heaven preserve me from these have-to dinners. I keep telling Jerry he better hurry up and make so much damn money that there's no one we have to be nice to. Come about seven-thirty tomorrow—and be casual, all right?"

Long streamers of smoke drifted back along the path of Grace's dash to the door. The sun glimmered through the smoke, making it look like solid bands of gray in the late afternoon dimness of the room. Through the veil of the smoke, Marguerite saw their two glasses, Grace's smeared with vivid red lipstick. She picked up the glass and tentatively put one finger in the middle of the red smear. And then she put the glass down, angrily wiped the red from her finger. What an idiot. Grace Whitman or no Grace Whitman, she wasn't going to lose sight of who she was. She was Marguerite Tanner. That was all she knew, and all she needed to know.

And so she waited until dinner was almost over to tell George, to watch with calm triumph the surprise and then the gratification spread over his face.

"That's my girl," George said. "I knew I could count on

you."

Neither of them asked what for.

She remembered how she had called Lorenzo frantically in the morning, did he know what Grace Whitman meant when she said "casual"?

"Come down here, dear," he said. She could picture him in his office, his ringed hand holding the pale ivory phone to his ear, the cigarette in the ebony holder smoldering in the heavy onyx ashtray on his desk.

She dropped the children at Polly's and drove straight to Lorenzo's. He didn't owe her anything. How could she pay for something new? Maybe a scarf to pick up an old outfit—she could have wept. What good did it do to get invited to Grace Whitman's house if you couldn't have the clothes to go with it?

But Lorenzo calmed her. He fixed her a Bloody Mary, carefully stirring in the vodka, rimming the glass with a bit of lime juice. He sat her down and disappeared into the shop; when he came back, he was carrying cream-colored linen pants and a brilliantly striped shirt.

"What do you think of this, darling, isn't it perfect? I just got it in, no one's even seen it. And it's perfect for you."

"But I can't afford it, Lorenzo. You know I could never buy your clothes."

"Some day you will. I saw in the paper that George got the contract for the new library—that should bring in something."

"Oh, he's getting jobs all right. But the house—and the furniture—and the overhead at his office. Lorenzo, I am so sick and tired of having to think about money all the time. Isn't it ridiculous, really, that a little amount of money like a hundred or so dollars stands between me and that gorgeous outfit? No, I came to get a scarf. I thought maybe a scarf to pick up the green in the navy outfit—you know the one."

Lorenzo was taking the pants off the hanger, holding them out to her.

"Try these on, dear, just try them on." And, of course, they fit perfectly, the long tailored lines fitting close to her long lines, the brilliant colors in the shirt picking up the green in her eyes, making her hair look blacker.

"You should never have had me try this on," she said. "Now I'll never be happy with that navy thing."

Lorenzo took her hand, kissed the palm. "But, dear, you may have it. Yes, don't argue, there's a newspaper campaign coming up. I'm going to need you to model, this is just advance payment."

She felt the tears come to her eyes. Why was Lorenzo so good to her? She had realized long ago that George was right; Lorenzo did like men better, but who was she to criticize him for that? At least it established the safety of her position. George could hardly complain about the long hours they spent together, knowing as he did that Lorenzo had no physical interest in her at all.

"Really, Lorenzo," she said, "you're too much. I'm going to have to stop coming in here if you give me something gorgeous and expensive like this everytime I do."

"You'll earn it, dear. You'll earn it. Now take it off, and I'll put it back on the hanger for you and you can dash home and do something about your nails. I do wish you could have a maid. It's ridiculous for you to be on your knees, scrubbing away like some captured elf."

"I hardly scrub on my knees," she said, and laughed.

"You might as well," he said. "Can't you talk George into getting you a maid?"

118

"Later. He says later."

"Well, for God's sake, wear gloves when you're working. I don't want two red paws sticking out from the sleeve of one of my creations."

He sounded cross, which unaccountably made her happy. There was, after all, one person in the world who saw her as she herself did, who saw her as destined for more than the suburban trap and the slavery of housework. She was buoyant; with the new outfit on, she would be as good-looking as anyone at Grace's party, they could hardly call her country come to town.

And when she walked into Grace's, she knew that she was right, that she was well up to the standard of dress here. She moved forward eagerly, her hand outstretched to meet Jerry Whitman's. Jerry surprised her, he pulled her to him and kissed her cheek, it was a light swift kiss, as light as the fall of a sword on a squire's shoulder making him a knight, but she felt that the mark of the kiss was on her, for everyone to see, and with it still on her cheek, she went to meet the other guests.

"Janet and Tom Baker, Becky and Jack Harris—this is George and Marguerite Tanner. Though you've probably met—the big style show last winter?"

Jerry handed out drinks, then commodored George aside, talking energetically about the shopping center, which had been open now for two months, and about plans for a new medical clinic he and his father wanted to build.

"George is that marvelous architect who did the center for Jerry," Grace said. She was in pants, too—light blue ones with a blue-and-yellow plaid shirt. Grace's outfit cost no more than her own; Marguerite ran her hand lightly over the silken sleeve of her shirt and picked up her drink.

119

"And he's doing our house," Grace went on. "Really, Janet, I think you're an ass to let Hoffman design your house. Every house he designs looks just like every other one—either it's fake Georgian or fake French. Don't you want something original?"

"I happen to like fake French," Janet said, and bit her martini olive in two.

"Oh, you do not. You're just mad because my house is going to be grander than your house. Well, don't blame me if you end up hating what Hoffman builds for you. I warned you." Grace picked up her glass and headed for the bar; the four men were gathered there, and Marguerite heard Grace as she approached them, heard her say, "Have you heard the one about playing highway?" And then her low voice as she told the joke, and the sudden burst of laughter from the men. "Don't tell dirty jokes, Grace," Jerry said. "You'll shock our guests."

"Who will I shock?" Grace stepped back, looked over the people in the room. "You, Jack? Or Becky? Or Tom and Janet? Maybe you think I shocked the Tanners. Well, Marguerite didn't even hear it. So George? Did I shock you?"

"Beautiful women make their own rules," he said.

Grace turned to Jerry, tossed her golden head. "You see, Jerry? I can make my own rules."

"Nice of George to approve," Jerry said, but he said it low, into his drink glass, and Marguerite thought that probably no one else had heard him.

They drank for almost two hours before going in to dinner; when the cook finally appeared and called them in, Marguerite wondered if she could stand up, if she could walk across the room. Then Jerry Whitman was there, offering her an arm; she clung to it, managed to get

120

to the dinner table, to sit at her place.

She couldn't remember later what they'd had to eat, or what they'd talked about. She had concentrated on acting sober, on hiding from the rest that the drinks had gone to her head. No one else seemed affected; even George, who had had at least as many as she had, seemed wrapped in sobriety. But her fear that it would show, that she would make a fool of herself and lose the opportunity this invitation had opened to her, was strong, stronger than the alcohol, so that by the time the meal was over she was feeling clearer. She drank her coffee and got a refill, and by the time they got up to go back to the living room, she was almost herself.

"I can't imagine why you'd want a new house," she said to Grace. "This one is beautiful."

"I'm tired of it. I've decorated it and redecorated it and changed the rugs and the draperies and the damn furniture and now there's nothing left to do. I need something to keep me going. I can play with that new house for a nice long time."

"And then you'll sell it?" She thought with a pang of the house George had built for them. A house like that was forever, she thought, but here Grace changed houses as casually as someone else might change a pair of shoes.

"Probably. Then George can design me another one."

"You're certainly sold on George," Becky said. She was drinking Drambuie, a faint sticky looking film on her mouth. Marguerite could imagine the soft sting of the liqueur as it entered Becky's mouth, feel that little stickiness it left behind it.

"You would be too if you had any taste," Grace said. Then she laughed. "Don't look like that, Marguerite, Becky knows I'm kidding."

"I think you're not," Becky said, but she didn't seem particularly upset about it.

"Early American," Grace said. "Becky likes Early American. They even built their garage to look like an old barn. I ask you!"

They were all looking at Marguerite, Becky and Janet with eyes that were as sharp as tiger's teeth, Grace with a curious kind of challenging look. "George does like to do things that haven't been done before," Marguerite said. "And I've come to like that kind of thing, too. But of course, we can't all live in the same kind of house. That would be monotonous."

"God save me from monotony—and speaking of monotony, did you all hear the latest Ruth story?" Grace turned to Marguerite. "That's Ruth McDaniels. Square with four square corners. Ruth's a Girl Scout leader, of course, what else? Anyway, she was having some kind of do, giving out badges, that kind of thing, and she sent a letter home with the kids saying if they wanted their badges, to bring the money. So some of the kids were getting out of Scouting and didn't want the badges, so Ruth thought nothing of it when the Lofton child didn't bring her money in. Ruth bought the rest of the badges, and the day of the deal was making sandwiches and baking cookies—God, with her money she's never heard of a caterer?—when the phone rings and it's Anna Lofton, saying what's this about a court of honor and her kid's not getting her badges, so Ruth explains, and Anna says, she says, 'My daughter's been in your troop for five years, and have I ever complained?' Hell! I'd have told her to go screw herself. But meek as a lamb, Ruth apologizes and goes down and buys the badges and gives them to the rotten kid."

122

"The meek shall inherit the earth," Janet said, and she laughed.

"Ruth has already damn near inherited the earth, and what has she done with it? That tacky house of hers—she did it herself, Marguerite, sewed the draperies, made the bedspreads—talk about loving hands at home."

Marguerite smoothed down the leg of her cream slacks. Thank God, this wasn't some outfit she'd just run up. And she would tell George, first thing in the morning, that she was not going to make the curtains for the den. They would just have to buy them. They could do it on time, why not? After all, properly made and hung draperies were an investment. She thought of the living-room draperies, of lying on her stomach measuring the material, of working to get the pleats just right. Well, she had had them professionally pressed. And everyone else thought they were lovely. She looked at Grace. Grace was watching the people in the room as though she were waiting to give them their next cue. She felt power there, and for the first time since she'd met Grace, she tried really to think about the future. What did a person like Grace want with her? But then Grace was there, organizing them, pulling them together. "I want everyone to tell their most embarrassing sex experience," she said. "Okay, Janet—"

"That was some evening," George said, driving with one arm casually dropped over her shoulders.

"Yes."

"Well, you're quiet. Didn't you have a good time? Or didn't the great Grace Whitman live up to your expectations?"

"I don't know. That game she had us play—"

"Oh, well, just for laughs. Everyone exaggerated, playing can you top this—you did all right."

Yes, she had done all right. She had told about the pre-med student back in college who had tried to seduce her by taking her up to see his skeleton and showing her drawings of intercourse in a medical book. They had laughed uproariously, and she had seen approval in Grace's eyes. So, why think of Polly, and wonder if she would ever tell Polly that story?

"She's sold on you, anyway," Marguerite said. "She kept raving about you all night."

"Those are our kind of people," George said. "We've got a toe in now—all we have to do is capitalize on what we've got. Okay?" But it was not a question; she knew it wasn't a question. She had noticed that George rarely asked real questions. He always expected her to say yes.

"It'll take a lot of money," she said. She thought of Lorenzo. "I don't even have a maid. People like Grace are free to go anywhere, do anything—"

"We've got the money. You can hire a maid tomorrow."

"How is it we have the money now? Just last week, when Ben Wilkinson asked for a contribution for his friend, that man who's running for judge, you told him we were broke."

"The money's been there for a long time. I was waiting for something to come along that was worth spending it on."

"And keeping up with the Whitmans is worth it."

"Isn't it?"

Again, she knew she was expected to answer yes.

CHAPTER TEN

For the first time in a long time she didn't know what to wear for lunch. They were going to Beechwood, which was elegant, but she was going with Lou Armitage, and he somehow was not elegant. She didn't know why he wasn't; heaven knew his clothes were expensive, and the two times she'd seen him, he was beautifully dressed, beautifully groomed. But not elegant. Perhaps it was his energy, the energy that was never quiet, that stirred the air around him, charging it, creating a tension in the room that she had longed to break. She remembered standing near him on the Bakers' patio; she had felt her hair rise gently off her neck, and when he had touched her arm briefly, pointing out something to her, her skin had felt charged, too.

She picked a yellow linen dress with long straight lines, a designer dress that she had found on sale at Neiman's, though she had learned long ago that Grace's friends did not buy things on sale, or, if they did, did not say so.

The dress was ladylike. She hadn't worn it all spring or summer. It had not suited her mood, but today she would be like the dress, and damn Lou Armitage to hell.

He was driving the Rolls himself; she felt a sudden weakness when she slid onto the soft gray seat. Why do I love rich things so much? It's ridiculous to be impressed by this car, a car is only a way to get somewhere, but still she did love it. She saw that though Lou Armitage might not be elegant himself, he appreciated elegant things. She was glad she had worn the yellow dress; when he smiled at her she smiled back. Phyllis would like Lou Armitage. Marguerite thought then that in a way Lou was very like those men who used to come to the restaurant and spend the afternoons with Phyllis, except of course that he had a great deal of money and they had, unfortunately, had none at all.

She could talk to him easily. She found that she was not flirting, that she was talking almost seriously, and mostly about herself. That bothered her, men like Lou Armitage did not take beautiful women to lunch to listen to a boring life story, but somehow she could not stop, and by the time they reached Beechwood, she felt that Lou knew more about her than even Grace did.

"Which edition is that?" he said. A man was waiting near the portecochere at Beechwood to park the car. He bowed and spoke to Lou, and whisked the car away. They stood for a minute before going inside. The crepe myrtle around the old house was blooming, painting large spots of pink, purple, lavender, and watermelon against the July-glaring white of the house.

"Which edition?"

"Everyone edits their life story for the audience. I just wondered which edition you were giving me."

126

Anger came hard and fast. She was right; men like Lou Armitage did not take beautiful women to lunch to hear a long, boring life story. She thought of Dr. Forrester, next Wednesday she would see him and he would listen to her, even if she had to pay him to listen, he would listen, and for the second time that day she confined Lou Armitage to hell.

But once inside, she forgave him. The doorman, the headwaiter, the busboy who poured their water, the waiter who took their drink order—they fell over Lou, hovered, drew almost a golden magic circle around their table that set them off from the other diners.

"You must come here a lot."

"Pretty often. I own it."

"You own it? But I thought—"

"Some mobster owned it? That what you heard? Maybe I am a mobster. You ever think about that?" Of course he wasn't. Mobsters didn't go to parties at the Bakers'.

"How do you know the Bakers, anyway?"

"Oh, here and there. How do you know them?"

"I don't know. I met them. Through Grace Whitman, I guess. Why wouldn't I know them?"

"Why wouldn't I?"

"No reason." But she still couldn't reconcile this man with the Bakers. Possibly, she couldn't reconcile him with herself.

"You're pretty impressed by all those people, aren't you?"

"Who?"

"The Bakers. The Whitmans. Them."

"I'm not impressed. I like them. They're our friends—"

"Crap. You like them because they're rich. And because they can help you get rich. And get the rest of the stuff you want. Bet you didn't belong to the country club 'til you got in with that crowd."

"You're a very rude man, do you know that?"

"Maybe. Maybe you're just a very fragile girl."

He beckoned to the waiter, ordered another drink. A man came into the dining room, saw them, walked over to their table. He was lean, dark, a small mustache forming a black crease just above his upper lip.

"Didn't know you'd be here today, Lou."

"This is pleasure, not business. You want a drink?"

The man sat down. His suit was not as well-cut as Lou's, not as definitively tailored. But he wore it with the ease that Lou did not have; when he sat down it was with one swift motion that suddenly melded him to the chair.

He smiled at Marguerite, held out his hand, and said, "I'm Johnny Roman."

He said it with much the same inflection that Lou had said, "I'm Lou Armitage." The inflection said that she should have recognized the name; she had not, she wondered how many worlds there were out there that she knew nothing about. With a panicky feeling she wondered how many there were that she should know about.

She was sorry that Johnny had joined them. She waited for the waiter to take his order, resigning herself to a lunch for pleasure turned into business, but he barely finished his drink before he was off, leaning over at the end to whisper something in Lou's ear, something that made Lou frown. And then he smiled at her, a hard, bright smile that at one and the same time looked through her and took her in completely, so that she felt their two faces were impressed on either side of a golden moment in time, and that she would never forget how Johnny Roman looked.

"Does he work for you?" she asked Lou, not really wanting to know.

"Sometimes he does." Lou's voice sounded closed. It made her laugh that a man like Lou, who apparently made his own world, was still like most of the men she knew, he did not want her to ask about his business; he assumed she was too stupid to understand it.

He didn't say anything else. She began eating the turtle soup the waiter had brought her; it was good, but maybe not as good as Galatoire's, and she started to say that, just to have something to say, but then she remembered that Lou owned Beechwood. If she said anything about the food, it should be good.

"This is delicious turtle soup," she said.

"Not as good as Galatoire's," he said. He was eating oysters, a heavy sauce covering them. "Damn chef can't get that flavor."

"I wouldn't like to work for you," she said.

"Why not?"

"You're too—I don't know. I just wouldn't."

"Listen, you know something? When I made you mad?"

"When did you make me mad?"

"Saying what I did about those people. That they impressed you."

"All right."

"That was a kind of compliment."

"It didn't sound like one."

"I wouldn't have said it if I didn't think you were really smarter than that."

"Smarter?"

"Smarter than to think those people—the Whitmans, the Bakers, that whole crowd—amount to anything more than a pile of chicken shit."

"Oh, Lou, for heaven's sake."

"Don't give me that crap. Look, I could buy and sell the whole crowd. Now, how does that impress you?"

She remembered how she looked then, remembered that she was after all a very beautiful woman, easily the most beautiful woman in the place, and that she was sitting with Lou Armitage, who owned the whole splendid building and apparently everyone in it.

"But it's not just money," she said. And then stopped. Lou was watching her over the rim of his wine glass. She had noticed, automatically, that the glasses brought to their table were of a finer crystal than those on the others. The wine itself was one that, as she had blurted to Lou, "I know people who would kill for a bottle of that." It was the private label, of one of the small California vineyards that had been steadily rising to star rank. She knew how few cases were sold each year. Some years, none were sold at all. When she tasted the wine, blushing over that comment, that impressed school-girl reaction, Lou had smiled, had said, "Well, is it worth killing for?"

"Yes," she said.

"Then there's no problem keeping you supplied," he'd said, and flicked a hand, and another golden bottle had appeared. She'd noticed that it wasn't just his hand that called a waiter over, a busboy to fill water goblets, clear ashtrays. It was his eyes. Eyes that belonged in one of those pictures that seemed to follow you no matter where you went in the room. Now the eyes were watching her, what had she said, something about it not being just money?

"It's not, you know," she said.

"What is it, then?"

She looked at his eyes then, really looked. And saw an

intensity, a gathering, a configuration, of many eyes, all of them male, that she had been looking into for a long, long time. Only where in each of those other eyes, there had been something missing, some small space where fear, where doubt, where hurt, could still come in, in Lou's eyes there was a wholeness that kept all of that out. And, if any of it had ever been there, had long since thrust it out, locked the door, and tossed away the key.

"Power," she said.

Lou laughed then, a laugh that made heads, not quite turn, but move, move restlessly as a herd of horses do when a sudden sweep of a coming chill wind first hits them. "Power," he repeated. "What the hell do you know about power?"

"I know people who have it. Jerry Whitman—"

"Whitman." The way Lou said the name wiped it out. "I've seen Whitman so scared he'd 've wet his pants if he hadn't been pissless already."

"Jerry?"

"So what, you think Whitman doesn't owe money? You think he doesn't depend on deals and cocksucking and all that shit?"

"But, Lou, everybody, I mean—"

"Everybody deals and sucks and lies and trades off everything they've got including their great-aunt Bessie. Maybe everybody you know. That's why you don't know one goddamn thing about power."

She was suddenly fascinated. This place, Beechwood, was a set. It had been created the night before, for just this scene, for just these two people. It was like the place that lay behind the overgrown and long-hidden wall in the fairy tale: if you could just find the place in all the brambles where the gate was, if you could just get through, if you just had the key—

"So what is power, Lou? What is it?"

He looked at his watch, and beckoned the waiter for dessert. "Power is never pissing when you don't want to. Power is also being in charge of your own crap."

"You say awfully vulgar things." She heard the prissiness in her voice, and the lie. George and Jerry and all the rest of the crowd talked the same way, using the same words. Wives who objected were told to have girl talk in the kitchen.

"You ever read that dirty Greek, that Aristophanes?"

"Some."

"A classic. So don't talk to me about vulgar." He looked at the dessert cart that stood now at his elbow. "So what do skinny sexy ladies eat for dessert?" he said.

"Strawberries with Devonshire," she said, and felt like a kitten that had just found a home.

Later, when she got home, she couldn't remember what they had talked about, not because she had drunk too much—Lou had said once, sharply, that he didn't like women who drank too much—but because the conversation after the first limping beginning had then settled into a smoothness that was like a walk in the country. She remembered only pleasant vistas and a feeling that something good had blown into her life.

For the first time in a long time, she'd walked through a room and known that nearly every man in it was undressing her with his eyes, and fucking her in his mind, and it hadn't made her feel dirty. Because when they'd reached the car, Lou had leaned over and taken her hand and looked at her and said, "Don't let somebody else's fantasies fuck your life, baby."

God, how she wished she'd heard that before! Wished

she'd heard it from George. And riding home, the smooth road, the smooth car, the smooth stream of air, the smooth stream of Mozart from the tape deck, riding home through all this smoothness she thought of the rough places other people's fantasies had made. When they were first married, and that awful thing had happened at the place where she worked. Funny, she hadn't thought about that in years.

She had almost given up on finding a job when she answered the ad for a typist-receptionist at Dawson Concrete. George hadn't been worried; or, if he were, he didn't show it.

"You'll find something," he said, and went on filling out his schedule for the fall semester.

But the limitations were stringent—at least, they appeared to be. She could type, but didn't know shorthand. And her typing, a skill acquired in high school, was hardly professional.

"You'll get a job on your looks," he said, and slapped her lightly on the buttocks.

"I can always clerk in a dimestore," she said, and waited for his reaction.

"The hell you say. It's one thing to work at a respectable job you can tell people about. It's quite another to take a job any illiterate can perform."

And then, just when she was ready to tell him to go to hell, that she would clerk in a dimestore or a department store, or any other damn place that would hire her, she saw the Dawson ad and went to see Pete Dawson and was hired.

Surprisingly, she liked it. The only other woman in the office was Gertrude Hannock; she was Pete's secretary and kept the books, and she accepted Marguerite the first

133

day with no more fuss than if she'd know her for years.

"This is a good place to work," Gertrude said, cutting her sweet roll in half and offering it to Marguerite. "Pete's a decent guy, the drivers are a nice bunch—you don't have to worry about any funny stuff."

It turned out that by funny stuff Gertrude meant passes. She was full of tales of other places she had worked where it was worth your life—or your virtue—to be caught alone in the office after five with one of the men. Marguerite thought that must have been years ago. Gertrude was now in her fifties, a happy size 20, with gray hair that kept springing up to cowlicks no matter how much she brushed it down.

So when the drivers came in and hung over the desk and looked at her breasts and made joking comments, she blushed and thought they didn't mean anything. Hadn't Gertrude said they were nice guys? One in particular, Al Martin, hung around the office a lot; he got into the habit of bringing her things, a bag of doughnuts, a small box of candy, and one day, a bunch of chrysanthemums he said he'd picked in his yard.

But even then she thought nothing of it; when the drivers stood near her desk and told what she knew must be dirty jokes in low voices that suddenly raised in raucous laughter, she kept her eyes on her work and tried not to pay attention.

Al found her alone one day; it was the lunch hour and both Pete and Gertrude were out. She brought her lunch, it was cheaper that way, and she rather liked being alone in the quiet, eating her sandwich, drinking milk from a Thermos, and then slowly enjoying a cigarette, with a cup of coffee from the office pot to blend with it.

"I got problems, doll," he said. He poured coffee into a

big green mug, stirred in sugar and milk. "You got time to listen to a buddy's problems?"

"Sure, Al," she said. She felt a small warmth that Al so easily accepted her, turned to her instead of to one of his fellow drivers.

"It's Harriet, see?" She knew Harriet was Al's wife, she had been down to the office a couple of times, a tiny blonde with large brown eyes and a somewhat shrill voice who was given to wearing clothes with tucks and lace and ruffles.

"Harriet decided I've been playing around with a girl on the bowling team—of course I wasn't, I never even looked at the dame, I mean she's a dog, right? who's going to look at her? But Harriet got this through her head, and she's put me on short rations. I guess you might say she's put me on no rations. So what I was wondering was, how about meeting me after work? We'll go to a bar I know, have a few drinks—who knows? We might really hit it off."

He was leaning over her desk, the heavy left fist clutching the coffee mug, the right hand resting next to her typewriter. She could smell his breath, it smelled of onion, and she could visualize Harriet making a meat loaf sandwich and slicing onion carefully onto it.

She knew that she had just been propositioned—curious word, no more meaning to it really than to seduced. Both words that strained out the terror and the sudden rush of fear, the realization that she was after all alone in the office with Al and that he was much, much bigger than she was.

"We're going out this evening," she said, and her voice seemed to stagger around the words so that the words came out bent, and out of shape. "My husband and I, we're going out with friends. So I can't."

135

Al put down his coffee mug, moved around the desk. "Okay, doll. Some other time, okay? But give me something to look forward to." His hands were on her before she could move, she felt the weight of them on her breasts as he lifted her from her chair; he pulled her to him, and she could smell the onion again and knew that she was going to be sick.

"I'm going to be sick," she said, and she jammed her hand over her mouth, twisting to get away from him. She felt the rush of undigested food in her throat. Something must have gotten through to Al, he let go of her and stepped back. She got to the bathroom, hung over the toilet. She thought Al was watching her through the open door. That was somehow worse than having him touch her had been.

When she came out, he was sitting near the desk, smoking. "I've never made anyone sick before, sister. What's the matter, don't your husband feel you up?"

She opened her purse, found a pack of Lifesavers, put one in her mouth.

"I want you to go," she said.

"Not until I hear what you're going to do."

"I'm not going to do anything."

"Not tell Pete?"

"Would he care?" She thought of the jokes they told, of the way they teased her. Pete wouldn't care, why should he?

"I don't know if he'd care or not. Just don't try him, okay?"

"Okay."

She leaned forward, put her head on her folded arms, listened to him leave. When she heard the door open again, she tensed, half-expecting Al to come back. But it was Gertrude, her arms loaded with packages, her leg reaching out to kick the door shut behind her.

"Hi, kid, taking a little nap?" She put down her packages, went into the bathroom. "Who's been sick in here?" she called out. "I can smell it."

"I was," Marguerite said. She'd cleaned up, but she knew the smell of sickness was still there, closed into the tiny room like the memory of yesterday's bad news.

"Well, it's not morning—officially, it's afternoon. But who said it was always morning sickness, anyway. You got anything to tell me?" Gertrude was smiling down at her. Marguerite knew that she wouldn't say anything about Al. Gertrude would believe it, and that would make it worse.

"Oh, Gertrude, for heaven's sake. I'm not pregnant. I just—ate my lunch too fast."

"Okay. No point in not telling though. That's one secret that's bound to come out—and out." Gertrude laughed and went on to her own desk. The routine of the afternoon set in; when four o'clock came, and the drivers came in to fill out their reports, she had almost forgotten about Al, and she looked up at him with the same smile she'd always had.

"Hey, you guys," Al said. "Anyone know what a cockteaser is? I mean a real, first-class, honest-to-God cockteaser. Anyone know?"

"Can it, Al, there's ladies here," Joe Turner said.

"Oh, you mean Gertrude. Gertrude don't mind a little education, do you, Gertrude? I'll bet Gertrude never was a cockteaser. You never made any promises you didn't keep."

He was swaggering over to the desk area now, his hands placed on his hips. Marguerite could see the anger, and the hate, in his eyes. She got up and went to the water cooler, poured water into a paper cup, lifted it to her mouth.

"Now you cut out that kind of talk, Al," Gertrude said. "It's ugly, and I won't have ugly talk in my office."

"But you'll work right along side a little whore, won't you? You'll have coffee with her and bring her dessert when you go to lunch and not mind at all, am I right?"

Marguerite knew that she was shaking. She could see the cup shaking in her fingers, could feel the vibrations that seemed to match the angry rhythms of Al's voice chasing down her spine and into her legs.

She heard Gertrude get up, heard the door into Pete's office open and close. In the sudden silence, she imagined that she heard the breathing of the men massed behind Al. She felt that if she turned, that collective breath, hot, angry, would shrivel the clothes from her and she would stand naked and defenseless before them.

"What the hell's going on here?" It was Pete, thank God, it was Pete. "Al, keep a damn civil tongue in your head, all right? I won't have these girls harassed, do you have that straight? Now sit down and make out your report."

He slammed back into his office; with the slam of the door Marguerite felt life slam back into her, she could move again, and she went back to her desk.

But after the drivers had left, after the office was quiet again, Pete came to the door and asked her to come into his office.

"Look, Marguerite, I don't know what started that ruckus with Al, and I don't want to know. But I don't want you flirting with these drivers or acting sweet and putting ideas in their heads, okay? You're a sexy dame, and I guess you know it. But try to forget it during business hours, see what I mean?"

Telling George about it later, she was still angry. "George, can you believe he would say that to me? That he would actually imply that it was my fault that horrible Al Martin humiliated me that way?" The tears that somehow had not come that afternoon came now; she put her head against George's shoulder and gave herself up to them.

"Well, it's what you should expect," George said. He didn't sound angry, he sounded—not amused, perhaps amused wasn't the word—did he sound proud?

She lifted her head. "You sound like you're glad it happened."

"Oh, baby, don't be silly. I'm sorry you got your feelings hurt. If it'll make you feel any better, I'll go see Pete Dawson and tell him he was 'way off base. But you've got to admit, Marguerite, the average Joe that looks at you is going to think about you. Of how he'd like to take your clothes off. And put you in his bed. And be inside you."

She felt then that George was not her husband, that he was just another man, like Al Martin or Joe Turner, or even Pete Dawson, yes, even Pete Dawson—and when she felt his fingers at the back of her neck, reaching for the zipper for her dress, she was overcome with shame.

"I can't," she said. "I can't let you do that."

But, of course, he did do it, did undress her, did carry her to the bed, did get inside her. And all the while, she wondered how cockteasers got away with it, how they could make men hot for them, and then laugh and not give it away after all.

A lot of people's fantasies had maybe fucked up her life. Not just George's. Those frilly blouses, lacy slips of Phyllis'. The wide eager eyes. The wide eager mouth.

CHAPTER ELEVEN

She checked the messages when she got home, though she didn't really care if there were any there or not. But one caught at her. "Mrs. Wilkinson called. Please call her." Polly Wilkinson—God, she hadn't talked to or seen Polly Wilkinson for months. The Wilkinsons hadn't come to their last big party—she remembered a little note from Polly, a formal little note, a mention of a previous engagement. She hadn't believed it then, and she wondered what on earth Polly wanted with her now.

She called Polly, and at the sound of the still-familiar voice said in a rush of remembered feeling, "Polly, it's so nice to hear from you! It's so stupid that it's been so long!"

And Polly, after a little pause, agreed that it was, and then in a quick, serious voice said she'd been put in charge of a style show for the auxiliary to the local mental health association and that she knew nothing about putting on style shows, but that she had read in the paper where Marguerite had put one on for some group just last month, so could she please pick Marguerite's brain, if that wasn't asking too much?

Could they meet for lunch? Marguerite said, because it suddenly seemed truly stupid that she never saw Polly any more, and then there was a confusion over when they were both free, but they finally settled on the next Tuesday at the country club, though Polly didn't like that, she was the one asking the favor, she should take Marguerite for lunch, and when it was too late to change, Marguerite saw her point and wanted to. Then she wanted to keep Polly on the phone, she asked about the children, and would have asked about Ben, but Polly was in a hurry, she said she would see Marguerite Tuesday, and rang off.

Marguerite stood there in the empty hall—strange, no matter how many rugs or expensive prints or decorator pieces you strew around a hall, it was still just an empty room—and thought about Polly Wilkinson, and she thought that maybe she would tell Dr. Forrester about Polly when she went to see him again, because once she and Polly had been close, and now they weren't, and she knew Polly had not changed.

She had met Polly the first awful week in Southport. It was July, it was hot, the apartment they'd rented had a window unit in the bedroom, and they could either keep the door closed and have a comfortably chilled bedroom or they could leave the door open and use a system of fans to waft the cold air to the kitchen and living room, and have the whole apartment then be a little below stifling.

She was happy when they moved to Southport, happier than she had thought she could be. Mrs. Tanner had lost the war, and she and George had married, but she had not lost a battle since, and the idea of leaving Texas, of moving

142

to a place that was far enough away for Mrs. Tanner to have to think before she came was pure heaven. Except that Marguerite was pregnant, and that the third day after they settled in the apartment she began to spot, and when she called the obstetrician the man in Austin had recommended, he's said to go to bed for a few days, to keep checking with him, just to be still and not worry.

George was worried, though, he came home that night to find her in bed and after fixing her soup and fruit and milk suddenly left the apartment. She heard him come back in some fifteen minutes later; he appeared in the bedroom door, a red-haired girl with him.

"This is Polly Wilkinson," he said. "She lives across the hall and she's going to check on you for me." And Marguerite had been embarrassed, for heaven's sake, what had George done, just barged over there and knocked on the door and captured Polly, and Polly had laughed and said just about, but after that she was in and out of the apartment a dozen times a day.

The luckiest thing was the way she and Polly got along. Polly's husband was a reporter for the afternoon paper, and Polly knew all kinds of funny things that happened down at city hall or at the jail or the courthouse that never got into the paper, but that Ben brought home for Polly to enjoy, too.

Polly had finished in English, she read all the time, and she brought books to Marguerite, not really asking Marguerite what she'd like to read, and not going on about any one book, but bringing what she called a smorgasbord, only occasionally saying, "This is really fine," so that Marguerite would read it. And then for the first time in her life she found that it was fun to talk about a book, that discussing books with Polly was nothing like

143

discussing "literature" had been back in high school, and finally thinking, with a kind of hopeful pride, that perhaps she did have a mind, after all.

"You can always finish here," Polly said, when Marguerite said she was sorry she'd only had one year at the university—she had said it with the kind of feeling she imagined Catholics must feel in the confessional, it was somehow a blot on the soul to be only twenty and to be married almost a year and not to have a college diploma.

The day Marguerite finally lost the baby, George had been out of town and Polly had driven her to the hospital, waiting until Dr. Harrison got there, putting a stack of magazines and a tin of peppermints on her bedside table. She had had a D and C the next morning—even though they put her to sleep, she dreamed of being emptied, of knives violating her. When she woke up, the first thing she thought of was that she was somehow enlarged, and that George, when he entered her, would be swallowed up by the vast emptiness inside her.

She remembered how kind Polly had been to her after the miscarriage. If she mentioned that to Polly next Tuesday, if she said, "I still remember how wonderful you always were to me," would Polly like her again, would the fear she felt in Polly's presence go away?

George was cross when he got home, a client had turned down the sketches that had taken him almost three weeks to prepare. "Well, but you didn't really do it. Wasn't it that young man, what's his name, he does the drafting?"

That made George furious. What did she think, that he'd let some kid, barely out of school, just finished in June, draw up the house for a client like Bill Stern? Hell, no, every drawing he put his name on was his, always had been. Didn't she remember the row he'd had at the firm where he'd worked before, he'd designed a house, a beautiful, fantastic house and Hoffman had expected to sign it?

She had forgotten that. She hadn't forgotten how she'd felt when George came home, stumbled home, really, still angry and already beginning to be scared, to tell her he'd been fired.

"George, you couldn't be!" she'd said. She was frying chicken, and she was eight months pregnant. The chicken was for a celebration supper with Ben and Polly Wilkinson because just yesterday they'd both found houses to rent, houses not three blocks away from each other in a quiet old section near the college. The houses were large and old and cheap; the cheap rent was the way the owner, a delicate widow whose husband had once been Dean of the Law School, had of helping university professors, who usually lived in the twenty-some-odd houses she owned. But the editor of the paper was a good friend of hers. He liked Ben and had spoken to Ben about the houses, and Ben had told George, and the four of them, the two girls pregnant, had gone to see Mrs. Atkins, and she had liked them—she must have, because she said she guessed you didn't have to be a teacher to need a cheap place to live, and had rented them the houses.

George had just begun to tell her what had happened when the doorbell rang and the Wilkinsons came in carrying a bottle of wine.

"You may as well hear this, too," George said, fixing gin and tonics for the four of them.

He had been working on the house for over a month, it was the largest job he'd had to work on since he'd taken the job with Hoffman. And he had been excited, because

145

his time of draftsmanship was almost up, and he was sure that if he did well on this house, Hoffman would give him a raise and more responsibility, all of which was just another step to the partnership Hoffman had promised when George had gone to work.

"That's why I took the job with Hoffman to begin with," George said, forgetting or not caring that the Wilkinsons had heard that part before. "Hell, I was damn near the top of my class, there were other places I could have gone. But this setup was so perfect. Hoffman the main architect in the firm, with just Sam Hammer as an assistant. And a respectable record of getting jobs. Good connections, all that. And idiot that I was, I believed him. 'Just come with me and I'll make you a partner in no time,' he said. 'I've made a lot of money and I'm getting an itchy foot. Mrs. Hoffman's been after me to ease up, get someone to take over. I don't mind telling you that Sam Hammer's not the man. He's good at design—but he's got no push. Can't get the work. I don't think you'd have that trouble.' So of course I listened to him. Of course, I went with him."

"Anyone would have, George," Polly said. She was almost as pregnant as Marguerite. Her glass rested on the shelf of her stomach, and her hand reached out to pat George's wrist.

"Maybe. But today. I was telling you about today. I'd finished the final drawings. And let me tell you, that house is something." For a moment, the anger faded. "He's really proud of that house," Marguerite thought. "He always has to be so proud of everything. Everything." And she reached around to rub her back that never stopped aching now—he would have to get his job back, he would have to, because if he stayed fired, what would they live on, her with a baby coming, and the lease on the new house signed? But she could hear the pride in his voice, and it was the same way he had sounded when he'd stood his mother down and told her, no, he would not go to work in Waco for Dorothy Hyland's father, that there were places he could make his own way, thank you, and the sooner she realized that, the better. Marguerite remembered that she had stood beside George while he talked to his mother. Their hands were clasped and she felt that she was an extension of George's power, that whatever he said to do with their lives, they would do.

"So I took the drawings in to Hoffman, really to ask if I should just call the client and go out and take them to him, and Hoffman looked at them, and then he said, 'Why is your name on these?' And I thought he was joking, my God, I'd been a month on them, he hadn't given me any other work, he'd wanted those done right and he'd wanted them done fast, and I said, 'Well, they're mine, aren't they?' and he looked at me. Ben, you've never met the S.O.B., you can't imagine how he looked, but he looked at me and he said, 'Everything that goes out of this office has my name on it. You know that.' I didn't know that. I had thought it was funny when an office building I saw going up had Hoffman's name as the architect, because I'd thought Sam had done it, but I didn't really give it any thought."

"But that's not honest!" Polly said.

"Well, I know it's not honest, and you know it's not honest, but I just lost my job for telling Hoffman that, because as far as he's concerned, it's perfectly all right."

"Did you really lost your job, George? He won't be sorry tomorrow and call you back?" Dim, a memory, her mother crying, a voice—was it Cissy's?—saying, "You've got to go back home."

"I wouldn't work for the bastard now for anything," George said.

"And you're absolutely right," Ben said. "The man obviously has no principles."

"That's it, Ben, that's it. I could work for Hoffman forever and no one would ever know how good I am. No one would ever see my name on a building design."

"George, do you really think Mr. Hoffman would keep on using you? Maybe it was just this once, maybe—" The baby kicked, hard. She thought of the fee scale posted on the obstetrician's wall, thought of the hospital room, the baby food, the pediatrician. A terrible feeling of being enclosed came over her; in that moment she hated George, because he was not keeping her safe, he was letting the world beat at her. How could he do that, how could he not protect her?

"Of course he'll keep using me. I talked to Sam. Well, he talked to me. I was clearing out my desk, making a hell of a lot of noise about it, when he came in. Asked if I wanted some coffee. Well, I didn't want any coffee. And I didn't want to talk to anyone. But he said it was important, something he should have told me a long time ago. So we went to the coffee shop and he told me I was about the fifth one in a parade of men through that office. Same offer to each one. And each one lasts a while before he quits. Only one who never quit is Sam Hammer."

"Sam Hammer? But that's ridiculous, George. He doesn't have any talent. Mr. Hoffman would never have offered him a partnership."

"I'm just telling you what the man said. Sam's got talent. All he lacks is push. Like Hoffman said. What he wants is impossible. He wants somebody who's good, with enough push to help him get work, and not enough to want to take over the whole thing. Crap. The hell with him. Marguerite, didn't you promise to feed us?"

They opened the wine anyway because, Ben said, they shouldn't let a bastard like Hoffman spoil their evening. And when they were drinking coffee he began talking about a Biff Roberts who was building subdivisions as fast as the plants brought in people to live in them, and that maybe George could get on with him.

"Doing what? That kind of builder doesn't want an architect. Just screw him up and cost him money."

"He's opening a big subdivision south of town in a few months, George. Editor of the business section was telling me about it today. Speculative houses, yes, but he does want an architect to design them."

"There's a catch somewhere," George said.

"Well, maybe there is. But it wouldn't hurt to talk to him. Being a reporter is my way of getting to where I want to go. This Hoffman thing might send you down a detour for a while. That's not to say you'll have lost the main road forever."

"You're damn right," George had said, and he sounded as he had the day he had asked her to undress for him, as though he were looking at the options ahead, and settling definitively on one. And then George had drunk his coffee and had put the cup down and shaken Ben's hand and said Ben was right, he needed a job, and if Biff Roberts would just build an honest house, there wasn't anything wrong in designing them.

But after the Wilkinsons had gone, and she and George had gotten into bed, and she had settled into the one position she could still sleep in, she thought of their arrival in Southport, of how the Hoffmans had had them to dinner as soon as she was over the miscarriage, of how carefully she had dressed, and how excited she had been, because she believed every word of George's future, and these people were the key.

They had gone first to the Hoffman house for drinks. It was a huge house, modeled after a plantation home that stood some thirty miles out from the town. Hoffman had taken her all over it, throwing open closets and opening pantries and bathroom doors, holding her by the elbow to steer her from room to enormous room.

"You'll have a house like this some day," he'd said. "You're married to a hell of a smart boy, and I promise you, I promise you I'm going to make a heap of money for that boy. You'll like that, won't you? All women like money. I've never seen a woman like money as much as my wife does. Lucky for me, I just keep raking it in. And so will George."

She had believed that. When she stood in the vast living room that would have held their entire apartment, she believed it. And when she finally sat down next to Mrs. Hoffman, after the tour, and accepted a drink, she talked as though she believed it. She was no longer scared, she knew that she and George had been picked by the Hoffmans as successors to all this, that in some way they had been touched with whatever magic the Hoffmans had that made all this money for them, and she felt safe.

She remembered that they had gone to the country club for dinner, and the Hoffmans had introduced them to several people there, and she had lapped it up, had lapped up being served by the red-jacketed waiters, had lapped up Mr. Hoffman asking her what wine she liked, had felt a surge of gratitude toward George for providing all this that had resulted in tumultous lovemaking when they got home, lovemaking during which for the first time she

150

sucked George, her loosened hair falling over his spread legs as his hard penis entered her mouth.

And now all that was gone, he would not be working for Mr. Hoffman, member of the country club and owner of a rich house and a rich wife, but for Biff Roberts, who did his own TV commercials, and was large and very sincere and who had always made her want to throw up. She didn't trust very sincere men, she didn't know why she didn't. But she had always felt far safer with men everyone else said were sneaky, because then she never let her guard down. With the sincere ones, there was a much greater chance of being taken off base and therefore destroyed. She didn't worry about whether George was sincere or not, that didn't seem to enter into it; they were married, they loved each other, and as long as they gave each other what they wanted, that was all that mattered.

The next day George had gone to see Biff Roberts with a large portfolio under his arm, and he'd come back with the job. The pay, surprisingly, was better than Hoffman's was, and George said that Roberts seemed to be a decent enough fellow. Marguerite didn't ask him about anything else. They had driven through a Biff Roberts subdivision when they were looking for a house, thinking perhaps to find one for rent, and there was nothing about any of the houses that made her think an architect had had anything to do with them.

She was embarrassed when there was a full-page ad in the next Sunday's paper, announcing George's association with the Roberts firm. George and Roberts were both quoted; George said something long and rather rambling to the effect that a home designed by an architect satisfied the aesthetic side of man as well as making him infinitely more comfortable, and Roberts followed with something saying that he didn't know anything about these aesthetics, that's why he had hired George Tanner, but that when the new subdivision was up, people in Southport would be struck once again with what a fine thing Biff Roberts always did for househunters.

"That's right," she said now to George. "No one can ever question your integrity. You were willing to lose your job with a pregnant wife and nothing to look forward to."

"I had myself to look forward to, baby. And it worked, didn't it? I had another job the next day."

"That's right."

"And that job worked out a hell of a lot better than anything I'd ever have done with Hoffman. Did I tell you I saw Sam Hammer at lunch the other day?"

"Is he still with Hoffman?"

"Where else would he be? He said the biggest kick he's gotten out of anything in years was when I beat Hoffman out of the Whitman shopping center."

"That was the beginning, wasn't it?" She waited for him to come to her and tell her, as he used to, that the beginning was when he met her. He didn't say things like that much anymore. She remembered that she had never demanded any kind of sincerity from George, that perhaps instead of that he had a kind of honesty that made a morality out of saying or not saying whatever he damned well pleased. It used to frighten her when they were first meeting important people, that George didn't kowtow to them, or soften his opinions, but charged ahead and said what he thought, and the devil take them if they minded. It had been years before she realized that those hard opinions of George's were eased into his listeners' minds with the film of dropped names, dropped places,

152

smoothing their ridges.

"What time are we leaving?" George asked, emptying his pockets and stripping off his shirt.

"Whenever you're ready. I packed for both of us."

"I'll just shower," he said. He was in his dressing room. She could hear him but not see him, and then he said, "Come here a minute, will you?" and she went in and saw him standing, his penis large and protruding, and he took her shoulders and pushed her gently, and she knelt and took it in her mouth and sucked and played her tongue along it until he came, and as she went to her own dressing room, her tongue gagging in her throat, to spit and brush her teeth and then use glass after glass of mouthwash, she wondered why in hell George had gotten to like that so much, that and other things that he said were all right as long as they both agreed. But did he ever ask her if she agreed, tell her that, did he?

"Who's going to be there?" he asked. She hadn't said a word since they'd left the house. They were going to the Whitmans' camp at the lake for the weekend, and she was trying to relax to prepare for that. Besides, she still felt his penis in her mouth, she felt that if she tried to talk, it would get in the way of her tongue, so she kept still.

Now she swallowed and said, "The Larkins, the Spencers, and Todd McDaniels."

"Just Todd? Where's Ruth?"

"Grace didn't say."

"Well, that's a blessing. Ruth isn't exactly the life of the party. Todd's wasting a lot of time."

"He is?"

"Sure. What do you think he gets from Ruth? Under the covers with the lights out." He looked at her. "She'd never do to him the things you do."

153

Maybe she's smarter than I am, Marguerite thought, but she felt herself smile and heard herself say, well, Ruth's mother couldn't have been much like Phyllis, catch Phyllis letting a daughter grow up a prude.

"Something else I have to thank Phyllis for," George said, and rubbed his hand along her thigh.

"Besides the house," she said. "House, wife, Phyllis did pretty well by you, didn't she, George?"

"She's been paid back," he said, and his voice was cold again, cold as it was most of the time if you got past that smile to hear it.

"Yes, I suppose she has."

"With interest."

"That's right, George, you always pay for what you get, don't you? Only I've always wondered how you knew Phyllis had that money."

"I didn't. Look, if you're going to be a bitch—"

"I'm not," she said, and turned to look at the pines rushing past the window.

The glass between her and the world was like the glass that had been between her and the world when they'd been living in Southport a while.

They had showed the house plans to her mother on one of her trips. Phyllis came infrequently, her suitcases still spilling out the frothy silks and flimsy chiffons that she always took to Houston. "I keep forgetting I'm a visiting grandma," she said, tying an apron over a ruffled dress.

"You should come more often," Marguerite said. "The children have to get used to you all over again every time."

"I will," Phyllis would say. But of course she never did. She still went to Houston at Christmas—she only had two days off, no time to come to Southport. But Marguerite knew that Phyllis would have gone to Houston anyway, to be with Cissy at the glittering party Cissy gave every Christmas Eve, to live, if only for two days, the brighter life that had somehow escaped her.

"I hope this place has more life to it than it seems to," Phyllis said after they'd gone to lunch and been by Lorenzo's.

"We're still getting into it, Mom. You know, meeting people, finding a group—with two little children, I can't exactly be a social butterfly."

"Fun. Everyone needs to have fun. I just hope you have enough of it." And then a long, piercing look. "Do you? Do you have fun?"

"Of course, I do," Marguerite said, and thought of the last dinner party they'd gone to, when the hosts' children had suddenly gotten sick, and the hostess had spent the evening running back and forth from the kitchen to the nursery. Well, it wasn't always like that. But she smoothed a hand over one of Phyllis' sheer nightgowns and wished briefly for a new beginning.

"I like these plans," Phyllis said, blowing a stream of cigarette smoke over them so that they were veiled and somehow out-of-reach. "What's it going to cost you to build a place like this?"

"Too much," George said. "More than I can afford, anyway."

He was watching Phyllis as he said this. Looking at her almost as though she were one of his sketches, those experiments, those ideas born from that busy, always busy brain.

Phyllis' eyes were still on the plans. Marguerite couldn't see her eyes, but she didn't have to. The house, already built, was in those eyes.

"How much?" It was Phyllis' voice and yet it wasn't

Phyllis' voice. It was maybe the third time in her life Marguerite had heard that voice. Just before she visited the Watsons'. Just before the summer she'd stayed in Austin to marry George. What was the prize this time?

"Ten thousand'd about cover it. I could handle the payments."

Phyllis leaned back and blew three perfect smoke rings in a row. Marguerite remembered the first time she'd seen her mother do that; she'd thought her mother was magic. "I can let you have that."

Wildly, Marguerite thought of two-bit and fifty-cent tips. Even after all those years, how much would that be? "*You* can?"

"Dad's insurance. With Mom dead, it came to me. It's sitting right there in the Grand View Federal Bank—ten thousand, free and clear."

"But it's all you've got—"

"Marguerite, it's not as though we won't pay her back." George's voice cut in. The sketch was fine, he was going to keep it.

"George, did you know Mom had that money?" she asked him when Phyllis had gone to her room.

"How could I have known? Did you know?"

"You know I didn't. I would have told you—" Or maybe I wouldn't, maybe I'd have been afraid that something like this would happen. Because George doesn't seem to see much difference between his and mine, mother's money and his need. It's as though the whole world is arranged for him, for him to use and take pleasure in. And maybe it is, maybe I'm the one who's wrong not to see things that way.

But as the house started going up, she forgot everything but her excitement that all the things they'd planned were

156

actually becoming real. She drove out to the lot every day, taking a lunch for herself and the children, making it a game for them.

"Not much to see yet," the foreman told her when the framing was just going up.

"I can see it all in my mind," she said. "And I still can't believe I'm going to have it. It's all I want in the whole world." She believed when she said that that she was speaking the truth.

They took Biff Roberts out to see the house when it was nearly finished.

"This the kind of house you want to design for my subdivisions, right?"

"This is for me to live in, Biff. Those houses of yours— well, they're not for me."

"I can see they're not. All this glass—it's interesting. I guess this is what you call an interesting house."

"I think it's beautiful," Marguerite said. "Of course, we can't begin to furnish it the way it should be. And I hate to think of the way it's going to look, us having to put in the stuff we've been using on Stephen Street." She sighed. "If I could just furnish the downstairs—the part people will see. If I could just do that, I'd die happy."

"Well, George, when a man builds a house, he's got more responsibility. I don't want you so worried over money that you can't do a good job for me. We'll talk about a raise tomorrow." Biff spoke to George, but he was looking at Marguerite.

"Oh, Biff, that's wonderful," she cried. She went to him swiftly and kissed his cheek. "George always has said you're the nicest person in the world to work for."

"I'm not just being nice. I'm trying to protect my investment. Even if this house isn't what I like, I know

157

enough about houses to know that George is one hell of an architect if he designed this. And that I better try to hang on to him, because everyone in Southport's going to be after him."

"Maybe you should look for another place," Marguerite said when they had dropped Biff off and were having a drink before dinner.

"I'm staying right where I am," George said.

"Oh, George, you heard what Biff said. You could work in a real firm, where you'd get to do things you like, not those stupid houses you do for Biff."

"I'm staying right where I am," George said again. "Until I'm ready to open up on my own."

"On your own? But, George—"

"Do you know how much prettier you are with your mouth closed?" he said. He reached for her drink, took it from her and put it on the coffee table. As he began kissing her, she automatically lifted her feet to the sofa and stretched out. She knew he wouldn't wait until they'd gone up to bed. He didn't understand how tense it made her, to make love in the comparative openness of the living room. Someone might come to the front door. Or one of the children, now happily ensconced in front of Walt Disney, might tire of the program and come in. She could feel the muscles inside tensing and she tried to relax; George hated it when she did that, when he had to almost force his way in. And it hurt, she tried to tell him that, but he said it couldn't, that she was just making an excuse. One-two-three, she counted slowly. Breathe deeply. Relax. Four-five-six. Another breath. And then she felt the sharp thrust and he was in, moving in her, reaching down for her hips, pulling them up toward him, getting her to move, too. So by the time it was over, and she was

158

dressed again, and in the kitchen frying chicken, she forgot what it was they had been talking about, and only remembered much later, when they were in bed and George was already asleep, that he had said he wanted to go out on his own. And that she had been frightened.

When they moved into the house, a card from Biff with a hundred-dollar gift certificate to one of the finer stores in town arrived. "I know enough to know I don't know how to pick out something you'd like," the note said. "Hope it doesn't offend you to get this instead of a present."

She went to the shop and bought a pair of crystal vases to put on the mantle in the living room—they were Swedish crystal, cut in the same kind of long lean lines as the house itself. George saw them in place and kissed her. She did, he said, have excellent taste.

CHAPTER TWELVE

And now her excellent taste and his excellent taste and the excellent taste of all the cocks that had been sucked to get them where they were had gotten them to this weekend at the Whitmans' camp. So why did she want to cry? Why did she want the camp without the party, the still blue lake and the dark black trees and the clean white sand, and no litter, no litter ever, ever again.

"I love it out here," she said to George, as the car left the main highway and turned onto the asphalt road leading to the lake.

"We always have a good time."

"That's not what I meant. I mean I love these woods. Sometimes I think I'd like to come out here with a tent or something, maybe not even that, maybe just a sleeping bag, and stay for a while. You know?"

The smile hit before the voice. Why was she always so goddamn dumb? Even though her ears tried to close, as her vagina tried to close, George got in. "Without your mirrors and your clothes and your maid—oh, sure."

"I'm sorry you think I'm so silly."

"Not silly. Civilized. Likes comforts."

"They're not the same."

"What?"

"Having comforts doesn't make you civilized."

"God, Marguerite, don't turn sociologist on me. What the hell are you reading now?"

"Roman orgies were comfortable—I wouldn't call them civilized."

"Hell of a lot of fun."

"Damn it, George, that's not what I mean! I mean, what lasted was the books, and the law, and, all right, the architecture. You still use those columns, don't you see—" She was excited, really excited, something was happening, she could feel some sort of flow, a flow she hadn't even been aware of. She turned to George, and stopped.

"It walks, it talks, it fucks—and now it thinks," George said.

Bastard, bad, you're a bastard, bastards are bad. "God, you can be a bastard," she said, and when they reached the Whitmans' camp a few minutes later, she jumped out of the car and ran ahead, leaving George to bring in the suitcases.

"You took long enough to come down," Grace said. She was standing in front of the large fireplace. She was wearing low-slung pants that hung below her navel, a brief halter that tied just beneath her large breasts.

"Some people still have to work for a living," George said.

"Forget it, sweetie. Have a drink. We were just trying to

162

decide whether to swim now or after supper."

"Depends on what you've got an appetite for," George said, going to the bar and fixing two drinks.

"How about it, Marguerite? What do you feel like doing?"

Going off by myself and having a good cry, she thought. But she went to George and took the drink and thought of the swim, of their naked bodies plunging into the pool, of sitting on the towels afterward, consciously not covering themselves, of the final walk up to the house, of how much more naked they all looked in the sudden clothed feeling of the furniture, and then of how silly, yes silly, they were, when, dressed, they settled down for cards and drinking.

"I don't care," she said, and walked to one of the french doors that looked out toward the lake.

In the morning, they would rise late and go down to the pier and perhaps even swim off it. She thought that she might slip down to the lake tonight when everyone else was asleep; she liked to swim at night, and the dark water would comfort her, it would make her forget how stupid and awkward she felt, walking to the pool with her breasts softly bouncing, the eyes of the men on her. She had been drunk the first time she'd spent a weekend at the Whitman camp; when Grace had said, "Let's go swimming," and everyone had started shedding clothes, she had shed hers, too, not even feeling naked, not feeling anything, really, but the liquor which clothed her. And the next morning, when she had remembered what she had done, it had been too late, it was accepted that she would go along with it. When she tried to talk to George about it, he had said, "Don't be a prude now. You had a good time, don't you remember?"

Todd McDaniels came and stood next to her. "I'm glad

you're here, Marguerite."

She hadn't seen Todd since that afternoon in his office. It embarrassed her to talk to him, and she wondered why Grace had asked him. She couldn't imagine Todd at their kind of weekend; maybe Grace was playing some kind of wicked joke, though that seemed dangerous rather than anything else.

"It's nice to see you, too, Todd."

"I'm going over to my place later. Got a lot of work to do. Thought I'd get it done in peace."

"I thought you were here for the weekend."

"I'm not quite in that league yet," he said. He knows, then, she thought. "Look, would you come for a walk?"

"A walk?"

"I'd like to talk to you."

She felt a laugh beginning inside. He probably wanted another time with her. She needn't have worried about Todd McDaniels. He was no different from any of the other men. That quiet act he put on, the solemn, gentlemanly manners—they were a front for the same kind of quick lust she'd found in so many other places. After all, that afternoon in his office, she'd hardly raped him. She thought of George. What a laugh he'd get out of that, her and Todd McDaniels.

"Sure," she said. "I'd like a walk."

They pushed out of the french doors, went down the broad wooden steps, turned off the path that led down toward the lake and onto one that twisted into the heavy woods.

"Where does this go?"

"Actually, it goes to my place. It's a couple of miles by the road, but not far this way."

"Are we going there?"

164

"It doesn't matter."

She waited for him to say something else. She hoped they would go to Todd's camp, she didn't feel like lying down in the woods, she was afraid of snakes, and as the night came on, she could hear the sound of mosquitoes in the trees.

"I want to thank you, Marguerite," Todd said.

"For what?"

"For what you did that afternoon. You know."

"Todd, you shouldn't even bring that up. That was terrible, I don't know what came over me, well, I'd had two martinis for lunch. I should never have—"

"It wasn't terrible. It was wonderful. You've no idea. You were so open, so generous. It made me think."

"Todd, look, that was just—"

"I'm not asking you for anything. I know that was an accident; I could tell that. After all, I'm not exactly your type. But it made me think about Ruth and me. You know Ruth, Marguerite."

"Ruth is a very nice person." Who hates me thoroughly.

"Yes, she is. Oh, she is. But, Marguerite, she's not like you. About sex, I mean. I know things go on at these weekends up here. Actually, Grace did ask me to stay for the weekend. I think she did it out of meanness. I know you like Grace a lot, Marguerite, but she can be very mean. She knew I wouldn't fit in up here."

"Nothing goes on up here that you wouldn't fit into, Todd. Now you're being ridiculous."

"Okay. But listen. I got to thinking, about Ruth and me. And then I remembered that clinic, over in Newellton. You know the one."

"That sex clinic?"

"Well, I don't think that's what they call it. But, yes,

that's what it is. And I thought, if Ruth and I went — well, wouldn't it change everything?"

"Todd, are you crazy?"

"Why?"

"Do you know what goes on there? I mean, what you have to do?"

"It would be worth it. I love Ruth, and I know she loves me, but we've never had a good time in bed. Not even on our honeymoon. Maybe especially not on our honeymoon."

"Todd, Ruth would never do it, not in a million years."

"Yes, she would. I asked her, and she said she would."

"She did!"

"Oh, she was upset at first. And I have to say she was hurt. I guess no woman likes to be told she hasn't given her husband much pleasure."

"I guess not."

"But I explained it to her. I told her I could have gone off and gotten a mistress. But I want it to be with her. Because I love her. You can understand that, can't you, Marguerite?"

"Sure." He's got to shut up, she thought. I don't want to hear one bit more of this.

"I told her we'd never do what the rest of the crowd does. It's all right, I'm not condemning you, but I know that would be too much for Ruth."

"For God's sake, Todd, all we do is a little skinny-dipping. I mean, hell, what's so awful about that?"

They had been pushing along the path; she saw a house ahead of them. A light burned inside and a car was parked in the turnaround in front of the camp.

"That's Ruth's car," Todd said. "What's it doing here?"

"Wasn't she joining you?"

166

"No, she was going to her mother's for the weekend. She does that a lot, she's a very devoted daughter—I don't understand."

"Maybe she decided to surprise you." I don't really care where Ruth is. I'm tired of Ruth and Todd and their dreary little problem. I hate thinking that every time I see Ruth from now on I'm going to know she's been to that clinic and had someone watch her and Todd make love, taking notes the whole damn time. God!

They had reached the front door; it was locked. Todd fumbled a key from his pocket, unlocked the door and opened it.

"Ruth? Ruth, are you here?"

And how is Todd going to explain having me along, we just happened to be walking in the woods, and we just happened to arrive at the camp, which we thought would be empty. Oh, boy, Ruth would love that.

She stood just inside the front door, leaning against the jamb. Todd moved ahead of her, switching on more lights. The camp looked like Ruth, it was neat and feminine. Pictures of the McDaniels children were on one wall; the three were smiling, eyes squinted against the sun. Marguerite remembered a dinner party at the McDaniels', the oldest daughter had helped serve, her entrances and exits smothering the conversation, while Ruth beamed and Todd poured wine, looking proud.

"The McDaniels are a very family couple," Grace had told her later. "But we all grew up together; you don't just drop people. And you don't have to go very often."

As it happened, they had never gone again. Marguerite had invited them back, dutifully, and Ruth had refused. She hadn't even made up an excuse, she had simply refused. And in that moment Marguerite hated her, too.

167

"We're not good enough for them," she had stormed to George. "Little snip. Just because her damn grandfather ran for governor or some such thing."

"That has nothing to do with it, and you know it. You threaten Ruth. She doesn't understand a woman like you."

But she'll have to, now, Marguerite thought. Oh, yes, she'll have to understand a woman like me now. Because that's what Todd wants, and oh, wouldn't it be fun, just wouldn't it, to be the fly on the wall at that place, and watch her? That's a bad thing to think. Now stop that. You're getting to be a tramp; you're thinking like a tramp. You should feel sorry for Ruth; that's going to be hard on her. Todd's an idiot.

She heard a noise from one of the rooms off the living room—it sounded like a scream that had begun deep within the walls of a body and then had not found its way out. It frightened her, and she called for Todd. Then the sound came again, but this time it was louder, and she heard footsteps and saw Todd come stumbling into view. He leaned against a chair and stared at her. A last fall of sunlight came through the dark pines and fell on his face. His face was terrible in that light, and she didn't know whether his face or the sound he made was the worst, and she moved forward, going to him.

"Todd, what is it? My God, where's Ruth?"

But he couldn't stop making that sound. It was turning to sobs now, explosive sobs that she knew must hurt his throat. She walked past him into the hall that led to the bedrooms. There was a light in one. She went into that and saw Ruth, her neck caught in a noose, her body hanging from a rope looped over one of the open beams under the roof.

She felt vomit rising in her throat and she lurched to the

bathroom that opened into the room and stood over the toilet, heaving and feeling the filth inside her come up. I wish I could faint, and have someone find me and pick me up and take me back to town and put me to bed, and then I could read about this in the papers, or maybe I wouldn't even read about it, because it's none of my business. I have nothing to do with this.

She heard a sound behind her and turned to see Todd standing just inside the door of the bathroom, watching her.

"Are you all right?" he said, and his voice did not sound as though it had been making those terrible noises.

"It was the shock. Todd, what—"

"There's some mouthwash in that cabinet. You must want to wash your mouth out."

He's gone crazy, she thought. He and Ruth both must have been crazy. He might have killed her himself. Who knows that it was suicide, these quiet people? Aren't they always the ones? And then got me over here to be some kind of witness.

"I did it, you know," he said. He was still watching her; she had turned to the cabinet and found the mouthwash and was using it. When he said that she lifted her head from the basin and looked at him. Her cheeks were puffed out with the mouthwash, her skin burned with it, and she thought, yes, he is crazy, I'll never get out of here alive.

"That's ridiculous, Todd," she said, spitting out the last of the mouthwash. "You've been with me."

"I don't mean it that way. I mean I'm responsible. Did you read the note?" He handed her a piece of paper. It was pale blue with Ruth's monogram across the top in darker blue.

"I'm sure Ruth wouldn't want anyone else to read that,

169

Todd."

"I want you to read it. I want someone else to know."

"Todd, let's forget about the note. Look, you go sit down. I'll fix you a drink. And I'll call the Whitmans. Todd, you're in shock. You're not thinking."

"Read the note, Marguerite. There's time to call the Whitmans. There's time for everything. Read the note."

She looked down. For a moment she couldn't read it; Ruth's handwriting was small and cramped, she felt a headache starting and her eyes ached; she wondered if she were going to throw up again.

"*Dear Todd,*

I have always thought we had a good marriage. We have three lovely children, and I've tried to be a good wife to you, just as you have tried to be a good husband to me. Now I know we don't have a good marriage, that it doesn't matter to you at all what kind of person I really am, because if it mattered, you would never have asked me to do what you have asked me to do. I know I'm not attractive like some of the other women. Men don't try to talk to me at parties, and when I take the children to the club to swim, nobody tries to look at me, but I thought you didn't mind. I mean, Todd, I guess I've read a few articles in the ladies' magazines about sex, so I won't say I didn't know we didn't have what everyone seems to be so worried about all the time. But I LOVED you, Todd, I would have done almost anything for you. I have to say almost because I won't go to that clinic. But I can't go on living with you if I don't go, because I'll always know how disappointed you are. I don't feel like a woman anymore, Todd, I don't know how I feel, but I don't feel like a woman. I thought about just leaving you, letting you get a divorce so you could marry one of those cute girls men seem to like to marry the second time, but I can't do that. I wouldn't know what to do, Todd. I went from living in my father's house to living in your house, I don't even know how to type. I don't want to work. I just

want to live with you and the children and grow my
flowers and do all the things I used to think pleased you,
only they don't anymore, so I'm leaving, but just in a
different way. I love you.

Ruth."

"Todd, she was out of her mind. You have to believe
that, she was out of her mind."

"I think what she says makes very good sense."

"It doesn't, Todd, it doesn't at all."

"This is all my fault, I don't know why you won't let me
accept the responsibility for it. All my life, I've always
accepted the responsibility for anything I've done."

"But, Todd, good God, you can't go around saying that."

"I won't. I won't dishonor Ruth's memory that way. But
I had already told you. You knew what I'd asked her to do.
And I thought it might do you some good to read that
note."

"Good?"

"To see what a real woman is like. I'm trying not to be
too hard on you, Marguerite. For that day in the office. I
know I met you half-way. All right, more than half-way.
And I enjoyed it. I won't deny that. But that's what started
all this. I won't forget that."

He's like every damn man I've ever met, she thought
drearily. It always turns out to be my fault.

"I'm sure you won't," she said. She pushed past him and
walked through the bedroom, keeping her eyes turned
from the figure swaying there. She found the phone and
dialed the Whitman camp. Grace answered. She was
laughing and there were voices in the background, they
sounded loud and close to the phone. Marguerite had to
shout, and God, the words were awful enough without
being that loud, there was an obscenity about the
loudness, it made the words go booming out into the

171

quiet night outside, hanging on the trees in long ugly shapes.

Marguerite was sitting on the low blue couch when they came, the Whitmans and George, eyes horrified, voices low. "Where's Todd, for God's sake?" Jerry asked. His light-green slacks had a sharp crease, the Christian Dior knit shirt above them was ivory, with a small band of the same green. He looked ready for golf, or a game of gin in the locker room, and Marguerite thought that, of course, none of them had packed the right clothes for death.

"With her. In there." She pointed toward the bedroom.

"Has he—cut her down yet?" George asked.

"I don't know. George, I need a drink. Fix me a drink."

"Sure, baby, sure." He went toward a small bar in the far corner of the room. She heard a door open, the sound of glass on glass. Ice falling into the liquid. A soft squirt of water. Then the paper-wrapped coldness in her hand, and the shock of the bourbon in her mouth, her throat. Her throat. Ruth's throat was bruised, bruised and marred by the heavy rope she must have gotten from the boathouse. She heard Jerry and George leave, heard the bedroom door shut, felt Grace come sit beside her.

"Jesus, what in God's name came over her? I mean, Ruth. People like Ruth don't hang themselves."

"She did."

"Okay. I'm not saying she didn't. But Ruth. What could have been bugging her? The last time I was up at the school, just before it was out, to see the principal about some damn scrape Jere had gotten into, I saw one of her kid's pictures on the wall. Student of the Month, some damn thing. Those kids were always doing stuff like that."

"That doesn't mean much."

"Well, it means *something*. I mean, it means she wasn't worried about her *kids*. And Todd—who in the hell would worry about Todd? Good old Todd, I saw him at Lorenzo's last week. Ruth's birthday was the next day. God, he was buying out the store. Picking it all out himself. Most of it was god-awful. Todd's got terrible taste, but it was kind of sweet, you know what I mean? Jerry just calls some damn clerk and tells her to choose something and wrap it up. He says I always take back the stuff he picks out. Which I do. Still."

Grace crushed out her cigarette, went to the bar, fixed a drink. "I really feel bad. God, this is terrible."

"I didn't think you liked Ruth that much, Grace. I'm sorry." She was beginning to shake now, the faint tremble in her muscles coursing down through her fingers to the glass she held; when she touched it to her mouth, she missed and hit her teeth with a small clicking sound.

"I didn't. Well, it wasn't that. Not much in common. You know. Still, she was a nice person. One time I said I'd be the girls' Brownie leader. I don't know why I said something dumb like that. I'm no good with kids, not my own, certainly not anybody else's. Well, the time came to get going, and I just couldn't. Mother wanted me to go to Europe with her, and I needed to redo the house—hell, I just didn't want to do it. I was moaning about it at a coffee one morning and Ruth heard me and said she'd do it. Just like that. Some bitch said later Ruth did it because she didn't think I was a good influence on the kids. I don't know. She did it, right?"

"Why are they taking so long?" Marguerite asked.

"I'm just not thinking about it. Jesus. Was it awful, Marguerite?"

"Yes. I threw up."

"What were you all doing over here, anyway?" Grace was looking at her now, her large glasses pushed back on top of her fluffed-out blonde hair.

"We weren't really coming here. We were just walking. When we got out of the woods, we could see the light. And Ruth's car."

"Damn bad thing to have happen."

"Yes."

George came into the room. His face had changed. He looked frightened and half-sick, and she thought of his strength on the tennis court, the long muscled legs carrying him through set after set, and she wondered where all that strength had gone.

"Did anyone call the police? Or a doctor?"

He was looking at Marguerite. She finished her drink and rose to make another one, and shook her head at him. "I didn't."

She could hear him at the phone; the strength was coming back now. She knew that he was standing easily on those long muscled legs, and that the strength in them was rising upward, going finally into his voice, so that the people at the other end of the line would know that he was in charge, that this was all being handled the right way.

"We can go now, can't we?" she said when he turned from the phone.

"Go? Of course not. You're a witness. You'll have to talk to the police."

"George, I can't."

"Don't be an ass. All you have to do is tell them what you told Grace on the phone. That's all."

"That's all?"

"Well, hell, what else could you tell them? You don't

174

know anything else, do you?"

"No. No, how could I?"

"Okay. So calm down." Now he was fixing some drinks. He drank from one glass and put the other two on a tray and went back to the bedroom.

"I imagine the chicken's burned up by now," Grace said.

"What?"

"Jerry had just put the chicken on the fire when you called. Guess it's burned up. Unless Joe Larkin got his head out of the bottle long enough to go watch them."

"I don't want to eat."

And then the police came, and the doctor, both coming from the small town not far from the lake where they usually went to get extra cigarettes and more beer and fresh vegetables. Only now the name of the town on the police car spelled death, and Marguerite sat and watched the uniformed men come in, terrified that they would know what she knew, and would get it out of her.

But they talked to Todd first, who came out of the bedroom when the police came, and sat in a large lounge chair that didn't really look well in that room, but that Marguerite knew Ruth had put there because it was comfortable for Todd and what did looks matter?

She saw Todd showing them the note, saw them reading it; she wondered if they would ask Todd what she was talking about, but if they did, she couldn't tell it from the way either they or Todd looked. Then they came to her, and it wasn't bad. She said she and Todd had just gone to stretch their legs a little before supper, it was only by chance they'd taken that path, and then they'd seen the light, and the car, and they had come in— She stopped then and had trouble going on, but she told them about

175

finding Ruth, and said she'd gone to call for help, and that she had been sitting right there ever since.

"You know Mrs. McDaniels well, m'am?"

"Oh, no, not well at all. Just at parties. We weren't friends, nothing like that."

"So you'd have no idea why she'd do a thing like this?"

"No." He'll see the lie in my eyes, I won't look at him. But then won't that make him suspicious, one way or the other, he'll know I'm lying.

"You saw the note, officer." That was Todd; his voice sounded hollow now. Perhaps those noises he had made when he'd first found Ruth had been like shovels or spades, digging a grave in his throat so that the sounds rolled around in its emptiness and came out sounding like that.

And finally it was over, and the ambulance came and took her away. Todd and Jerry followed it in Ruth's car, and Marguerite and George and Grace walked back to the Whitman camp, where the others were waiting, frightened out of their early-evening boozing and offering great mugs of hot black coffee.

They had all left the camp within half an hour; Grace poured water over the blackened chickens on the grill and slammed the lid down.

"I'll send Tim out tomorrow to clean this mess up," she said, and Marguerite thought, yes, tomorrow there'll be no mess, it will be in the papers, but I've talked to the police. I'm not going to have to talk to them again, tomorrow I can start cleaning this mess up.

"Some weekend," George said as they drove back down the road to the main highway.

"I'll never get to sleep."

"Take a pill. I've got some if you're out."

176

"I don't think a pill will help. I'm all right as long as my eyes are open and I can see other things. But everytime I shut my eyes I see her hanging there. Oh, George, it was awful!"

"Okay. I saw her. It was awful. But you're not helping matters going all to pieces. She's nothing to you, anyway."

"Maybe she should have been."

"What?"

"Nothing."

She scrambled eggs and fried ham when they got home, and opened a jar of the blackberry preserves Phyllis had sent. "I still can't see Mother making preserves," she said.

"Face it. Your mom's getting old. Can't be flirting around in that café forever."

"She doesn't flirt around in that café."

"'Course she does. Well, hell, what difference does it make? She's not going to get in any trouble."

"I won't have you talk about my mother that way, George."

"You've said it yourself. Teased her, I've heard you, about how she gets all dolled up and goes down and hands out the smiles and the sweet talk."

"I do no such thing." And then she began to cry, her head down on the maple table that she'd found in an antique show and paid someone the earth to refinish because she'd ruin her hands if she did it herself as she used to, and while she cried the thick sweet smell of the blackberry preserves on her plate filled her senses and she thought of Phyllis and Ruth and that it wasn't fair—none of it was fair.

The funeral was on Monday. They went to the funeral home first, and that was the worst, the very worst. Marguerite had tried to talk George out of going there.

Why couldn't they just go to the church service, but he said, hell, there wasn't a book to sign at the church, and they'd never see Todd there. How would Todd know they'd even gone if they didn't go to the funeral home?

She had a black linen suit and she'd put that on first, but it looked ostentatious, as though she had a right to mourn Ruth McDaniels, so she changed it for a navy silk that she'd ordered from Neiman's and then hadn't liked and had forgotten to send back, and she thought that perhaps it was right after all that she not look her best, going to Ruth McDaniels' funeral.

Everyone they knew, practically, was at the funeral home. Grace detached herself from a group and came over and said, "God, did you ever see so many flowers? The Henderson wedding is tonight, and they've run out of flowers and are having to send to Tarlton for more."

"How is Todd?"

"Holding up. His brother flew down from Wisconsin, and, of course, he's got a sister—you know Maureen Hamilton?—living here. She took the kids right away. I took some food over there this morning, and she's got them pretty well settled down."

Marguerite felt the door shutting in her face again. She kept forgetting, perhaps she needed to forget it, that Grace had been born here and lived all of her life here. Of course, she would know that Todd had a brother in Wisconsin, she'd probably met the damn plane, and the sister, no, she didn't know Maureen Hamilton, she wouldn't know her if she fell over her.

"That's good," she said, and took George's arm to walk to the front and speak to Todd.

He did look all right. He shook George's hand and took hers briefly, and then he introduced his children, who

178

were spotlessly clean and pressed and whose red-rimmed eyes were the only disordered thing about them.

"When Alan and Sue get back from camp, we'll have to have your children over," she said.

"Fine," Todd said, but he was looking past her, looking, Marguerite was sure, at the coffin, and she thought that in that moment, Todd was making a private vow to Ruth never to have anything to do with any of the Tanners again.

"Let's go grab some lunch," George said to the Whitmans as they began walking from the gravesite back to their cars.

"We're going on out to Todd's," Grace said. "I promised I'd help get food out. You know."

"We can still go somewhere," George said to Marguerite as he backed the car off the grass onto the gravel cemetery road.

"This isn't a party, George."

"Hell, I didn't say it was a party. We need to eat, don't we? Okay, we'll go home. Lora Mae can fix me a sandwich. I'm just trying to be nice. You've been in such a foul mood all weekend, I thought a nice lunch might cheer you up. Isn't that one of your favorite things, to go to lunch?"

"I have not been in a foul mood."

"Okay. You haven't. And what about last night, what about last night, you weren't in a foul mood then? God, one look at your face and I shriveled."

"I just didn't feel like it."

"You just didn't feel like it. Why not?"

"It didn't seem—right."

"Right?"

"With everything that had happened."

"You mean Ruth?"

"Maybe."

"Good God. If there was one thing I thought when I married a girl from East Texas, it was that she would have good sense. Not go on in some goddamn mysterious way. What in the hell does Ruth McDaniels being dead have to do with you and me?"

"We were there, George. We were there."

"Yeah, and I was there when my best buddy in high school was killed in a car wreck. In fact, if you want to know the truth, it was my car, that's right, my car, and I should have been driving, but I was too drunk to do it, and the kid that took the wheel didn't know shit about driving, and he ran us off the road and Harry got thrown out and slammed his head up against a telephone post, and let me tell you, that was it. But I never went around after that carrying on the way you are, like the whole damn thing had been my fault. Jesus!"

"I'm not carrying on like it's my fault. Don't say that, George, I'm not."

"Okay. But cheer up, will you, I don't ask a hell of a lot, but I damn sure like a cheerful face to look at."

He followed her upstairs after lunch, and she knew he would take her to bed. She stripped off her clothes and got under the sheet and waited for him, and when she could feel him come she moved faster and clasped her legs harder around him and let the sounds come out of her throat, because of course he liked a cheerful woman. All men did, hadn't Phyllis always told her that?

She had been about nine, that was right, because that was the summer she had the flu, and out-of-season flu that the doctor thought might be polio, and the whole house had been quiet and frightened, with even her grandfather forgetting to quote the Bible to her, but coming in to take

180

his turn at fanning her to keep her from being so terribly hot. He would sit in the low chair next to her bed, with the direct draft of the electric fan across her, and to that he would add the breeze of a large cardboard fan that said "Hammill's Funeral Home" on the back, and a picture of a basket of lilies on the front, and she noticed that he kept the side with the words turned away from her, so for that reason she thought she was going to die. But she didn't die, she finally got better, and began eating the food her grandmother cooked.

"Decent food, for a change," said her grandmother, who had frowned and fussed each time Marguerite had asked for another Coke, but had given her one anyway, because the doctor said she needed lots of liquids.

"Anytime you want a Coke, you just come down to the café and ask for one," Phyllis said, sitting by the bed in a loose pink robe and blowing cigarette smoke into the draft of the fan.

"Don't you be tempting that child to walk in this heat down to that café, Phyllis. No such thing. She needs rest and quiet. This child's been sick, even if it weren't polio. Anyway, that café's not a fit place for a child."

"For the love of Pete, Ma. What does that say about me?"

"You know what it says about you. I saw you, sitting there laughing and talking with a bunch of men last week, when your child was lying here, burning up with fever."

"I was sitting there, laughing and talking as you say, because that's part of my *job,* Ma. That's part of my job. You think those men want to be waited on by some old sourpuss? They like a cheerful woman. All men like a cheerful woman. Hey, Marguerite, honey, you remember that now, you hear? All men like a cheerful woman."

181

"That's the first thing I didn't like about Nancy Roberts," she said, as she watched George dress. "She wasn't cheerful."

"Nancy *Roberts?* What the hell made you think of her? She was crazy, anyway."

"It would have helped if you'd told me that, at the very beginning."

"For God's sake, Marguerite, will you ever give up on that?"

Only when I stop paying for it, she thought. Because no matter how many times she ran the reel, her lines were never any better.

She met Biff Roberts and his wife Nancy when Alan was three weeks old. They came to see her in the house on Stephen Street, carrying a huge box that contained a cashmere carriage robe.

"It's lovely, it really is," she said, and tried to forget her stitches, which still hurt, and made her twist in her chair. Her breasts ached, too, it would soon be time to nurse Alan—they shouldn't have come, why would perfect strangers come see her when her baby was just three weeks old?—she heard George offering coffee and the Roberts accepting. She excused herself to nurse the baby and sat tensely in the rocking chair upstairs, hearing Biff's great booming voice careening off the walls of the stairwell. It still hurt to nurse, the doctor had said that would wear off, but it hadn't. She wondered if there were anyway to satisfy men's appetites that didn't hurt.

And then when Alan was older, and she had gotten her figure back, the Roberts had had them to dinner. She hadn't wanted to go.

"Just because you work for someone doesn't mean you have to socialize with them," she said.

"Come off it, Marguerite. This man is paying me more than Hoffman did, giving me total responsibility for design. If he asks us to dinner, we say, 'Thank you very much,' and we go."

"I don't know what to wear."

"Christ. You saw Nancy. Wear something like she'd wear."

But that was the whole point. She didn't want to wear something that Nancy Roberts would wear. She didn't want to eat with the Roberts, to be identified with them and their tacky subdivisions and their careful manners. George had never looked back, once he'd left Hoffman. And she—she was having a hard time looking forward.

The dinner was heavy, with too much food. Nancy looked tired, she'd probably spent the whole day cooking all that—as Marguerite tried to swallow the candied yams and the lima-bean casserole, she felt a heaviness that was like the heaviness of the food. This, then, was to be their fate.

Not to be with people like the Hoffmans, who served delicate French food with chilled white wines, or took you to the country club where you sat in private splendor, but to be associated with the Roberts, who lived in a big tacky house that had big tacky furniture, and to force heavy meals down a reluctant throat while Nancy Roberts sat wilting at her end of the table, and Biff, gesturing with his fork, held forth at his end. Marguerite stopped trying to talk, she played with her food and occasionally looked at Biff to see that he was still talking, and then finally they were finished and could get up, could leave the chocolate cake to crumble under its thick layer of frosting, could leave the weak coffee to cool in the cups, could look at a watch and think, "Half an hour, half an hour for politeness,

183

and then we'll go."

Biff took them out to the patio, it was nice out, he said, they could sit and enjoy the night air. George sat down in a chair near the pool, he looked perfectly comfortable and at ease. He smiled at Biff's jokes and offered some of his own, he included Nancy in what he said. He was acting, Marguerite thought, in a servile and humble manner that made her sick. She got up abruptly and asked Nancy about a bathroom, then headed for the house. She took her time, freshening her makeup and watching herself in the mirror; what a waste, she thought, the silk dress, the long flowing hair, the bright young face—all wasted on dinner at the Roberts?

George was standing in the hall when she came out of the bathroom. She almost walked into him and felt the shock go down her spine.

"Are you ready to go?" she asked.

"Not until you've mended your manners," he said, and he took her roughly by the arm. "You're acting like a bitch."

"I am not, I'm trying very hard. Is it my fault Nancy and I don't have anything in common?"

"You have a hell of a lot in common, the way I see it. For starters, your husbands work together. How's that for having something in common?"

"You know what I mean."

"I know what you mean. Now, let's see how well you understand what I mean. Biff is really touchy about Nancy—God knows why, I can't figure it out, she seems ordinary enough to me—but as far as he's concerned, she hung the moon. And so when little Miss Bitch here gets on her high horse, Biff notices it. And guess who he can take it out on."

184

He'll bruise my arm, she thought. Thank heaven I have long sleeves. What could I say to explain that bruise?

"Okay, okay. You've made your point."

"Now you get out there and make up to that woman, do you hear? Just make up to her."

He pushed her down the hall, turned and went into the bathroom. She could picture the thin yellow stream coming from his limp penis, God, if it would only stay limp. She was tired of listening to George, she was tired of fucking with George—maybe she was just tired of George.

When she got back to the patio, she tried to concentrate on what Nancy Roberts was saying, but there was no getting around it. Nancy might be nice, but she was a bore, she knew nothing outside of her kitchen and her home. The greatest challenge of her life, it seemed, was deciding to teach a class in Bible study at her church, she went on about this at some length. And Marguerite thought hollowly of all the times ahead when she would listen to this woman, and nod her head, and make assenting noises, and grow thick in the middle, like Nancy, and gray at the temples, like Nancy, and never, never know what was going on in the wonderful big world outside.

After that, they saw a lot of the Roberts. They went out on the Roberts' boat, they ate dinner together, they even spent one wretched weekend together, going to the Roberts' camp, Biff and George going off to fish, leaving her to endure Nancy. She came to hate the sight of Biff's signature on the checks she took to the bank; he was paying for both of them, she thought, and she, at least, wanted a raise.

She had finally found out why Biff was so touchy about Nancy, found out too late for the knowledge to do anything but load guilt on her. Nancy had been in a mental hospital for two years; when George went to work, she had only been out two months and hadn't yet picked up the threads of her old life. Biff had seen in Marguerite a chance for Nancy with someone new, someone who didn't know her, someone whose approval would be real.

"But you should have told me," she raged at George. "God, how did I know she'd been sick? All this time—"

"Biff thought it better if you didn't know. He didn't want you playacting, he wanted you and Nancy to have a real relationship."

"But, my God, George, you knew I couldn't have a real relationship with her. There's nothing there. I mean, she's a hole, just an empty space, she talks and nothing comes out. Oh, hell, George, all the times I was rude, all the times I was bored—Christ!"

This, after Nancy had gone under again, had sunk gently beneath the surface of whatever it was that had kept her going for a while, had sunk and been sent back to the hospital.

"What you did or didn't do made no difference," George said. "You didn't push Nancy over the edge."

"But I might have been the last straw. Don't you ever think that, when you're about to do something? That it might be the last straw for someone?"

"Everybody's got a life to live. I'm responsible for myself—that's all."

"And for me and Alan."

George didn't say anything then, he just looked at her, and then he smiled slowly and came over to her and held her and whispered against her forehead, "In a way, I am. In a way."

Certain panic rose in her, fought against the closure of

his hands on her back. George was denying her, denying that he after all had the shaping of their lives in his hands: he was the one who had accepted the job with Biff Roberts, he was the one who made most of the big decisions—he wasn't responsible for her "in a way," he was totally and completely responsible for her. Except that if he didn't feel that—if he didn't feel that, then she was free, after all. Free to be responsible for herself, to be beholden to no one. She felt the panic go, to be replaced by surging strength. She was Marguerite Tanner, and she had something good in store for her. She would make that true, she would make it happen.

And lying in bed, she thought—well, she had made it true, it had happened. Look where they were now, and where they still could go. She stretched her length against the smoothness of the sheet. She had it all going for her now. Nothing could stop her, nothing.

She heard George leave, the door closing behind him, the quiet coming back into the house. Funny how some people pushed quiet out, held it away. Phyllis had done it with energy, kinetic motion, frantic motion. George did it with—power? No, George's pants were probably as wet as anybody's. George did it with lies, lies that so astonished the quiet that it withdrew, ashamed to have recorded on its surface the lies he so easily told. The big lie he'd told to get the Whitman shopping center. And made it sound so plausible, so reasonable, just as he made everything he did sound plausible, reasonable, how could she not view the world in exactly the way that he did? When he had joined the Southport Health Club soon after it opened, and she had complained about the expense. When it didn't even have a place she could go to for lunch, much less use any of the male-only exercise and massage rooms.

"Good business contacts," he'd said.

"It's Biff's business, what do you care?"

"I care," he said, and he took to dropping in there every evening after work and spending several hours on Saturday jogging, playing handball, getting a massage.

"It's not exclusive like the country club is," she said on a Saturday when she'd been cooped up by rain with the two children all day. "Who can you meet there who'll do you any good?"

"The sons of the men who use the country club. People like Jerry Whitman, for one."

"Did he remember you?"

"Said he did. Anyway. He and his father are about to build a big shopping center and office complex south of town."

"He told you that?"

"I listen. Pieces here and there."

"Well, you can bet that he won't hire Biff Roberts to build it. So that pretty well lets you out."

"You say," George said; oddly, he did not seem angry at her disparagement of Biff.

"I had lunch with Sam Hammer today," George said one night a week later.

"Still slaving at Hoffman's?"

"Of course. That's what Sam's cut out for. But, thank heaven, there's no love lost."

"What does that mean?"

"It means I got a good look at Hoffman's plans for the Whitman job."

"I don't see what good that does."

"It means I now know the dimensions of the plot—and how many stores and offices they're planning to build."

"But if Hoffman has the job—"

"They haven't accepted his work yet. He's still just in the design stage."

"And you're going to try to get it away from him? Oh, George."

"I'm not going to try. I'm going to do it."

When he came home from work the next day, it was with the news that he had asked Biff for a week to ten days off to get some medical tests run.

"Medical tests?" She was alarmed. Then she saw his smile. "You're going to use the time to draw your plans?"

"Now you understand."

"George, is this really the right thing to do? I mean, isn't it a little like cheating, seeing Hoffman's plans?"

"Stop worrying about old Hoffman. God, he's screwed so many people in this town—including your husband, don't forget what he did to me—I should get a prize for getting something back from him."

"If you get it."

"I'll get it."

And, of course, he did. Even thinking about it now, it still seemed incredible. He had come home late, to find her putting up peach preserves, her hair pulled back from the sweet-smelling steam, the kitchen heavy with the smell of boiling sugar and juice-filled fruit.

"When will you be finished with that stuff?" he said as he came in.

"Oh, George, I didn't know when you'd be home. I've got a plate for you in the oven—are you hungry now?"

"When will you be finished with that stuff?"

"Well, in a while. I don't know. Half an hour. Why?"

"I'll go up and shower. Hurry, you hear?"

She only noticed then that he was carrying a bag behind his back, a bag which he maneuvered so that she couldn't fully see it.

"George?"

She decided that it was some anniversary of theirs that she had forgotten. First date? First kiss? Silly, George wasn't like that. He wouldn't remember either one. The preserves boiled up to the top of the pot; she grabbed a spoon and stirred air into them, then began ladling them into the sterilized jars.

She was sealing the last jar when George came down, a thin seersucker robe wrapped around him. His legs and feet were bare, she knew that he had nothing on under the robe, and with a small grab at her back, she hoped that he would give her time to change, to wash the stickiness from her hands and arms. He was still carrying the bag. Now he reached in and pulled out a bottle of champagne.

"Run on up and take a shower, comb your hair. But don't take long, all right? I'll be chilling this." He patted her bottom swiftly, pushing her out of the kitchen.

She put her Mother's Day robe on, it was sheer and graceful and completely impractical; there was no danger of there being a smear of baby food or a stain of cod liver oil on its impeccable folds. It was not the kind of robe to be a mother in.

But she felt shy about it; the opaqueness of the robe's sheerness veiled her flesh like a final layer of silvery paint, but the pink of her nipples showed through, the dark tangle of pubic hair. She might as well be naked. Suppose Polly arrived to borrow something? She had kept George waiting long enough, she pulled the brush through her hair once more and then went down the stairs, purposely avoiding looking in the mirror at the foot of them. It was too ridiculous, they were like characters in a bad play, making a public exhibition of their private intensities. But it wasn't public, this was the privacy of their own home. Why shouldn't they walk around as dressed or undressed as suited them? She thought of her grandmother, of the fact that she had never seen her in a robe, much less more undressed than that. She shivered, feeling the long finger of disapproval draw a line of cold down her spine.

And then there was the chill of the champagne glass in her hand, the cold tickle on her tongue. She listened to the toast George was making, but she didn't believe it, she couldn't believe it, after so many years she had become resigned to Biff Roberts, what was George saying?

"We're drinking to the Whitmans' new architect, and to the beginning of the firm of George Tanner, sole proprietor, senior partner, junior partner—everything—so how about that, baby, what do you think of that?"

Of course, she thought it was wonderful, and when George took the robe away from her and shed his own robe and pulled her to the thin green rug on the floor, she let him dribble champagne across her breasts and belly so he could lick them clean; in the first riot of joy that assailed her, she forgot whatever limits she might have ever imposed. Whatever George wanted was all right, hadn't he proved his right to her, to all that she could give him? The Whitmans. Not unknown entities to dream over, to make wishes about, but here, practically in her hands.

And then he told her all about it, how he had gone up to Jerry after the game, had gone up and said that he had some plans he'd like Jerry to look at, if Jerry had a minute—knowing that the first look must draw him, that the weight of that first look could tip the future in his favor, or lock him forever in the present confines of Biff Roberts, Inc. But Jerry had liked it after one swift look at the overall design, and had then sat down and gone over the plans page by page, asking questions, probing.

"He's smart," George said. "He may be inheriting money and a business from the old man, but he's well able to handle it himself. If I hadn't known that, I'd never have tried to get the center in the first place."

She could see that. If Jerry were stupid, were his father's pawn, the older Whitman wouldn't care what Jerry liked; his opinion would have no value. But Jerry wasn't stupid; his opinion did count. He liked the plans and so would his father.

"But will his father like them? Oh, George, if he doesn't!"

"Jerry's pretty sure he will. I've done a couple of things that are innovative, and Jerry likes that. He very much wants to be ahead of everybody else. One thing he didn't like about what Hoffman was doing is that it's similar to a place Hoffman designed on the coast a couple of years ago."

"How did you explain having the plans to begin with? I mean, you had to tell him something."

"I let him think one of the girls in Hoffman's office slipped a copy to me."

"One of the girls?"

"I couldn't get old Sam in trouble."

"But one of the girls?"

"He thinks I'm sleeping with a typist or something. Who cares? If that's what he wants to think—"

"But it's not true. And it makes you look bad."

"Not in Jerry's eyes. Oh, come on, Marguerite, what the hell difference does it make? Do you know how much money this is going to make for us?" And then he told her how much money, and she felt—like a pulse, like a pulse of his penis—the excitement gathering in her and exploding.

And he had opened his own office, small at first, later moved to one of the choicer locations in the new Whitman center, and she supposed that they—or at least she—had never looked back. The junior Whitman home had followed the center, then a small city contract, nothing large, but a beginning. And then—and then the jobs had come in so fast that George had hired two assistants, and had begun to get what she called his sleek look, a look that she no longer liked. Except that now she couldn't remember how George had ever looked before.

CHAPTER THIRTEEN

She woke to rain on Tuesday morning, rain and a feeling of apprehension that she couldn't place, until she remembered that she was to meet Polly Wilkinson for lunch at the club. But Tuesday was Ladies' Golfers Day. When it rained, they couldn't play golf; they played bridge instead and she knew the club would be overrun with women, all, she thought, talking about Ruth. She went to the phone and called Polly and asked if they could meet somewhere besides the club.

"It's Ladies' Day. There'll be swarms of women there and we won't be able to hear ourselves think."

Polly said that was fine, she didn't care, and then they talked about where to meet. Finally Polly suggested the new lunch place at the museum, it was quiet, she said, and had a lovely view of the park next to the museum.

"Only they don't serve drinks," she said.

"That's all right," Marguerite said, and tried to remember when the last time was when she'd gone out to lunch at a place that didn't serve drinks.

"I've never been," she said. "What do people wear?"

She heard Polly laughing. It should have made her angry, but it didn't, because of all people in the world, Polly Wilkinson cared less about clothes than anyone she'd ever known.

"Gracious, don't ask me, Marguerite! You're the expert. I don't know. A summer cotton. Anything. I'm the one who should worry."

But Polly wouldn't worry, she would put on something ordinary, probably a shirtwaist, and she might remember to screw summer-white earrings in her ears, and her bag undoubtedly would not match her shoes, because she said—or used to say—that once she packed a bag for a season, it was too much trouble to keep changing to another one. And still, Marguerite remembered, still, there was that night at the Foremans' when Doug Foreman, who taught history at the college and was attractive, and yes, sexy, had been sitting with Marguerite and then he had said, watching Polly across the room talking to George, "Polly Wilkinson is the sexiest woman I know." Marguerite had looked at him thinking this was some line that she was expected to toss back, but he didn't look at her, he just watched Polly, and said, "She's so supportive. I've never heard her say anything to cut a man down, or make him feel foolish. She seems to understand that men and women are good for one another, that the battle of the sexes, if that's what you want to call it, is the most destructive thing there is. And she understands that without asking that either side surrender."

So when they met in the museum foyer, Polly wearing a light-blue shirtwaist dress that did nothing for her hips and made her eyes look enormous, Marguerite tried to see

196

her as men might see her, and still couldn't see it. Surely anyone looking at them would have to say that she, Marguerite, was beautiful, beautiful and exciting, while Polly looked exactly what she was, a woman in her early thirties who undoubtedly had children and a husband, and spent most of her time on them.

The woman at the desk called Marguerite by name. "Oh, Mrs. Tanner, how nice to see you. We've relighted the West Gallery where your picture is. You really ought to go see how nice it looks."

"What picture is that?" Polly asked, and Marguerite answered that it was just an old thing George's mother had had and hadn't wanted and given to them, so they gave it to the museum—loaned it, anyway.

"But I want to see it!" Polly said, and walked away toward the entrance to the West Gallery, while Marguerite followed, wondering why in hell she should be so embarrassed.

She remembered asking George to buy a picture to give to the museum. That had been two years ago, when he was beginning to make a lot of money, and she was finding ways to spend it that would, as she told George, "do them good."

"There's a picture for sale at the Cartwright Gallery that I happen to know the museum would love to have," she told George. "It's fifteen hundred dollars, but it's a good investment, George. It's going to go up, and, anyway, all kinds of important people are giving pictures to the museum, they've just added that West Gallery, and they're trying to fill it up with local donations and loans."

"I'm not about to spend fifteen hundred dollars on a picture for that museum," George said.

And she had cried and said what good did it do her to

197

join the Friends of the Museum and try to get active in the community and get to know all these people if he wouldn't cooperate? "There's going to be a special party for the people who give pictures, George, not just the big reception that all the Friends will be invited to, but a special party. Mrs. Altman's planning it, George, it's going to be lovely, and I want to go, I want to go to that party."

He had said, God, he wished her father had been a judge so she could have had her fill of all that small-time society stuff growing up, as he had, when would she find out that those women were no different from any other women, why in the hell did it matter so much to her that she be seen with them?

"Because their husbands are rich," she said. "And they can give you expensive jobs, jobs that you can really do something with. That's why I care, and you should, too, George, you should want to do just as many big important jobs as you can."

He hadn't said anything else, but that weekend he'd gone to Waco alone to visit his parents—he said it was just a quick trip—and too much trouble for her to pack up two kids. When he came back he carried a large flat package heavily wrapped in brown paper into the living room, carefully untied it, and stripped away the paper, and there was a large painting of a woman—she was not nude—she had some kind of Spanish shawl draped around her, but the flesh that showed was luminescent and seductive, and her eyes held a knowledge more naked than the shoulders and legs that gleamed with a pearly light.

"George, what is it? What on earth is it for?"

"It's a painting, obviously. For the museum."

"But, George, they want only very good things. Where did you get this? How do you know they'll want it?"

198

And then he had told her that the painting was by an artist who had by now built up quite a name for himself. He had a studio in New York, and hung in the best galleries there, and was in museums in the States and abroad, and that the museum would be damn glad to get this painting, which was an early one, but which nevertheless had all the characteristics that made his style notable.

"But where did you get it? You must have paid the earth!"

"It was Mother's," he said, and he smiled, the smile said that he found this all very funny, though Marguerite didn't see the joke.

"I never saw it in your house."

"Wasn't in the house. The woman in the painting is Mother's younger sister. This artist, this Thompson, spent a summer batting around Texas. He came to Waco and met my aunt some way. And painted her. She spent every afternoon for three weeks in the garage apartment where he lived, being painted. And, Mother was sure, doing other things as well. When the family finally saw the painting, Mother looked straight at my aunt, and asked, 'Do you have anything on under that shawl?' and my aunt looked straight back and said, 'No.' Mother marched out of the room and didn't speak to her sister again, which was a damn shame, because she was thrown from a horse a couple of months later and broke her neck. When her place was cleaned out, of course the portrait was there, Thompson having left it with her, and Mother couldn't bear to look at it, but somehow she didn't want to get rid of it, either, so she packed it away. She was glad enough to give it to me, but she made me promise I wouldn't tell anyone that was my aunt."

"Your poor mother," Marguerite said.

"What?"

"Well, she's got everything, doesn't she? Her husband's a judge, and known everywhere. She's got money. Lots of money. Oh, I don't know. You'd think there'd come a time when you could just tell everyone to go to hell. You'd think she could say, 'Yes, that's my sister, isn't she lovely?' I mean, my God, George, isn't there ever a time when you don't have to worry about what people say?"

"I don't worry," George said, but that was a lie, because she watched him at the museum party given for donors, and he was lapping it up, he loved having people go up to the painting, and read the card. "Loaned by Mr. and Mrs. George Tanner," and then come to him and say, "A Thompson! My God, a Thompson! It's great, it really is."

She came up to Polly, who was looking at the picture with her hands crossed behind her back and her head lifted, tilted slightly.

"It's lovely," she said. "Really lovely. I've seen it before, of course. But I didn't read the card. I didn't know you and George had given it to the museum."

"Loaned," said Marguerite, thinking how like Polly it was not to have read the donor cards; she would not give a fig who had given what. She cared about the pictures, and that was the extent of her interest.

The lunchroom was pleasant, with a lot of glass that gave the good view of the park that Polly had promised, and Marguerite sat down and ordered Gazpacho and a cream-cheese sandwich, feeling very virtuous that she wasn't beginning lunch with a couple of vodka martinis.

"Do you come here often?" she asked Polly.

"Oh, sometimes. Mostly when the museum exhibits

200

change. I like to get a quiet look myself before bringing the children down."

"Do they like to come here?"

"It's like anything else; they like parts of it, parts of it they don't. But they're too young to make up their minds about what they will see and what they won't. If I bring them often enough, I guess it'll sink in."

"You always were a good mother, Polly."

"I like doing it."

Marguerite thought of Alan and Sue, off at camp. She had heard twice from each of them, the dutiful letters that the counselors forced them to write. And she had written back, hasty notes that said very little about anything, because what was she doing that they could possibly be interested in?

"Remember when Alan and Tim were babies?" she said suddenly. "How many mornings and afternoons we spent, watching them? We must have drunk a hundred gallons of iced tea."

"And then when the girls were born—it was like having our own nursery."

"Funny how our babies were born so close to each other."

Polly laughed. "We always used to tease Ben and George about that."

They both laughed then, and the moment seemed caught in the kind of clear light that they had left in the West Gallery, Marguerite could see them sitting there laughing, and she thought, "Portrait of Two Friends Having Lunch."

"We had such fun then," she said to Polly.

"Yes, we did."

"Polly, what happened to it?" But she knew what had

happened to it. Those times with Polly belonged to another century, another time. Now there was Grace, a different kind of fun, a new kind of excitement. She bit down on her cream-cheese sandwich. It was, after all, very bland. She should have ordered pastrami on rye.

"I don't know. People get busy," Polly said.

"But I'm not that busy."

She thought about that. It was true. She really wasn't busy. She paid membership dues to almost a dozen organizations, but she rarely went to the meetings. Lora Mae did the housework, the children were either at school or at gymnastics or basketball or summer camp or talking in covert voices with friends and George, of course, had his work, and she—she wasn't busy.

"You must be busy. I'm always reading about you in the paper."

"Oh, Polly, you're not."

"Sure. There was that article on your patio. That was nice. The pictures were lovely. You must be very proud of it. And I imagine that takes some time, keeping all that up."

But I don't do it, she thought. The people from the landscape service take care of it; the day they came and found out I'd gotten out and dusted the roses, they had a fit. She remembered when Sue was an infant. It was spring. Sue woke around five in the morning, she picked her up and carried her to the kitchen to cook the egg yolk and then took Sue and the egg outside to feed her. Then she laid Sue in the center of the old chaise lounge they'd bought at a second-hand furniture place and fooled with the rose bushes, pulling the weeds that clustered around their trunks, dusting them gently with the fine yellow powder that puffed softly from the hole in the can.

202

"I'm not nearly as busy as I used to be," she said. She felt a surge of panic. If Polly faced her down and said, "All right, what do you do, what do you really do?" what could she say?

"A different kind of busyness," Polly said. She looked at her watch. "But I am a little busier today than I thought I'd be when we planned to meet. Tim's swim meet's been moved up to three o'clock, so I'll have to get home and change and pick up a bunch of kids—well, you know how it is."

"He doesn't go to camp?"

A shift of light that looked like a blush crossed Polly's face. "You remember how I always was about the kids. I like to have them around me. And Ben—well, he counts on the summers to see more of them. He's got such a crazy schedule, sometimes in the winter he goes a couple of days without much time for them."

"George told me that Ben's city editor now."

Again the shift of light, the pale blush. "Yes. He's very pleased. We both are."

"George said to tell you he's mastered his barbecue. He hopes you and Ben will come sample it some time."

"Oh, fine," Polly said.

But Marguerite remembered the little note, refusing their last invitation. Would Polly come if Marguerite called and said it would just be the four of them, like old times, bring the children, they'd drink beer and eat popcorn and play Monopoly until one in the morning? She felt tears, and she blinked her eyes rapidly, willing the tears to go away. She swallowed some tea and wished that it were vodka; she needed something strong to hold on to, to surround herself with. She felt open and vulnerable, and she wondered why she now saw Polly as an enemy.

Polly had taken out a notebook and opened it to a blank page. "Now let's talk about that fashion show. I really don't know where to begin."

They talked for half an hour, Marguerite referring to the notes she'd brought, Polly writing quickly. She didn't really need this information. This is easy, anyone as smart as Polly would know how to put on a dumb fashion show, so why did she really call? Was it to see Marguerite as she might go see a new exhibit at the museum or take the children to the zoo to behold a rare and exotic beast?

"I hope this has helped," Marguerite said.

"Oh, it has."

"Though almost anyone could have told you this."

"Well, maybe. But then, I know you." Polly's eyes were clear; Marguerite thought guiltily that, of course, Polly had had no other reason for calling than the one she had given. Polly, she knew, had never done a devious thing in her life. She hadn't known what to expect, seeing Polly again after all this time. And now she didn't know how she felt—maybe diminished was what it was. Because Polly had not commented, as Grace would have, on her outfit, or noticed how carefully the peach in her scarf picked up the shade of blush she'd rubbed into her cheeks. I might as well have worn a gunnysack, she thought. The knowledge that Polly thought her a silly, vain woman hit her like an anvil falling.

She heard herself asking, "Who are the models, anyway?"

"Mostly members," Polly said.

"I'm a member."

"You are?"

"Well, not too active. But I am a member."

There was a silence. The ice in Marguerite's tea glass

shifted position as it melted; the sound was loud and unbearable.

"We'd love to have you model, then. I know you're almost professional."

The old pleasure came over her. Yes, she knew that; she knew how good she was. She was the darling of the buyers. They loved to have her model. When she'd finally been named to the Best Dressed list, Lorenzo, the owner and buyer of the best specialty shop in town, had hugged her and told her that it had just been a matter of time; he had been pulling for her all along; there wasn't a woman in this town who could wear clothes the way she did. Happy, she had repeated that to George, and he had laughed and said, "If I were Lorenzo and getting thousands of dollars a year out of you for clothes, I'd have said the same thing."

That was so like George, he managed to spoil anything she really enjoyed. He'd tried to spoil her enjoying Lorenzo from the very beginning. They'd still been living on Stephen Street, only now she had two babies, Alan and Sue, and now they had lived in Southport for three years, and still, she thought, still she was nobody and there was nothing in the future that augured that she ever would be anything but a nobody.

And then the note from Cissy had come, the handwriting sprawling across the page, almost undecipherable. "Sweetie," the note said, "a darling friend of mine is moving to Southport, taking over a dress shop there. He's really good people, so be nice to him when he calls. His name is Jim Davis, but he might call himself Lorenzo, so if he does, you'll know who it is. Love, Cissy."

And Jim Davis had indeed called, had indeed called himself Lorenzo, and had been duly invited to dinner. He arrived wearing skintight trousers with a white linen double-breasted blazer, a soft silk ascot knotted at his throat. He brought wine, really excellent wine, and Marguerite liked him at once. George, she thought, did, too, until Lorenzo left, and George prissed around the room on his tiptoes and squeaked, "My, ain't he *sweet!*" It had taken Marguerite a minute to understand what George meant; when she did, she felt as though she herself had been attacked, felt that the whole lovely evening, the talk of clothes and Lorenzo's shop— "My dear, I inherited this dreary place from my aunt, you wouldn't believe the lines she carried, it's all too depressing, but I've got marvelous ideas, simply marvelous ideas, in no time, I mean in no time, Lorenzo's will be the *dernier cri,* absolutely the *dernier cri*—" was all being besmirched by George. She ran to him and begin pounding on his chest with small clenched fists.

"Stop it!" she said. "Stop it right now! That's mean, and I won't have it!"

And George had stopped. "Good God, Marguerite, I was joking. Though really, don't you think your friend Lorenzo is a bit much?"

Her friend. Of course, Lorenzo was to be her friend. George would have nothing to do with him. Which was all right with her. The next day she packed Sue into her carryall and stuffed Alan next to her in his carseat, and drove to Lorenzo's shop. He was hauling out trash, dressed that day in an alpine green jumpsuit, and he had kissed her hands and chucked the babies under their chins and made coffee well-laced with brandy that they drank out of thick porcelain mugs.

After that first day, she went to the shop at least three times a week. She helped Lorenzo haul the old merchandise to the Salvation Army, helped unpack the boxes of

206

fresh new clothes, helped him hang them up, modeled some of them for him.

"My dear, the perfect job for you. The absolutely perfect job. All you have to do, all you have to do when I get this tiny place open, is just do some modeling for me. I've talked to the manager of that pretentious French place next door, and he wants me to show my things there. And there'll be a few other places. You're perfect, you're gorgeous, I wouldn't have anyone else, not if they'd modeled in New York. You're just exactly what I need. And because I know you want decent clothes, my dear, what you've been wearing is—well, between you and me, it's a good thing you're so elegant-looking, I mean, to look at your clothes—well, bargain basement can't look like Dior, can it? Anyway, instead of money, money that would just go on cod-liver oil and strained spinach, isn't that right? I'll give you clothes, yes, dear, some of the prettiest that you model. Now, doesn't that please you?"

And, of course, it did. She traded off baby-sitting with Polly and some of the other girls in the neighborhood, and would leave, beautifully free, to go to Lorenzo's where he would fuss over her hair and carefully paint her face and zip her up into one creation after the other. George walked in one day while Lorenzo was putting her hair in a French twist. Marguerite was sitting in a bra and half-slip, and George had given her the dickens later on, what did she mean, sitting there in front of that man half-naked? Only then he'd laughed and said, well, I guess you know what I mean about him, and slapped her on the buttocks, and asked to see the dress she had earned that day.

She had thought George might not like her getting paid in clothes. She had been prepared to argue about that, but he had agreed at once, no income tax, he said, and

207

besides, he liked Marguerite to have pretty things. The other girls in the neighborhood envied her; it wasn't only the clothes, though of course that was part of it, it was the fact that she was doing something, had something to look forward to other than cooking and cleaning and minding babies.

At first, she had been scared. The beautiful world that Lorenzo held up like a screen, a screen that she could weave herself into, become part of, would fold up and present its dark side again, because she had never modeled. She had practiced those funny swift turns at home, patting a baby's back mechanically while she did it, but that wasn't the same as training. She knew she'd fall flat on her face.

"I've never done this before," she'd said to Lorenzo.

He slipped the black silk over her head, settled the ruffles that fell from neckline to hem, stepped back and looked at her.

"My dear, you've been on for years. Don't tell me that a woman as beautiful as you are doesn't enter every room as though it were a stage, a runway, with gaping admirers around her. You were *born* to model, absolutely born to it."

And she did look good. The soft black ruffle just covered the top of her breasts—the hint of a swelling made the dress that much more seductive, that much more elegant. And then she thought of the crowd in the restaurant, looking up from their steaks or chicken or shrimp to watch her move through the tables. Or maybe not looking. Maybe not caring whether she was there or not, whether she was wearing the black silk or wearing nothing at all.

"I don't know what to expect," she said. "From the

people, I mean."

"Marguerite, darling—you just walk around, be sure you pass each table; if someone comments, you can tell them about the dress. And smile, sweetheart, smile. You are not Marie Antoinette going to the guillotine."

"I still think you should have gotten a professional model."

"Dammit, what's the matter with you? Don't you think I have enough sense to know what pleases me? You please me, not some goddamn professional model who's had all the humanity trained out of her. You look beautiful, beautiful and vulnerable—you'll make every man in that place want to buy the dress just to help you out."

"If you say so." She put her makeup on, the eyeliner, the mascara, the frosted pink lipstick Lorenzo wanted.

There was a private entrance to the restaurant through the manager's office. She went there, feeling with every step away from Lorenzo that she was entering a no-man's land of fear, and that she was armored with nothing more than a fragile shield of silk.

The haze of smoke, the smell of food, the sudden sharp whiff of bourbon as she passed the bar—and the noise, the noise of voices and of knives and forks, and of waiters picking up plates and putting down plates—she knew that no one would notice her, that she would be a terrible failure, and that Lorenzo would get someone else.

She began her slow walk through the room, pausing briefly at each table, turning, moving the ruffled skirt with her hand, trying to remember all Lorenzo had taught her about how to move, how to make the fall of the dress a part of her, so that her bones and muscles and the fabric of the dress were somehow melded into a whole picture of grace.

"That's a lovely dress, isn't it, Edna?" The voice caught her by surprise. Someone had noticed her; she stopped and smiled at the two older women who sat beside her, small glasses of sherry in front of them. "Not for me, of course, but for Bettina? Don't you think that would look lovely on Bettina? How much is it?"

"It's one hundred eighty-five dollars, but of course it's a lovely fabric, and a very special design—Lorenzo has only one like it." She held her breath, she didn't have to sell the clothes, that wasn't part of the bargain, but in a rush of loyalty and gratitude to Lorenzo, she felt that she very much wanted to sell everything she modeled.

"It is her birthday. And my only daughter—I'll stop in next door after lunch, look at it some more."

What a nice woman, what a very nice woman! She moved on, feeling better now—people probably did enjoy seeing pretty clothes while they were eating, my God, there were enough fashion shows every year. She could remember lunch at Sakowitz' Sky Terrace with Cissy, and how pleasant it had been to see all the clothes, even if she couldn't afford to buy them.

Then the hour wove itself together in a tapestry of wool sweaters and flannel skirts and soft crepes and shimmering velvets, until finally she had shown the last dress, and she was sitting wearily in a chair in the big dressing room at Lorenzo's sipping a glass of red wine and eating the chop he'd had sent over from the restaurant.

"You were a marvel, darling, I knew you would be. We've got five customers out there who came over just because they saw you. Oh, this is going to be good, I can tell how good it's going to be. Now come see what I've picked out for you to take home, you were such a good girl; I've got something really lovely."

It was a cashmere sweater with a Pendleton wool skirt, the plaid in thin blues and greens reflected in the fine pastel sweater. She loved it immediately; it brought to mind large fireplaces with logs tumbling in a blaze of fiery death, and herself sitting on a fur rug, sipping something very good and very hot from the large mug.

"It's far more elegant than anywhere I'll ever go," she said. "But I love it anyway."

"Just because those dreary women you know don't dress well doesn't mean you can't," Lorenzo said. "You'll come into your own, don't worry about that. There'll come a day when you'll have a closet full of clothes just this lovely, and your calendar will be crowded with fun places to wear them."

"Is that a prophecy or a wish?" she asked, but his words wrapped themselves about her nicely; they kept her almost as warm as would the sweater.

She went to the shop one morning to find Lorenzo in a state. She felt the warmth of being there; he would tell her what had him so wrought up; he would take her into that special world she lived in when she was with him.

"My dear, you'll never believe it, here I've been open—what?—not two years, and already I seem to have arrived. Mrs. Clarence Logan, surely you know who she is, you've read about her, she's constantly in the newspaper. Anyway, she called me, just now, just a minute ago, my dear, the phone rang, I answered it, how was I to know what a moment this was? Anyway, she asked me to provide the clothes for the big fashion benefit that opens the fall season. My dear, do you realize, do you know how I've worked and waited for just such a chance. *Everyone* goes to that benefit—and the models—well, suffice it to say the *crème de la crème!*"

Marguerite felt her own excitement die as Lorenzo's rose. Of course, it was wonderful for him, she had read about the benefit every year, read the names of the women modeling, had even thought last year of going, but she had no one to go with—it had not seemed worth it. And now, just at first, when Lorenzo had told her about it, she had thought—well, not thought, nothing as conscious as a thought, she had felt—that she was part of what he was saying, and that she should be glad, too. But she was not a part of it, she was, after all, a paid model, and the models for that show were, she knew, drawn from the city's leading group.

"That's wonderful, Lorenzo, I'm so pleased," she said, and kissed his cheek.

"You should be, my dear, you should be. Because you, my own Marguerite, are going to be the absolute star of the show. Yes, you are, I insisted. I told Mrs. Logan, of course I'll be happy to use the models you choose, providing, of course, that they are a decent size, I can't clothe fat ladies, you know that, but I reserve the right to have one model of my choice, a girl who is fantastic, you wouldn't want to have the show without her. She didn't know what to make of that, but of course she gave in, I know her type, they like to think they rule the world and actually they're just waiting for someone to come along and stand up to them."

"Lorenzo, you didn't tell her that," she said, but she knew that he had, that in his own way, Lorenzo understood her very well, and that he had done this for her.

So that even though she was nervous about the other models, even though she wasn't sure what you said to a Janet Baker or a Grace Whitman or a Ruth McDaniels, she knew that she was as good as the best of them when it came to wearing the clothes and showing them off. The fact that Lorenzo considered her the star, and gave her all the prettiest things, heightened her own awareness of herself. It was possible to be graciously silent when all around her the other models were complaining because they didn't like what they were wearing, or a certain cut of dress showed their stomachs too much, or, in the case of Ruth McDaniels, the dress was cut too low. Her clothes fit her perfectly, she looked, she knew Lorenzo would say, like an angel, and looking that good was a help in remembering that these half-magic people, these denizens of the world she so much wanted to join, were, after all, flesh and blood, like herself, and not possessors of some secret that she would never know.

Her first time on a runway was a revelation. She expected to be nervous, a little frightened—the spotlight, focused as it was, blinded her, and she could see nothing of the runway beyond about two feet in front of her. But around her, on either side, she was aware of people, of people turning to look at her, at her, Marguerite Tanner, and in the moment of that knowledge an exultation swept over her so that she forgot that she couldn't see the end of the runway, forgot that she was nervous, that the back of the dress dipped down below her waistline, and that the halter front barely covered her. She forgot everything in the warmth she felt coming to her from those beautiful people; that and the fact that George was in the audience, and that he must be proud of her.

Her exhilaration lasted into the party after the show, when models and husbands gathered in the suite Lorenzo had taken and ate pâté and caviar and drank champagne.

"You were the hit of the show," Janet Baker said to her, passing by with two glasses of champagne in her hands.

213

"I'd be jealous, but we all know Lorenzo likes you best, so what's the point?"

"Did you hear what Janet Baker said?" she asked George. It was cold in the car. She wished the heater worked better, but by the time it began to come on, they would be home.

"I hate to see you impressed by all those people," George said.

The fun began to drift out of the evening; just the smallest thing George said could do that. She tried to fight it, tried to see it as George being contrary, but then, George knew about people like that. Wasn't he one of them? Or had been, back in Waco.

"I'm not impressed," she said. She was lying. She was impressed. Impressed by the fact that most of the girls could afford to buy everything they modeled. Impressed by the fact that they could discuss the quality of the caviar, because they had eaten it often enough to know. Impressed by their money, and who they were, and what they had.

"I'm not impressed," she said again. And inside, there was a little fall of belief, a fall that told her that Lorenzo might very well be wrong, that she might never reach the spot so happily inhabited by Janet and Grace and Ruth and all the rest of them.

"But you want what they've got."

"Who wouldn't? Can you sit there and tell me you'd rather live in a rented house and drive an old car and wear suits off the rack? When if you were rich—"

"If I were rich—" George didn't sound angry, but she knew that he was. And that his anger would come out in another time, and at another place, so that she could never really have a fight with him, because by the time he

214

allowed her to know that he was angry, she wasn't angry anymore, and could only feel miserably attacked.

"I shouldn't have said that. I didn't mean it."

She thought of Phyllis' warning, "Never complain to a man about what he can give you. Worse thing you can do. Always act like you're happy with what you've got, but do everything you can to get more." She felt that Phyllis had been talking to someone else. She was happy with what she had, this was just a game she was playing, she and Lorenzo, making believe that something wonderful waited for her.

"Of course, you meant it. And I agree. It would be nice to be rich. Very rich. Which we will be. Do you really think I enjoy playing golf at the public course? Or care for the people we see, all those college professors who work half a week and think they're exhausted? Shit. I grew up with the best. Do you think I'll settle for anything less now?"

She should be happy, George agreed with her, but he didn't make it sound like Lorenzo did, Lorenzo with his shocking-pink boxes spilling out those lovely goodies— no, George sounded grim, dead serious. It occurred to her that perhaps it wouldn't be much fun to be rich with George.

But the next day Lorenzo's truck arrived with the green backless dress she'd modeled. She wore it to a faculty dance at the college that Saturday night, and watched the men's faces and the women's eyes with a kind of triumph that she had never felt before.

"I could never model or do anything like that," Polly said. But she didn't sound as though she cared very much. Marguerite remembered that she'd just said to Polly, "It's a kind of hobby." She thought of the hobbies they'd had when they had been close, all those years ago, exchanging recipes and patterns, making needlepoint pillows, and one long cold winter, even braiding rugs for their children's rooms.

"I'll be glad to model if you really want me to," she said, and she heard the ice in her voice, it had somehow shifted from its place in the tea glass and had gotten into her throat, so that every word passed through its chill.

"Yes, of course we do. I'll call you and fill you in," Polly said. She had the check in her hand, was opening her purse for money.

"This is on me," Marguerite said. "We were going to the club. I'm the one who changed it, let me—"

"Marguerite," Polly said, and she looked at her with those clear blue eyes. "I've never had enough money really to make any difference. But one thing about it, I won't fight over it. I asked you to lunch and I'm paying for it." She grinned then. "Ben doesn't mind eating red beans for supper."

They used to joke about that, that if they entertained someone at a meal, they had to eat beans to make up the cost. And here was Polly being so friendly, why couldn't she be friendly back, why this feeling that she didn't know who Polly was, or perhaps being with Polly made her not know who she was—she thought of Dr. Forrester, and that she was to see him again, and she thought, "I'll tell him about Polly, I'll tell him how it was." But she knew that telling Dr. Forrester about it would not bring it back, that if she and Polly sat here and had lunch every day for a month, that wouldn't bring it back, either. But why should she want it back? Did she really want to be poor again: did she really want to pinch pennies and stretch dollars, and do all the little demeaning things you had to do without money, all the things that Polly did, but which did not

216

demean her?

When she got home, home to a house that was cool against the July sun, she went to her room and carefully hung the linen skirt and the pima cotton blouse in her huge closet, put the peach scarf and the coral earrings away, and eased the shoe trees into her new soft kid pumps. She lay down on the chaise in her slip, letting the cool draft of the air conditioning blow over her skin, and she thought of Polly, going home and changing into whatever for a swimming meet and picking up a carload of bathing-suited little boys, all squealing and all excited, and then sitting in the hot, hot sun, getting freckles and wrinkles and dry hair. And it sounded terrible, of course, it sounded terrible, but it had for her the kind of fascination anything Polly had ever done had for her, and she wondered for perhaps the ten thousandth time if she had changed because she couldn't stand not being like Polly, if she had changed because she had finally known that she would never be like Polly, or if their friendship all those years ago had been phony after all. Because maybe she hadn't changed, maybe she had been this way underneath all that time, maybe she had always been a bitch who slept around and couldn't get through lunch without three martinis and pushed her husband to buy her every goddamn thing in town.

Though there had been a time, when they still lived on Stephen Street, when she had been told, almost guaranteed, that she didn't have to push. It was all out there, waiting. Doug Freeman had just had a paper accepted by a prestigious quarterly, and he'd bought half-gallons of California burgundy and called them over. The Wilkinsons were there, Tim already asleep in the bedroom, and the usual crowd of neighborhood academics had gathered. She remembered that in those days, Ben and George had sparred with these inhabitants of the ivory towers, forcing them out into the real world. She remembered that Ben seemed to love the arguing for the sheer energy of the thought and the words. George liked to win.

But that night, nobody argued with Doug. He was high on the red wine of California, with the sheer height he now had reached. He stood in the center of the room, thick-stemmed wine glass in hand, telling them they were going to get a preview of a paper that would be even better than the one just accepted, create far more of a stir.

"And not just in academic circles," he'd said, looking through his wine glass at Ben. "You might just run excerpts of that paper, Ben. And be run out of town on a rail."

"Now, Doug," Madge said.

"I love to hear stories introduced by someone saying 'Now, Doug,'" George said. "I gather even the lowly layman will like this topic."

"I am only expressing what everyone here has observed, but has been too nice, or too shit-scared, or too optimistic to say. That what we've got here, in this little ole Southern town with its little ole Southern customs and its little ole plantation houses is a grand and glorious fake—a facade, if you will. A set by Cecil B. deMille—or Walt Disney, depending on your point of view."

Someone across the room snickered. Someone else clapped and said, "Amen, brother!" Marguerite looked at George. He sat, relaxed, spine straight against the newel post, the rest of his body curved like the curve of the balustrade—the taut lines and seductive curves of his own buildings. No facade here, it was George Tanner, through and through.

218

She became so fascinated with the lines of her husband's body, with the way his light eyes fastened on first one speaker, then another, that she heard only the top words—"money, just a lot of jackasses fighting over money"—"no grace, no breeding, hell, is there any family here that can get beyond grandpapa?"—"a local intellegentsia that asks if *exodus* isn't a little pro-Jew"—"brains and genitals in their wallets." And George just sat there, a statue, even the light eyes blank like a statue.

"Now, hold on," Doug said. He was really tight now, swinging the half-empty jug in an ever-widening arc over the heads around him. "You're all missing the point."

"So what is the point?" George's voice, coming in now, startled Marguerite. Why is he asking, he always knows what the point is. Always.

"The point, my friend, is that this is a wide-open town. Anybody, I kid you not, anybody, can come in here, and if they make enough money, and know how to splash it around, they'll get in, get knighted and crowned, or whatever the crap it is. The whole merry-go-round. Brass ring, brass tune. The whole thing." He was drinking from the jug now, a trickle of burgundy ran from the corner of his mouth like fake blood from a fake hero in a fake town in a fake world.

"Luckily," said Polly, laughing, "Ben and I are in no danger of making any money. And neither are you, Doug, unless you turn that paper of yours into a sex-filled tale of life in the old South."

"You read my paper?" Doug's eyes were suddenly focused.

"You don't mind?"

"Hell, no." He was moving toward Polly now. Marguerite remembered he'd called Polly sexy. Was that what made her sexy? And then they were talking, heads nodding, close, intimate.

She turned to George. "Let's go home," she said. "Doug is a funny man," she said to George when they got home.

"Funny?"

"All that talk about what kind of town this is. He must care a little, or he wouldn't have thought about it so much."

"He really doesn't care. He doesn't have to."

"Because he's a professor?"

"What the hell does that have to do with anything? He doesn't care because he's the real thing. The Freemans have been in Mobile forever. Old money, old blood. The very things he said this place doesn't have."

Doug had a passport and didn't even use it. For that moment, she thought she stood before a door, a door that she could finally open, could finally walk into the place where there were no passports, and where the people who were born with them burned them and scattered their useless ashes over the verdant ground.

The moment shifted like the small writhing of a leaf that hides the sun telescoped by distance into a pin-bright dot. She shivered, the sun had gone out.

"But he did say this town is wide open. He did say that."

CHAPTER FOURTEEN

"Sure." She watched George pull his shirt off, throw it across the chair at the foot of the bed. As he lifted his T-shirt over his head, his body looked suddenly vulnerable. The bones, the muscles, the skin could not be strong enough for what it was she needed him to do; she would somehow find a way to strengthen him, to make him see, as she saw, where their future lay.

"Doesn't that interest you at all?"

"What?"

His eyes were on her now. She stopped in the act of unbuttoning her blouse, she didn't want to talk as she undressed, her undressing would lead to sex, or if it didn't that would worry her. In any case, she would be distracted.

"That we can go anywhere we want to."

"Where is it you want to go, Marguerite?"

The wine, which had not affected her earlier, seemed to suddenly gather all of its potency and rise to her tongue in one swift burst. She stood up, arms flung wide, almost touching the wall beside her.

"I want—I want a big house, and Louis XIV chairs, and a big flashy car and so many clothes it takes me an hour just to decide what dress to put on. I want to go to New York for plays and to Europe, not when I'm old as a sop to having hung on that long, but *now, now,* George. I want people to look at me, and to know who I am. I want—" She moved to the window and looked down at the backyard, its scraggly shrubs and slightly leaning fence turned into a theatrical setting by the strong moon that governed the night. "I want everything."

Her back was to George. She couldn't see his face. When she heard his laugh, she felt caught between two forces, the force of that strong light before her and the force of his—what? derision?—behind her.

"Don't laugh at me, George." She still was turned from him. The back yard was wide, threatening. She couldn't see Alan's sandbox and wading pool; they were hidden in the shadows from the large azalea bush at the corner of the garage. The world beyond the back yard was wider still, more threatening still. She felt a strength rise in her. If George chose to laugh, she did not. If George chose not to care, to accept whatever he could get, she did not. He was, after all, managed easily enough. She turned and moved to him, thrusting out of her clothes.

"I'm not laughing at you," he said. "All this time I thought I was married to a nice little girl from East Texas. Now it turns out I'm married to some kind of tiger who wants to devour the world."

"I want it for you, George," she said. She had stepped out of the last of her clothes, she went to him and unsnapped the grippers at the top of his shorts. "You're a

222

very good architect, you know that and I know that. I want more for you than designing those houses for Biff Roberts. I want you to design big office buildings that people will stop and stare at. I want you to design big expensive houses that people will call the Tanner house, and forget even who owns it."

He let her pull off his shorts. He rolled them both back onto the bed. "The fact that I'd make a hell of a lot of money doing all this is incidental, right?"

"Don't you want money, George?"

"Not the way you do."

"But you've always had it."

"Maybe. You haven't done so badly. All right, Marguerite, I'll do the best I can. I don't think designing houses for Biff Roberts is the be all and end all of existence. But I will not be pushed."

He was on top of her now; she could feel his penis hard against her thighs. He's not going to try to get me ready, she thought, it will hurt, but I'll smile anyway, because he must not be pushed, he must not be pushed, but if I please him enough—

So George could never accuse her of pushing him. He had opened the office, he had taken the risk, and she—she had gotten what she wanted, yes, she had, and one lunch with Polly Wilkinson was not going to make her forget that. Polly had just wanted to check her out, to see if all the wild tales she probably heard about Marguerite were true. Looking just as she had looked all those years ago, with her red hair and big blue eyes. Well, she, Marguerite, didn't look the way she had way back then. No, she looked a hundred, a thousand times better, and so much for Polly if she didn't like it. Fuck Polly. Fuck her and Ben and that whole stuffy crowd.

When the phone rang, she almost said, "Fuck you," when she picked up the receiver. And then Lou Armitage's voice came over the line, to ask her to lunch tomorrow.

"As long as it's not at that goddamn tearoom at the museum," she said.

Lou laughed. "You got a private fight going with the museum? I'll buy the fucking thing and you can burn it down," he said.

"I think you would," she said. "I think you really would."

"Okay. So you want me to send a car, what?"

"No. I'll use my car. Where are we going?"

"Come to my office. We'll go from there."

"I don't know where it is."

"Top floor of the Castillian Hotel."

"Do you own that, too?"

"Why not?"

She was to see Dr. Forrester at eleven; she could go from there to lunch with Lou. As she dressed, she felt foolish. She didn't need a psychiatrist, it was only a whim, a wanting someone else to give her answers she was too lazy to find out for herself, like asking a friend to copy the answers to algebra homework.

But she went. She had, after all, made the appointment; his time was worth money. It would be rude not to show up.

"I really don't have anything to talk about," she said. "I'm beginning to think even more that this is a mistake—I probably just need a vacation, or to take up needlepoint or something." She tried to laugh and was surprised to hear a near-sob.

"There's nothing current bothering you?"

"Well, my children are at camp, how could there be?" She did laugh then; at the same moment, she thought of Ruth. She said again, "How could there be?"

"Last week you were telling me about your family. You mentioned a brother—Bill, I think you said?"

"Oh, Bill. Well, there's nothing there. Bill's in the Air Force, he's a career officer, I never even see him."

"He is younger than you are?"

"He was born when I was four. After my father died. Bill is the only man in the whole world I've ever gotten along with so well. Except for my husband, I mean. Of course, my husband. But Bill—"

He had been a small baby, rushed into the world by her mother's desperation, coming several weeks too soon, so that her mother came home from the hospital without him—the baby, she said, was still too small to be with them.

And when he did come, still tiny, still red, wrinkled, bald—still ugly, Marguerite thought—she had been drawn to him and to his bed, and to everything about him, so that her dolls lay in twisted piles on the floor, her crayons melted forgotten in their box. And she dogged her mother's footsteps, handing her diapers, handing her powder, handing her bottles, wanting only to be near that small brother.

"Marguerite is such a wonderful help," her mother told friends, and Marguerite felt the beam of warmth that circled the baby swinging out to take her in, too.

She remembered almost no one else from her childhood. There had been, she supposed, girlfriends. She must have had teaparties, jumped rope, played hopscotch. But she could remember none of that. Only the long summer evenings when she was Aleta to his Prince Valiant, the shiny silver sword and shield their grandfather had made him glimmering in the strange dusk. Only the evenings in winter when they lined up his toy soldiers and sent marble cannonballs crashing into the troops so that her smallest doll, in nurse's gown, could go among them. The time when that queer boy in high school had taken to her, had called her, come to see her, and tried to walk home with her. She hadn't been able to discourage him, had taken the whole thing lightly, until one night when she was alone in the house and he came to see her, determined to speak, angry because she wouldn't let him in. Bill had come back from a baseball game to find her crying. He had listened to her and had then lifted the bat and swung it slowly, slowly, saying in his young voice, "If he bothers you again, you just let me know. I'll take care of him."

"Why should that make me cry?" she said to Dr. Forrester. She fumbled at the box of tissues he held out, pressed one to her face.

"Perhaps you feel a lack of—caring—in your life now."

"Oh, no, that just isn't so! George—well, George cares for me very much." She held out her arm; a heavy gold bracelet circled her wrist, the finely etched design catching at the light. "He brought me this just last week. For no reason. I mean, it wasn't a birthday or anything. He just knew I would like it." Her arm looked suddenly grotesque. Dr. Forrester leaned forward, nodded at the bracelet. "Bill gave me a bracelet once. It was a charm bracelet. All the other girls had one. I thought I'd die if I didn't get one, but it was forever until Christmas and I'd already had my birthday. Anyway, Bill had been saving up for something. I don't know. He took the money, went down to the store, and bought me the bracelet and one

226

charm. It was a little horseshoe; I'll never forget it." Now she was really crying, great sobs that tore up through her—she listened to herself and thought drearily, I really will have to stop coming if all it does is make me cry.

"Do you think there is any difference in your brother giving you that bracelet and your husband giving you this one?"

"Well, of course this one is worth so much more. I mean, this is real gold, and Bill's little bracelet, well, it wasn't even plate, it was just—" That's not what he wants, she thought. "All right. When Bill gave me that bracelet, it—it took everything he had. He had to really give something up. I don't think George had to give anything up to give me this bracelet. Now that I have it, I don't even want the damn thing."

"What is it you do want from you husband?"

"But there's nothing to want. He gives me everything. Everything."

"Will you think about that? Between now and next week?"

"Dr. Forrester, are you going to make me cry every time?"

"Only if the tears are there, Mrs. Tanner."

The elevator was a special one. It rose straight to the top floor with no stops. The corridor was carpeted in a plush maroon that picked up the thin maroon stripes in the gray wallpaper; there were groupings of chairs and tables along the walls. Marguerite had priced the whole thing by the time she reached the receptionist's desk at the end of the hall; it was the first indication she had seen of Lou's taste, and she felt flattered; he considered her as choice an item as the Chinese porcelain sitting on a low table, as the English chair standing next to the elevator doors.

"This is a fantastic place," she said.

There was a view of the whole city from his windows. She had seen the view from the restaurant on the floor beneath this one, but there were skylights in this room. You were, you knew, at the top of the world.

"I thought we'd eat here," he said.

"In the Matador Room?" I can't eat there with him, too many people I know have lunch there, I'll have to tell him I'm sick—

"I've got a little suite up here. We'll eat there." He opened a door in the far wall, she could see a small hall, and beyond that, a room.

As she walked ahead of him, hearing the door close behind them, she felt a panic, a panic she hadn't felt since the time she'd dated a football player with a reputation for refusing to take no for an answer. For the first time, she forced herself to think about what she had agreed to in saying she'd have lunch a second time. I ought to be laughing at myself, she thought. How many times have I slept with men I hardly know, anyway? So what's different about this one? It'll make a wonderful story to tell Grace, she'll appreciate it, and when I tell her about it, I will, too. But would she tell Grace? There were things she didn't tell Grace, even when they were part of the game they were playing.

Just last month. "Let's go some place, get out of town," Grace said. They were lunching, sometimes it seemed to Marguerite that they spent their lives lunching, dressing late, drinking their two or three or four martinis, eating food that they could hardly taste, spending a long sleepy afternoon.

"Can't. George is up to his ears. He hardly has time to

come home and eat dinner."

"I don't mean with George and Jerry. I mean us, just us. We'll run down to New Orleans for a couple of days. Shop—go to the races—put a little life into things."

"The children—"

"The children can stay with my kids and good old Mrs. Broom. God, Marguerite, you ought to get a live-in housekeeper. It's gorgeous. She's taken over completely. I don't even have to go to the grocery for a loaf of bread."

"George doesn't want to give up his privacy."

"Well, it's not as though she'd be sleeping on a cot in your room, is it? Keep talking it up, sweetie. You really don't know what you're missing."

And yet Marguerite felt that this very superiority of Grace's was part of what kept their friendship going—that Grace enjoyed being the one with more furs, more jewels, a bigger house, a fancier car, a live-in housekeeper—that part of Marguerite's use for Grace was to be a mirror, faithfully showing her just how great she really was.

"I'll talk to George."

"God, Marguerite, you don't *talk* to George. You *tell* George. George, Grace and I are running down to New Orleans for a couple of days. Suck him, or something." She casually waved a hand at the waiter, made motions over their empty glasses.

"I never ask old Jere anything. He minds very well." She plucked the olive from her empty glass, twirled it a moment and then opened her mouth and popped it in. Grace's mouth mesmerized Marguerite: she tried to tell herself that it was just an ordinary mouth, but it seemed larger, somehow, than other mouths, and the words that spilled from it seemed to have a special kind of fascination. She would watch the pink tongue dart out, watch it go back behind the barrier of white, white teeth, and right now, just because Grace had put the idea in her head, she could see Grace's mouth opening wide to receive a penis, and she wondered if Grace did indeed suck Jerry. At that time, she thought she was the only woman whose husband liked it—or, at least, whose husband asked his wife to do it.

George favored the idea. She should have known he would. She was going with Grace, and anything that bonded Grace and Marguerite more closely together was fine. So she packed the children up, filled a suitcase with her best clothes, and put on a fine linen suit that she had wheedled out of Lorenzo at cost, and drove to Grace's.

"We'll take my car," Grace said, and they crammed themselves and their suitcases into her sports car and took off in a spray of flying pea gravel, the four children and Mrs. Broom dutifully waving until they were out of sight.

"Pour me a Bloody Mary from that Thermos," Grace said as they left the highway and climbed up to the interstate.

She had three Bloody Marys in the time it took them to drive to New Orleans. Her driving didn't noticeably change, the car simply hurtled forward, taking a straight line down the concrete road, pointed like a dart at its destination.

"I hope a policeman doesn't stop us," Marguerite said. She was drinking, too, and the vodka, so early in the morning and on an empty stomach, was insulating her away from everything but the frightening speed of the car.

"Think I can't handle a policeman?" Grace said, and Marguerite hoped that she wouldn't have the opportunity to show how she did it.

230

But they arrived in New Orleans easily, Grace slowed down as they hit the midtown traffic, and took them to their French Quarter hotel as sedately as though they were both old ladies in their seventies out for a Sunday afternoon ride.

"If I didn't know better, I'd think you were trying to scare me," Marguerite said.

Grace flashed her a glance. "How well do you know me, sweetie?" And then she laughed and leaned over and kissed Marguerite's cheek and said, "Don't look at me with those great big eyes," and swung herself neatly from the car, handing the key to the attendant.

The room was lush: two large double beds, a chaise, a sofa, upholstered chairs—and on the low dresser, an arrangement of flowers, the yellow picking up the yellow of the print of the draperies.

"From the manager," Grace said, breaking off a flower and sticking it in her hair. "He likes to do these nice little things." And Marguerite felt a tiny nudge of envy that Grace always had good things happen to her, that her life was filled with flowers and wine and baskets of fruit. She had seen, last Christmas, the amount of presents that flowed into the Whitman house, flowed from all sorts of people. Grace hadn't cared for any of it, she had given most of the fruit to her maid and yardman, and kept only the wine that she said was drinkable—the rest, several cases full, she stuck in a closet to be given to the milkman and the postman and the garbage collectors at some later holiday.

"So shall we go to the races? Or go shopping? What?"

"I've never been to the races. That might be fun."

"Never been? Lord, I keep forgetting what a sheltered life you led before you met me. I swear, I have a ball just

231

showing you around. Okay, the races it is. I have a pass to the clubhouse. We'll eat there, okay?"

Grace bet seriously, studying the program, consulting the tip sheet, reading the racing form. "Steve Manchester's riding today, that's good, I'll bet on him. If he rides a horse nearly as well as he rides women—" She laughed, her mouth wide open and moist, her eyes watching Marguerite.

"Have you—"

"Slept with him? Sure. One winter down in Florida. Met him at some horsy party—never got out to the track, but we were together a lot. Funny little bastard. He really wasn't that great in the sack, but it was the novelty, you know? Somebody that small. Anyway, he's riding a pretty decent horse; I'll take a flyer."

By the end of the afternoon, Grace had won $1200 and Marguerite, following Grace's lead, but more cautiously, had won $400. Grace seemed to think little or nothing of it, she stuffed the money into her purse, slung her purse on her shoulder, and moved off. But Marguerite felt the excitement of winning going all through her. She patted the purse where the $400 was and thought of all she could do with it. She was still excited when they got back to the hotel and Grace suggested stopping in the lobby bar for a drink before they went upstairs.

There were several couples sitting in the bar, a few lone men, and at one table, two men who looked up when they came in, rose, and came to them. In the confusion of greetings Marguerite caught that one of the men was Ron Alford and the other was Hank Stern, and that Grace had apparently known them for ages, known them well. So, of course, they sat down, the four of them, and had drinks, several drinks, that added to all the rest of what she had

had today put Marguerite in a fine mood, a mood to take risks and to have dinner with these two nice men who just happened to be in New Orleans the same time they were. Which, when she thought about it, seemed like a strange and perhaps not to be believed coincidence.

"Did you know they'd be here?" she asked Grace, watching Grace pull her dress off when they'd gone upstairs to change for dinner.

"Who? Ron and Hank? You think I arranged that little meeting?"

"I don't know. It's a kind of funny coincidence. Their just happening to be in town."

"They travel a lot. And maybe I did know they'd be here. So what's the difference? Now we've got escorts for dinner, okay?"

Is that all we've got, she wanted to ask, but you didn't ask Grace anything, not if you wanted to stay on her good side.

And dinner was fun. They went to an elegant restaurant on St. Charles Avenue and worked their way through seven courses and several bottles of wine, and by the time they got back to the hotel, Marguerite decided that she was almost drunk, and she wanted nothing so much as to go upstairs and fall into bed and sleep the day off.

But Grace, after herding them all upstairs, stopped at the door of the room only a moment, and then took Ron's arm and moved off down the hall.

"Where—where are they going?" she asked Hank. She kept thinking that if she could only close her eyes, she could see things clearly, because as it was, she couldn't seem to focus, and nothing that she saw or heard made very much sense. She felt Hank take the door key, heard it scraping in the lock, felt herself gently pushed into the room. She stood just inside the door, heard Hank close the door, and was aware that he walked ahead of her into the room and dropped the door key on the dresser.

He sat on the sofa and took out a cigarette. She tried to focus on the tiny flame at the end of the match, but it was out before she could quite do it.

"I've had too much to drink," she said.

"Going to be sick?" He was there, a hand under her elbow, moving her softly forward.

"I don't think so. I just can't focus very well. And it takes forever to say something. But I want to know. Where's Grace?"

"Down in our room with Ron."

"I can't do it, she thought. Drunk as I am, I can't take off my clothes and get into bed with this man I didn't even know six hours ago. Grace shouldn't expect me to; Ron may be an old friend of hers, but Hank isn't a friend of mine, and I won't sleep with him.

"I won't sleep with you," she said.

"Good. Because I have no intention of sleeping with you."

His words tunneled their way through the thickness in her brain. She wondered, should she feel insulted, or glad, or relieved, or mad or what?

"Because I'm drunk?"

"Look, why don't you get undressed, get comfortable. I'll call room service, have some hot tea and toast sent up. Think you could get that down all right?" He was lifting the receiver as he spoke, giving the order.

She got her nightgown and robe and went into the bathroom. The face that looked back at her from the mirror didn't look drunk, it looked sleepy, maybe, but not bad, not puffy, the way it felt. She brushed her teeth, hard,

234

and went back into the room.

"Good," Hank said. The tea and toast had arrived. He poured out a cup and handed it to her, asked, "Apple or orange marmalade," and then nodded and spread some marmalade on a piece of toast and handed that to her, too.

"I'm glad it worked out this way," he said, drinking from his cup. "If I'd gotten Grace, I'd have trouble on my hands right now. But I kind of steered things so Ron would take Grace and I'd take you. I didn't know how you'd take it, my not sleeping with you. But I had rather try my chances with a stranger than with Grace."

"You didn't want to sleep with anybody, is that what you're saying?"

"It's not just you. You're right, I don't want to sleep with anybody. Which Grace might not understand. Because we've been having these little meetings for a couple of years now, always a lot of laughs, a lot of swapping around. But I'm through with all that."

The tea tasted good; she let it lie gently on her tongue, warming the inside of her mouth. Even the toast, thick with marmalade, was good. She hadn't thought she'd be able to eat, had thought the liquor would make it impossible to eat, but she could eat, she thought that with any luck, she wouldn't even have a hangover.

"Want to hear why? You're a nice lady, a pretty lady. I guess you ought to know why I wouldn't jump in the sack with you. It's my wife. 'Bout a year ago, she had surgery, had a breast removed. So it really got to her, you know? She was sure I wouldn't want to go near her. And I won't say the scar isn't bad—it took some getting used to. But she's my wife, right? And I owed her something. So right then, I told myself that if I could convince Anne I didn't care about the goddamn scar, I'd keep away from other

235

women. She never knew I'd cheated on her, so it wasn't that. But I felt—I don't know—kind of like if I cheated on her now, it'd be different. Know what I mean? Oh, hell. It's too complicated. I don't even understand it myself."

"But it's not complicated. It's beautiful. I think it's beautiful." She felt the easy tears, but held them back. She poured more tea into her cup. Now she felt at home with Hank; they could sit here and drink tea and tell each other secret things. The bad feeling she'd had when the door closed behind Grace and Ron would stay hidden in the corner where she had pushed it.

"Well, beautiful, not beautiful—that's the way I feel. So you can go on to bed, doll, if that's what you want to do. I'll wait for Grace to call and then I'll clear out, okay? And, look—not a word to anyone. I only told you because—I don't know. You're a different breed than what Grace usually turns up with. I thought I owed it to you."

But Hank must be mistaken. Grace hadn't done this before, hadn't had some other woman along. She tried to focus on that thought, but it slipped away from her, gliding easily down the path that liquor had so smoothly made past her brain. "I won't tell anyone."

The thought of bed was overpowering. She put her cup down, slipped out of her robe and into bed. Hank carried the tray to the door and put it outside. "Can't have them knowing we sat here and had tea," he said. He pulled the covers up to her chin, leaned over and kissed her lightly. "I think I'm missing something good," he said. "But let me tell you something, honey. Save it for your husband, all right? These little games—they have a way of catching up with you."

The next morning, she could remember very little of the evening—only that Hank had not slept with her, and

236

why. "Hank was fine," she told Grace over a late breakfast. "Very good."

"Yes, but they're leaving today." Grace looked at her watch. "Correction, have already left. Blast Ron anyway. I told him to plan on tonight, too. That's what happens when you get mixed up with men who don't run their own businesses."

"I'm kind of tired, anyway," Marguerite said. She leaned back in her chair, stretched. "I feel like I could sleep the rest of the day."

"Sleep, hell. We've got to find some prospects. You're not running out on me, are you?" Underneath the light tone lay the hard metal that frightened Marguerite into doing whatever it was that Grace wanted.

"Certainly not. Let me shower, I'll feel tons better."

But an afternoon at the races and a couple of drinks in the hotel bar produced no one but a fat drug salesman who lugged his sample case with him when he tried to pick Grace up. Grace had given him one look, and he had retreated to the bar, shakily picking up a beer and carefully turning his back to them.

"I can't believe this," Grace said when they went alone to dinner at a Chinese restaurant across the street from the hotel. "Either I'm losing my touch or I've gotten so damn discriminating I'm passing up people I'd have chosen a year ago."

So Hank was right. Grace had been doing this a long time. Why had she thought it had only begun with their game? She didn't like to hear Grace talk that way; it made her sound common. And if Grace were common, what did that make Marguerite? She was relieved and happy; as each hour of the afternoon and evening went by, and no men had appeared that Grace considered worth fooling with, she had felt better and better. She was able to steel herself to sleep with men she knew; she could laugh at the thought of Tom Baker having her quickly in the Bakers' guest room while a party raged drunkenly downstairs. And it added a piquancy to dining with the Harrises when she knew that Jack Harris had visited her earlier in the day for a luxurious hour in her bed. She was sure Janet Baker and Toni Harris slept around, too. They never said anything, but didn't everyone? But strangers—that was something else again. She ate an eggroll, dipping it into the hot mustard and feeling the tears start in her eyes.

"The next trip will be better, I promise you," Grace said, driving home the next day.

"This one was fine," she said, and she got out of the car at Grace's house with the feeling that she wanted nothing so much as to gather her children to her and get home and shut them all in and lock up the doors, tight.

CHAPTER FIFTEEN

This room she was in now, with Lou, gave her a feeling that maybe she at last had found a place where doors would lock, and never, never have to be opened unless you really wanted them to.

The table was already set, there was a pitcher of martinis on a large silver tray, and Lou poured one and handed it to her, his other hand coming down on her wrist in a small, fleeting touch. But he didn't touch her again. They ate crab salad and crisp pieces of freshly made Melba toast, drank a cool Rhine wine, and finished off with strawberries and Kirsch.

"You want coffee?" The sound of his voice seemed loud in the room. They hadn't talked much during the meal. She was too nervous, and hadn't been able to think of anything to say. Lou had not tried to talk, had eaten his salad, crunched his toast, drunk his wine.

"No, this was wonderful, lovely, I'd better be going—"

"Now, Marguerite."

I hate these silences, she thought. I always feel stripped and bound and helpless.

"All right." She stood up, looked vaguely around. The sofa? That seemed ridiculous. But he was ahead of her, he was opening another door, a door that led to a bedroom, and she walked through the door and stood in the middle of the floor, waiting.

"Would you like me to help you undress?"

"Yes. No. I don't know."

"Why don't I go back in the other room for a minute. You can undress and get in bed, okay?"

"Okay." Her voice was low, deadened by the tears that lay just under it.

She felt the obscenity of the marks of her bra and panty hose on her skin. People should either stay dressed or be naked all the time, this memory of clothing when you had shed it was like an accusation.

He came back when she was in bed, undressed carefully, turned from her so that all she saw was his chunky back and his surprisingly narrow buttocks. He was easy to move with, he seemed, in fact, to be always a little ahead of her. She did not have to work so hard, though it seemed to go on a very long time, longer, certainly, than George, longer than most of the men she had had. When he came, she was almost too tired to remember to cry out and clutch his back and even scratch a thin long mark across his shoulder.

He rolled off her, reached to the table beside the bed and lit two cigarettes. "So why didn't you like it?" he said.

"But I did, Lou, it was wonderful. What's the matter, didn't you enjoy that?"

"We're not talking about me. We're talking about you. You didn't like it. So why not? Did I rush you?"

240

"No, Lou, really, I—I liked it very much."

She wouldn't look at him, she looked instead at the tip of the cigarette. Her breasts were still uncovered, though the sheet was over the rest of her, and she hoped that the smoke would drift down and cover her. She had never gotten used to nakedness; it seemed to her by far the worst part of the whole thing.

"Crap. What are you, a whore? I'm not just using you. You didn't enjoy it. So all right, we don't know each other very well; I didn't go about it the right way. Tell me, okay?"

The tears came with the same ease as the smoke drifting from her nostrils. Men don't like women who cry, she thought, but she didn't care, she didn't. Lou was right, of course he was right, she hadn't enjoyed it, what was there to enjoy?

He pulled the sheet around her and turned her to him. Her face was close to his neck, she could feel the soft hair on his chest tickling her, he was patting her back, patting it rhythmically; she could smell their cigarettes burning in the ashtray where Lou had put them.

"I never do enjoy it," she said. The tears were stopping now, with the lightness of a spring shower that gently falls and then as gently stops, they quit. Unlike other times when she cried, she had no headache, she felt only a soft relief.

"Then your husband is a son-of-a-bitch."

"Oh, no, it's not George's fault."

"Then whose is it?"

"Well, it's mine, I mean, there's something wrong with me—"

"Crap. You read French? Some old guy, I don't remember who, he said anytime you find a frigid woman you find an incompetent man. Okay?"

241

"I don't want to talk about George."

"So. Neither do I. Look, you feeling any better?"

"I feel all right."

"I want to do something, okay?"

She moved slightly. They always wanted to do something, okay?

"All right."

"Turn over on your stomach."

She could smell her own perfume on the pillow as she turned; there was a small smear of mascara just beneath her cheek, and she thought that she would have to try a new brand. She felt Lou pull the sheet away from her, and she waited. When his hands began to touch her, to rub her back, working gently and then more firmly at the long tense muscles, she tightened up.

"Don't fight me, baby," he said. "Think of something quiet. What is it? Black velvet? Some damn thing. Anything that quiets you down, all right?"

She waited at first for the attack, the sudden move into her privacy—and then the long strokes began to force Lou's own ease into her, she felt the muscles loosen, she was aware, mixed in with the smell of her perfume, a strong clean smell coming from Lou.

As she slept she thought absurdly of her sweetheart in kindergarten, a little boy who had stolen flowers from a neighbor's yard to bring to her every morning until one day he had been caught and whipped, his legs reddening under the lashes from the thin willow switch. She woke to the smell of coffee; Lou stood beside the bed, dressed, a small tray in his hands.

"I didn't know how long to let you sleep. It's only two o'clock—"

As she sat up, the sheet fell from her. She felt his eyes on her breasts, and she sat straighter, lifting them. An illumination of the whole room seemed to happen as she watched him—the tray, the cup, the bowl of sugar, the pitcher of cream, Lou himself—all seemed bound by some kind of pouring light.

"I feel wonderful. I haven't slept like that in—oh, years."

"Good. Look, there's an elevator in the hall here that goes right down to the parking garage. I thought you'd like to use that."

"Fine." She drank the coffee, got up, and began to dress. She didn't mind that he was watching her, it was her that he was watching, not just any woman, not just any body. She pulled her slip over her head and then went to him, kissed him.

"Thank you, Lou."

"Okay. I'll call you."

She drove home through the slow July heat; the radio was tuned on to an FM all-music station, and she let the music envelop her, wrap her in a cool cocoon, safe, safe. She was aware of the length of her back against the car seat. If she concentrated on relaxing, on just feeling, then the long strokes of Lou's hands on her came back—did not come back, had never in fact left.

"I liked that," she thought. "I really liked that." A small nestling of hope. The way she had felt, lying under Lou's hands, might grow. It might someday be expected to soar, so that she would be like other women, women who still smiled the morning after, women whose meetings with men were compliments, not confrontations.

Again she thought that she wouldn't tell Grace about Lou. Let Grace think what she wanted, that Marguerite wasn't able to compete or that she didn't care. She could always make up a man. Though that was cheating. She and

Grace had both agreed, at the very beginning, that they wouldn't cheat that way. Still, she did not want to laugh at Lou Armitage over a long lunch with Grace. The way he had offered her the whole thing—the lunch, the view, the—she might as well say it, it was the second time today she had had to think about it, she might as well get it out in the open, yes, the caring. If both Lou and Dr. Forrester make me cry, she thought—watching the windshield blur as though the watery mist were on the glass and not in her eyes—if they both make me cry, I'll have to stop going to both of them.

The stillness of the house made her restless. Two months is too long for the children to be at camp; I should never have agreed to it. It had sounded so wonderful, back in March. Such a nice group of children going. The Whitmans' children, of course. And the Bakers'. And others of that crowd. And the prospect of two months of freedom from car pools and loud wrangling and from peanut-butter-smeared table tops and grimy baseball uniforms had sounded wonderful, too. But the stillness made her restless. She needed to fill up the house with people—the people her own thoughts cast up bothered her. Thinking now about her children, she knew those thoughts bothered her, too.

She had named Alan for George—George Alan Tanner, Jr.—and Sue for her grandmother, Sue-Ellen Marguerite. The name had always seemed too elegant somehow for her grandmother, yet she couldn't imagine anyone calling that thin stern wisp of a woman Susie, or Peggy, or by any other diminutive. She herself sometimes called Sue Susie; it made her furious, she wanted to be called Sue, only Sue, even when she was quite a little girl—she had made that clear.

Somehow the children had begun embarrassing her. One day they were toddlers under foot, having a screaming fit once in a while, but usually amenable, usually pretty nice, and then the next day, or so it seemed, they were ten and twelve and turning ugly. There was the time they had gone for a family dinner to the Roberts'—it was one of Nancy's good periods, she was out of the hospital and "doing things" as Biff put it.

As they sat at the table, Alan picked up the wine bottle that stood at Biff's place and said, "This is very cheap wine." She was horrified. But Biff had laughed and said that Alan was probably right, that he knew nothing about wines, and should have asked George's advice. If it were undrinkable, he would put it away and they could have iced tea. No, she had protested, it's fine: we love a good domestic wine, they're every bit as good as the imported. And she had shot Alan a look which promised retribution.

But on the way home, when she remonstrated with Alan, George had laughed. "The kid was right. It was a cheap wine."

"But he didn't have to say so," she said. "That was rude."

"Oh, right, he shouldn't have said so," George said, winking at Alan in the mirror. She had seen the wink, and had felt with a plummeting of her stomach that nothing she said to either child was going to matter too much anymore.

And then there was the way Sue had behaved when she was getting ready to go to camp just this summer. They had spent days buying the clothes she would need, and Marguerite had spent more days sewing on the name tags. "Don't cover the label in that sweater," Sue said, coming in and standing idly near the door.

"Why ever not?" Marguerite asked.

"Well, don't you think I want the other girls to see what kind of sweater it is? I mean, we paid a lot for it; I might as well show it off."

Again the cold clutch at her stomach, the cold clutch that was becoming more frequent as she tried to find her way through the maze the children had raised between her and them.

"Sue, that really doesn't matter, does it?"

"Matter? Of course, it matters. Do you know that June Atkinson bought all her stuff at Sears? Sears! Can you imagine?"

"I think Sears has some nice merchandise," Marguerite said. "We bought your baby furniture there."

"Oh, mother, that was eons ago when you were poor. But I bet there isn't one thing, not even one thing, in this house now that came from Sears—or Penney's, or any of those other dreadful places."

"You're turning into a terrible snob," she said, biting the end of the thread.

There was a sudden sharpness in Sue's face, a sharpness followed by a look of almost—contrition. Then, with a toss of her head she said, "Who's always talking about the 'right' people? Who, just last week, told daddy it didn't matter if you canceled a dinner date at the last minute because it was 'just the Crosbys?'"

"I didn't mean it the way you took it, Sue. I meant that—" But, of course, she had meant it in just that way. The Crosbys were leftovers from an earlier time; they tried to hang on to the old relationship, but it was becoming harder and harder to meet them, to find any common ground. "I meant that we were going out to eat. Of course, if Mrs. Crosby had spent all day fixing a meal, we'd never dream of not going."

246

"Oh, that was it," Sue said. Marguerite had noticed that the children had picked up George's way of smiling, that terrible secret smile that was becoming more and more unbearable.

"Don't be impudent," she said. "And stop lazing around. You can start folding these things to put in your trunk."

She talked to George about it later that night. "Sue's awfully snobbish," she said. "And I can't do a thing with Alan any more. He just gives me a look and goes right on with what he wants to do."

"But they're not doing anything wrong," George said. "We don't have two delinquents on our hands. They're clean, nice kids."

"I don't know about nice," she said.

"You've just never been around rich kids before," George said.

"What?"

"You've just never been around rich kids before. If you had been, you'd have known that rich kids are quite different from poor ones. They've got more confidence, for one thing."

"I call it arrogance," she said, but she kept her voice low.

"They're surer there's a place for them in the world, and that that place is a good one. Hell, you don't want the kids growing up like you did, do you? Wearing homemade clothes, never going anywhere. What do you think I work for, anyway?"

"Your own satisfaction," she said, but again she said it too low for him to hear.

"The kids are all right. I've watched them out at the club. They're just like the Whitman kids, or the Bakers'. Your friends' kids."

247

"Then God help us all," she said, and this time he heard her.

"You're a funny one, Marguerite. For years you give the kids everything they want, and now you complain because they're a little spoiled."

"Everthing they want—what does that mean, after all? Not much."

"The kids'll be all right. They're growing up. You can't expect them to act like sweet babies forever."

It was a few days after that that she found Sue's birthday ring lying on a table by the pool. She picked it up, thinking that she would return it, until it struck her that perhaps it would be better not to—let Sue miss the ring, hunt for it, worry a bit. It really was a lovely ring; she wouldn't mind having it herself. Old, it was old, and the soft gold of the setting gleamed with a patina that seemed made of all the twistings and turnings of the ring against the soft skin of the women who had once wore it. She had tried to convey something of what she felt about the ring when they'd given it to Sue. Sue had half-listened, not trying to understand.

"All you're saying is that other people before me have had this ring," she said. "Well, I know that. That's what an antique is—something that's been used, only it's so fine that instead of just getting to be used or second-hand, it's an antique. This is an antique, isn't it?"

"Yes," she'd said.

But Sue had not missed the ring, or, if she had, she said nothing about it. So that the day before she left for camp, Marguerite had said, "Why haven't you been wearing your ring?"

"I don't know where it is," Sue said. She was eating a bowl of cereal, there was the small crunch of the crisp flakes between her teeth.

"You mean you've lost it?"

"Well, I don't know where it is. I guess that means I've lost it."

"Sue, do you know how much that ring cost?"

Sue looked up from the cereal, her eyes like two small transoms opening up the dark reaches of her mind. "You never would tell me. Was it a lot?"

"It was enough." She didn't feel the familiar coldness now, only a hot anger that burned up through her, caught in her throat, and prepared itself to rush out and overwhelm the girl opposite her.

"Well, it must have been insured. It was, wasn't it? So you can collect the insurance and get me another one."

"Is that all you have to say?"

"What do you want me to say?"

"That you've been careless, that anyone who leaves their ring on a table outside deserves to lose it."

"On a table outside—did you find my ring?"

"I found it four days ago."

"And you didn't give it to me? Oh, that's mean." She tossed her head emphatically.

"Why should I give it to you? You should have asked for it; you should have told me it was lost."

"And get a long lecture? No, thanks. Anyway, I don't want to take it to camp, so you can keep it until I get back, okay?" She pushed her cereal bowl back, got up, and started to leave the room.

"Sue, come back and put your bowl in the dishwasher."

"Lora Mae can do that."

The anger was no longer just in her throat, it was all through her. It propelled her out of the chair across the room to where Sue was, it guided her hand to Sue's arm, it

249

tempered the strength of her voice.

"Come back and put that bowl in the dishwasher, do you hear me? And do it right now."

"Did you ever ask your doctor about the witch syndrome? I understand some women have it when they get their period."

She watched Sue walk across the kitchen, the long blond hair falling down her back, the pert swing of the buttocks as she walked. "She's lovely," Marguerite thought, "lovely and ruined."

When she went upstairs to dress for lunch with Grace, she opened her jewelry case and looked at Sue's ring. And her mind went tumbling back, to the first ring she had ever had.

She had been about eight, she supposed—a lanky quiet child—Phyllis chided her about that, saying why didn't she put a little life into the house, for chris sake, she was already like a little old lady. But she liked being quiet; between Phyllis' tempestuous chatter and her grandmother's long complaints, she found that silence was a cloak she could pull around her and keep both of them out.

The ring was lying on the sidewalk near the school, a silver circle with a small silver sombrero on the top. She had picked it up and slid it on her ring finger, it had fit with a perfection that made it from that moment hers. It was a magic ring, she decided, and when she got home, she had gone to her room and twisted the ring three times and waited for something marvelous to happen.

Nothing marvelous did happen, but then the ring was marvelous in itself, and she could make up enough dreams, wishes, and tales to satisfy any magic. She had not worn the ring down to supper, had in fact worn it only in her room, until on Sunday, as she was dressing for Sunday School, she got it out of its secret place and put it on her finger.

And, of course, at breakfast her grandmother saw it right away and wanted to know where she had gotten it.

"I found it," she said, knowing somehow that that was the wrong answer, but knowing too that it was the truth, so that it should be the right one.

"Did you try to find out who lost it?" Her grandmother seemed to fill the room. Everywhere Marguerite looked there seemed to be a lavender-dressed old woman, with streaked gray hair and hard steel glasses.

"No." Now she knew why it was wrong to say that she had found it; she should have said that someone had given it to her.

"That's as good as stealing, to find something and not try to find out who lost it," her grandmother said.

"Now, Ma, for God's sake. Leave the kid alone. Ring's probably not worth ten bucks."

"Stop taking the Lord's name in vain, Phyllis. And since when is honesty to be counted by worth in dollars? The commandment doesn't say, 'Thou shalt not steal anything worth over ten dollars.' It says, 'Thou shalt not steal.'"

"Marguerite didn't steal it, Ma. I won't have you saying that."

"Good as, if she doesn't try to find out who it belongs to."

"All right, all right. Where'd you find the ring, honey?"

But her mother's kindness, as always, was too small to overcome the desolation of being judged a thief by her powerful grandmother. Through the tears that she hated, because she knew her grandmother hated them, she said she'd found it near the school.

251

And so on the next day Phyllis had gone with her to the principal's office, and they had turned in the ring. A few days later, a girl claimed it, and the ring was lost forever.

A week later, Phyllis came home from work with a small ribboned box, which she had given to Marguerite in the perfumed sanctuary of her room.

Inside was a small silver ring with a turquoise mounted in the center. "One of my buddies picked that up for me in Houston," Phyllis said. "See, it's got a stone. That's better than an old sombrero, don't you think?"

"Much better," she said, and put the ring on.

But her grandmother had something to say about that, too. "Giving the child a ring for no good reason. Not her birthday, not Christmas. You'll spoil that girl, Phyllis, sure as I'm standing here, you're going to spoil that child."

"Nobody ever got spoiled over one silver ring," Phyllis said. "God!"

And she had swished out of the room, her silk print skirt moving the air behind her with a soft stirring.

But it had made Marguerite feel funny about the ring, and when her birthday came, she asked only for small things, and told herself that the ring was her big present.

Well, she'd do something about Alan and Sue later. For now—the restlessness seized at her, moved with her. She needed something. Grace would say she needed a good fuck, that was ridiculous. She needed love, approval, admiration. They were giving a party, she would talk to George about it tonight. The patio looked splendid now; even if it were hot, she could rent those huge fans and put them around—she felt a spurt of happiness. "Marguerite's parties are always wonderful," people said, and they were. That was something she did very, very well. And she would buy a new dress for it, something marvelous that would make everyone look at her, and remember her.

She went to her room and undressed, moving to her huge closet with her dress over her arm. In the quick flare of the light as she flicked the switch, she felt immersed in color. Row upon row they hung, heavy linens, graceful silks, fine imported cottons—she hung her clothes by color, so that in one part of the closet the blues shimmered, ranging from almost black navy to a fragile dress in blue so light it was almost white. And then the greens, the scarlets, the yellows and browns, the pristine whites, the weighty blacks. She went deeper into the closet, stood close to the rack of clothes, pulled their softness around her. She pressed into the colors, and the fragrance that puffed out from the pomander balls hanging on hooks high above her. "I am Marguerite Tanner," she said aloud. "I am Marguerite Tanner and I can have any damn thing I want."

She pulled a caftan from its hanger, dropped it over her head, shoved her arms through the sleeves. She still had on her jewelry, and she took it off as she went toward her jewel box, a massive case of fine leather that stood on her lingerie chest. And there was more color, and textures with substance—the thin etching on bracelets, the solid heft of her gold charm bracelet, the comfortable weight of the rings on her hands. She placed the topaz ring she had worn in its slot—it was the first piece of jewelry besides her engagement and wedding rings that George had ever given her. He had bought it soon after he'd gone to work for Biff Roberts, she remembered that George had gone to Mexico on a fishing trip with Biff, and she had begged him to go to the market at Matamoras and buy her a ring.

"They don't cost much," she had said. "Really nothing, compared to what you have to pay here. Oh, George, if I can just have a pretty ring, I promise you, I won't ask for another thing this year. It can be Christmas and birthday."

"And Halloween and St. Patrick's Day?"

But he had brought her the ring, a really lovely one, so nice that she had caught her breath and said, "But, George, it must have cost the earth!"

And he had smiled at her—funny how she preferred George unsmiling—and said, "I got lucky at poker."

Which statement had almost ruined the surprise of the ring for her, because what if he had lost? "I don't lose," George said, and that night he took out a Polaroid camera he'd borrowed from the office and took pictures of her, using lights to throw shadows across her nakedness, or to bathe her in a wash of warm brightness that made her feel she was blushing with shame.

Now there was a respectable amount of jewelry in the case. She never wore costume jewelry anymore, unless it was spectacularly suitable. She sank to the floor with the case in her hands and let the long gold and silver chains, the gleaming circlets of the bracelets, the finely crafted earrings, spill from one hand to the other. The light slanted off the stones, their color changed, deepening then becoming brighter, as she dropped them from hand to hand. "Lou could buy every bit of this and never even miss it," she thought. And thought again of his hands on her. He wore a gold ring on one hand, and she could remember now the small cold nudge of the metal on her back.

She almost didn't like being able to remember so much about Lou. When you remembered all those small things about people, they had a hold on you. They were part of your thoughts, part of your days, and of your nights, and the tightest wedge of your being was threatened by the

254

lever of their hold. "I won't think about Lou anymore," she said, murmuring the words into the open case before her. "I'll think about those jade earrings down at Williams'. I'll get George to buy them for me, and then I'll get a party dress to go with them, I'll wear them for the first time at our party, and I'll be tall and cool and green and almost every woman there will hate my guts." But she didn't laugh at herself as she usually did, even the thought of the jade earrings was pale in the afterglow of the glittering jewelry before her. She had, after all, had much the same kind of thought about every piece of jewelry in this box, and they hadn't worked, either, had they?

"I'll just do a steak for supper," she thought, and she put each piece of jewelry back in its place. Funny, the light had changed or something, the stones and metals looked duller now; it was as though something had pierced through the center of each piece and let all the sparkle out.

She was tearing lettuce for a salad when George got home; he looked, as always, spotless,—a quality George had, even when he put on work clothes and went out to a building site and stood in the heat and the dust, he managed to look clean and wonderfully important.

"Steak again? What's the matter, have you forgotten how to cook?"

"What's the matter with steak? My God, it's a rib-eye. I paid enough for it."

"You haven't cooked a for-real dinner in what? two weeks? Either we go out or you do a steak, or maybe broil some fish—"

"And you want what?"

"Food. Something that takes hours to cook. Gumbo. Or a chicken pie. Something."

"I've asked you to let me hire a cook."

"Cook! Crap. You can cook. You're a damn good cook. You used to cook all the time. Now you can't be bothered. You're so busy all the time."

"I am busy." She was quartering the tomatoes now; what if I turned and pushed this very sharp little knife into George; would he bleed redly as the tomatoes do? What kind of noise would he make?

"Sure. The checkbook shows how busy you are. So what did you buy today?"

"Nothing. I didn't go shopping."

"You were out. I called around one-thirty. Lora Mae said you'd been gone."

"All right. I was seeing my psychiatrist."

"Your psychiatrist? Since when have you been seeing a psychiatrist?"

"Since last week." She concentrated on the tomato in her hand. George would laugh, she already knew that. She thought dully that that was perhaps a reason for seeing Dr. Forrester at all.

And then he did laugh. The terrible thing about George's laughing at you was that it did not seem cruel. He laughed so openly, so freely, that even if he were laughing at you, you sensed a very good joke going on, and you wanted to share it. Nothing so appealing could be cruel.

"It's not funny, George."

"Of course, it is. Only unhappy people go to psychiatrists. And what do you have to be unhappy about?" The laughter seeped from his face, going in tiny riverlets that left the skin behind arid and lean. "What in the hell do you have to be unhappy about? Unless you want to cry on some goddamn expensive shoulder that I won't pay sixty-five thousand dollars for a lot you want."

"That's silly, George. I'm not going to a psychiatrist to talk about that lot."

"But you want it, don't you? Just like you wanted the lot this house is built on, and then the house, and then the big patio, and then the landscaping for the patio—Christ! You're a bottomless pit." He flung himself into one of the Windsor chairs at the refectory table. She winced and closed her mouth on the quick warning that rose; those chairs were antiques, they weren't meant for people to fling themselves on. She sometimes thought that if she lived in a museum, she would be perfectly happy. Surrounded by authentic things, perfectly valued, perfectly cared for—and the public allowed in only under the most rigid and limited circumstances.

"I am not a bottomless pit, just because I like nice things—"

"Nice things! That's a laugh. Do you ever, just out of the slightest curiosity, or maybe the tiniest interest in the amount of debt you've gotten your husband in, do you ever open a bill and just glance at it? Oh, I wouldn't expect you to do more than that, I don't want to upset you, of course not—but goddamm it, do you have any idea of how much money you spend?"

The salad was ready for the dressing now, she looked at it a moment as though she didn't know what it was she was looking at. It was, she noted wistfully, a new and expensive salad dressing that almost but not quite duplicated a recipe of her own that she could have made for about half the cost.

"But we have the money. We do, don't we, George?"

"And that's all you really care about, isn't it? That we do have the money. Have it, so spend it."

"I don't see what else money is good for."

She saw George watching her, a look, finally, of astonishment freezing his face into a parody.

"My God. My God. You really mean that."

"Don't look at me like that, George. What else would you do with money?"

"Save it. Invest it. Little things like that."

She saw towers of money, thin green and light silver, stacked, hovering over her. "But we do save money. You have your life insurance—and stocks. You told me you buy stocks."

"I could do a hell of a lot more of that kind of thing if you didn't put so much on your back."

"But you never tell me not to buy things. You never do, George."

"More's the pity. Well. Want a drink?"

He seemed cheerful. She couldn't understand it. She had thought they were having a fight, would say at last all the things she was sure they both thought, but did not say.

Reluctantly, she moved away from the fight. "I'd like a gin and tonic."

He went to the wet bar in the big room that stretched across the back of the house. She could hear him whistling, could hear the ice falling into glasses, could almost imagine that she heard the soft gurgle of the gin as it splashed down the ice cubes to rest finally in the heavy-bottomed glass.

He came back and handed her her drink. "Okay. So why are you going to a psychiatrist?"

"If I knew, I wouldn't have to go. Would I?"

"Hell, how should I know? Don't go all complicated on me, Marguerite. Your big virtue, as far as I'm concerned, has always been that you're the most uncomplicated woman I know. It's like living with a beautiful baby. Keep

258

you fed with pretty things and you stay happy. And I like a woman to be happy."

"You make me sound so stupid."

"Stupid to be happy? Listen, you've got it all over those women who forever want to prove themselves in some goddamn dumb way. At the Bakers' a while back? Hank Hopkins' sister was in town—did you meet her? She's got four kids, the youngest is ten, and she's in law school. Law school! And it's not as though she has to work to put food on the table. Her husband makes a lot of money. God, she was boring. Went on and on about it. How she'd never been alive until she started law school. How she'd wasted years. That kind of crap."

"Maybe she really had."

"What?"

"Wasted years."

"Like you have, huh? That what you mean? Listen here, I can provide you any goddamn thing you want, all right? You're Mrs. George Tanner and by God, that should be enough for anybody."

She took a long sip from her drink. George hadn't bothered to cut lime for the drink. She thought back to the perfect martinis Lou had given her at lunch, the lemon peel thin and twisted, lying lightly on top of the heavy drink.

"Oh, it is, George, it is. Sometimes it's more than I can handle. So I certainly wouldn't want to take on anything else."

"If I didn't know you better, I'd think you were saying that sarcastically."

She felt sex powerful in the air between them. She withdrew into her caftan, surely the wide swath of its material would be protection for her. But it wasn't, of

259

course. George unzipped it and dropped it to her feet in one movement; he unhooked her bra, pulled it from her, slid her panties down over her hips and let them fall to the floor. "Go on," he said, giving her a small push toward the back room.

"George—" George, what? Don't do this? Don't fuck me? Because that's what you do, you fuck me, you don't make love to me, have you ever made love to me?

But she didn't say his name again. She said nothing as she walked ahead of him into the room and lay down on the couch. This will ruin the upholstery, she thought. And as he got out of his clothes, she picked up his discarded shorts and placed them under her.

For the second time that day she remembered to move and cry out and even scratch the shoulders rising above her; this time no one caught her at it, this time the man was cheerful, this time the man was George.

"Max Farris was bragging the other day," George said, rolling off her and reaching for two cigarettes from the pack in his shirt pocket. "He was pretty stoned and he started telling us about him and Alice. How she is in bed. He buys these sex manuals, see, and gives them to Alice to study. It was all I could do to keep from laughing. Can you imagine Alice? God, the woman's got no breasts at all. Bony. You'd get bruised just lying on top of her." He handed her the lighted cigarette and moved to the end of the couch.

"But that's sad, don't you think that's kind of sad, George? That he would tell you about it?"

"Men talk. What's sad about that?"

"But you don't, George, you don't—"

"Let 'em imagine what it's like with you—I don't tell 'em a damn thing. And don't think they don't try to imagine. Hell, do you know what happens when you walk into a room?"

It would be a long walk back to her clothes. She might as well get started.

"Don't be silly, George. I'm an old married woman with two kids, nothing happens, nothing at all." Then she turned and looked at him standing there, that little smile watching her. "You're a little young to have to start fantasizing, George." The smile vanished; she did not like the look that replaced it.

She turned away, and as she began to pull on her clothes, heard George go upstairs. If she turned the broiler on now, the steaks would be ready when he got back down from his shower. She washed her hands and began seasoning the rich red meat. She became aware of tears on her face. For a moment she thought water had splashed up from the sink when she'd washed her hands, but then she knew that she was crying, and she thought back to the morning, the morning of crying in Dr. Forrester's office, and she heard again that slow voice saying, "Perhaps you feel a lack of—caring—in your life now."

CHAPTER SIXTEEN

She was sitting at the breakfast table drinking coffee while George ate his eggs when she saw a face staring up from the folded newspaper on the table. She put her cup down and turned the paper so as to see the picture better; with a start she saw that it was Johnny Roman, that friend of Lou's she'd met. She read the caption under the picture and gave a half-scream that resounded sharply off the polished surface of the table, off the glasses and cups. George looked up.

"What?"

"Nothing. A murder. I don't know, it just surprised me."

George reached across and picked up the paper. "Who? This Johnny Roman?" His eyes scanned the newsprint. Johnny Roman wasn't even important enough for George Tanner's eyes to focus on.

"Police suspect it's a gang killing." When George's smile became vocal, became a laugh, it made her want the smile back. "Suspect! That's a laugh."

"Why?"

"Because, of course, it's a gang killing. My God, the company Roman keeps—"

"What do you know about it?"

"Roman's murder? Not a damn thing." He was turning to the sports section: obviously, there were better wars to follow.

"No. Not the murder. Just—him. I mean, you sounded as though you—knew him."

"Good God, Marguerite, I'm in business here. You think I don't know who runs the town? Fortunately, I'm not in a sensitive business. But I know, of course, I know."

"Know what?" She heard the rise of her voice. If it kept rising, it would be a perpetual scream, screaming at George—what, why, why, not really what, but *why?*

"It's nothing to do with you," George said. "Just don't think about it." He put down his cup, looked at his watch. "Did I tell you I'm going to Washington? About a week, I guess." He got up, leaving his napkin crushed near his plate. The slow drift of smoke from his half-stubbed-out cigarette faded across that end of the table; it caught the empty chair, the empty place—how nice if it could catch George, bear him away, not just to Washington, but away, away, to join all those smiles that still caught at her and all those penises that still pushed at her—how nice if he were just gone.

"You could have told me."

"Why?"

"Well, the children are gone, you'll be gone—I could even have gone with you."

"I imagine you'll find enough to keep you busy." He looked at her then, the light eyes coming in fast from behind the screen of smoke, hooking her. The look was so full of knowledge that Marguerite thought, with the skin chill that accompanies truth, that George did know what she and Grace did, knew and was not going to say one damn word about it.

"Any suggestions?" She watched the light eyes go blank.

"I can't tell you what to do," he said. "That's not really up to me."

"No, it isn't, is it?" she said, and took a cigarette from the pack on the table and lit it.

She waited until George had taken his suitcase and gone, and Lora Mae was audibly vacuuming the living room before going to the phone to call Lou. When he came on the line, his voice coming over the wire harsh and somewhat loud, she was frightened. She started to hang up without saying anything; then the feel of his hands on her back was suddenly there, and she almost whispered into the phone, "Lou, it's Marguerite. I read about Johnny Roman, I—"

"Yeah. Tough break."

Silence. Then, "I just wanted to say I'm sorry, that I—"

"Sure. Okay. Listen, Marguerite, I'm going out of town, I'm kind of in a hurry, got some business to wind up—"

"You're going, too?" She hadn't meant for the wail to sound in her words.

"What do you mean, too?"

"George left this morning. He'll be gone at least a week."

"Okay. Good. You come with me then, all right?"

"Come with you?"

"Right."

"But, Lou, I can't just walk out of here for a week, I can't—"

"Okay. You can't. I'll talk to you when I get back."

She thought of George. I can't tell you what to do, he'd said. "Wait, Lou—maybe I could go with you. Where are you going?"

"Just places. Around. Houston—New Orleans—Biloxi. So what is it, you coming or not?"

"I'm coming," she said.

"They're warming the jet. Get on down here."

The phone disconnected. The cord that tied her to Lou's voice became just a cord. She put the receiver down and just as quickly picked it up. She heard her voice ask Lorenzo to cover for her, her voice tell George's secretary she was going on a buying trip for Lorenzo—Would the secretary call the children's camp and leave her mother's phone number? Then she called Phyllis.

For just a second, when that eager lilt filled her ear, she wanted to tell Phyllis the truth. "Hey, Mother, guess what—I've finally gotten the gold ring. I've found what you sent me out to look for all those years ago, only you sent me to all the wrong places—" Shit! Don't make some big romance out of this, Marguerite. Lou Armitage took you to bed the second time he took you to lunch—that's no gold ring.

But Phyllis heard it in her voice. "You sound pretty excited over an old buying trip. I'd think you'd be sick of looking at clothes. Now, if you were going to a resort. Cissy was telling me about a place down in the Yucatàn, it's—"

"Mother, I'm late. Look, I'll call you, okay?"

She packed swiftly, trying to calm herself by the careful attention she gave to folding her clothes just right, by the careful attention she gave to selecting the jewelry and the scarves and the ribbons and the shoes. She thought what had passed between them might somehow be engraved on the phone—Lou's astonishing invitation, her even more astonishing acceptance. Where did this trip fit into Grace's rules? In one freeing rush, she knew that it fit nowhere.

In a little over an hour from the time she had spoken to Lou she was easing her car down the ramp into the grey darkness of the parking garage. The ceiling pressed low over her; such places made her claustrophobic, the weight of the building overhead was large on her. One day surely it would collapse, surely a day when she was in the garage, her steel car roof helpless against the crashing brick and concrete.

But the ceiling remained firm. She locked her car and went to the elevator. A man was waiting there. He spoke to her and asked about luggage. She gave him the keys and waited while he put her two bags in the trunk of Lou's car, then rode with him up to Lou's floor.

Lou's jet was silver and blue; it was lovely against the hot July sky. She felt the excitement of knowing that she was right to do this. The hell with George, she was right to do this.

She didn't ask where they were going. It was enough to sit beside Lou, feeling the sudden lift of the plane, the almost straight climb, the gentle leveling off, the final turn as it settled on course. Lou put glasses on and began reading a paper he had taken out of his attaché case. The paper was long, with closely typed lines, and he squinted slightly as his eyes moved across it. He looked different with glasses on, more believable, somehow, so that the trip seemed almost normal. It was like going with George on one of his trips when he read and worked, and she was left to amuse herself.

She reached into her large bag and pulled out a paperback; it was a book Polly had mentioned at lunch, and which Marguerite had not even heard of. She had seen the surprise in Polly's eyes, and then a kind of—what?—a kind of sadness—that was it, sadness—which was silly. Why should Polly be sad because Marguerite hadn't read a book? But she had picked it up yesterday at the bookstore, and now she opened it to the first page and began reading. She didn't have to read more than two paragraphs to know that it was good, and she felt a kind of excitement she hadn't felt in a long time; she saw suddenly that Polly still knew her, knew her in a way that other people did not, could not, and she wished then that other people could know her in just that way.

"Don't you even want to know where we're going first?" Lou asked after they had been flying perhaps half an hour.

"I'm going with you. That's all that really matters," Marguerite said, and then she blushed, because what a stupid thing to say, how dumb could she get, she sounded like a schoolgirl. But Lou smiled and put his hand over hers. She could feel the ring again, and this time the small gentle nudge made her think of something.

"I never asked—is there a Mrs. Armitage?"

"Would you care if there were?"

"Not really."

"You don't mind sleeping with married men? Don't worry about breaking up a home?"

"That's nonsense. Either the home's already broken up, or it can't be broken."

"So which is yours?"

"Mine?"

"You and friend George. Already broken up, or not able to be broken?"

"George and I get along very well."

"That's why you sleep around, huh?"

"Don't say it that way."

"How do you want me to say it?"

"You make it sound—sordid."

"I don't make it sound any way. Just stating a fact. You do sleep around. So is it you don't get along with George, or you just like variety, or what?"

I wonder if I should tell him, she thought. That crazy day at Grace's. I'd only known her about six months, but already we were great friends. We talked on the phone every day, had lunch several times a week—and every day I thanked Fate or God or whoever for Grace. And every day I prayed that she wouldn't guess how grateful I was. But that day. That particular day we were lying out by the pool. We were both in bikinis, maybe one thing that drew us together is that we are both really beautiful, really great to look at, so there can be no jealousy, no envy, between us. Anyway. We were lying there, and then Grace said, "God, am I bored!" And then she sat up and looked at me and said, "Aren't you bored?" I could never be bored around her, but I knew she didn't want to hear me say that, so I said I guessed maybe I was, and she said we'd have to think of something, something we could do to wake our lives up. And she lay back and thought a while, and when she sat up again, she was smiling, it was her cat smile, long and thin and just a little frightening. And I was right to be frightened, very right, because what she said was that we would have a contest. We would see how many men we could sleep with, and she got very excited, and began making rules, and saying how a certain kind of man

269

counted more points than the others.

And I just lay there, thank God I had huge sunglasses on that hid most of my face. I couldn't believe what I was hearing. How could Grace Whitman be talking like that? I remember that I decided it was a joke, it had to be, so I sat up and began playing along, talking as though I thought she meant it. And then we went inside and showered and dressed and had a couple of gin and tonics, and I went home, and two days later at lunch Grace told me about her first one, and I knew it wasn't a joke. Only by then it was too late to do anything about it, because Grace would be furious if she found out that I hadn't meant it, hadn't meant that I thought it was a fine idea. And above all else, I couldn't afford to have Grace furious at me. No one else in that crowd was as nice as Grace was. No one else saw to it that George and I were included in the parties, taken in as though we belonged. So I couldn't help it, I had to go along with Grace. It doesn't really matter, anyway. The men who sleep with me are getting nothing, nothing but a lot of fake acting. They're not getting anywhere near *me*, near where I am. George doesn't even do that. No one does. Except I think maybe Lou will. And that's why I took the terrible risk of coming on this trip. I think finally I've met someone who will know me, will know me and like me—maybe even love me. The rest of it doesn't matter.

"I belong to myself, Lou. If I want to sleep with someone, I'm the one who's doing it, right? So it has nothing to do with George. Nothing to do with him at all."

"That's an interesting viewpoint. I wonder if friend George looks at it that way."

"I really don't care whether he does or not," she said, and she was proud of the firm voice with which she said it.

"That's my girl," Lou said, and she heard approval, and something else. Was it doubt?

They were descending now, going lightly down the cloud-filled sky as though on stepping stones. She saw an airport beneath them, and the letters spelling Houston, and she crossed her fingers and hoped not to run into Cissy.

A car was waiting. It wasn't a Rolls, but it was long and elegant and expensive, with a short dark man at the wheel who hopped out and held open doors, and made almost a ceremony of putting their luggage in the trunk. He didn't ask where they were going. Everyone, it seemed, knew where they were going except her, but she didn't care. It was gladly out of her hands, all she had to do was sit back and be pampered. It was something she knew very well how to do.

The hotel was tall, with an almost fortresslike front. Inside, the lobby ceiling soared some forty floors above them, with glass-fronted elevators climbing like beetles into the heights. Lou steered her to an elevator, this one in a bank of elevators that rose steeply on the outside of the building; through the glass front she could see the sidewalk diminishing, the fountain across the street throwing up smaller and smaller spray.

The suite was large, with a well-stocked bar set in a small alcove just past the entrance. Marguerite followed Lou into the bedroom; when the bellhop arrived with her bags, she waited for him to put them on the luggage racks and then began taking dresses out, fitting them carefully on the hangers in the closet.

She heard Lou say something to the bellhop, saw a flash of money out of the corner of her eye, heard the door close as the boy went out. Lou came and put his arms

271

around her from behind, catching the linen suit she was hanging up against her.

"Glad I don't have to pay your clothes bills," he said.

"With your connections, I'm sure you'd get a better price," she said, giving him the look that said: take care of me; you're so big and I'm so little.

"What connections?"

The voice, heavy, rough, rubbed against the weave of the linen. She actually looked down to see if a thread were pulled. That was the first really foolish thing she'd said today. Much more foolish than saying she'd spend a week in the company of another man.

"I'm sorry, Lou. That was stupid, tacky—"

"You ever think about the difference between real crooks and pretend crooks, Marguerite?"

He was moving toward the living room of the suite, going to the bar, fixing two gin and tonics. She followed him, held out her hand for the glass, sat on the long red couch that took up most of one wall. I'll be serious, she thought. She looked up at him; this time the look measured neither of them. "No."

"Real crooks have phony fronts. They make their money one way, but everyone thinks they make it another. They have their letter in the right church, their names on the right lists, belong to the right clubs. Their kids go to fancy schools, their dogs have fancy pedigrees, their wives have fancy tastes."

Somehow, this sounded familiar. A nudge at her memory, like the nudge of Lou's ring along her spine.

"Whereas pretend crooks are making money out of drugs, prostitution, gambling, extortion, murder."

"Lou?"

"I'm a pretend crook, baby. Everybody in town knows

where my money comes from. So it's laundered. They know it started out dirty; I know it started out dirty. And still I get invited to the Bakers'. Got that?

"Now Whitman, he's a real crook. People think he makes money from real estate and a couple of food-processing plants, nice clean business, right? Except all the while old Jerry is using drugs, prostitution, gambling, extortion—I suppose he does stop short of murder. If he can get what he wants any other way."

"Lou, look—"

"You want to know what I'm talking about? Jerry Whitman doesn't import the damn drugs—but he sure as hell buys the coke for his parties. He sure as hell pays the girls to entertain in those little apartments he's got set up everywhere. He sure as hell knows how to put pressure on—extortion pressure, baby. And you know what? He'll have dinner with a known crook like Lou Armitage anytime he can sweat the invitation—but he and that fancy whore of his couldn't be bothered to go to the class picnic at his kid's teacher's house."

The gin must have somehow separated itself from the tonic; something was choking her. Lou's last words had meaning at the same time they didn't have meaning. Jerry and Grace hadn't gone to some school thing?

"How do you know that?"

"Because my niece is the goddamn kid's teacher. Nice girl, married to a nice young engineer, so she teaches math or something at that fancy school because she can teach just in the mornings and be home with the baby, you know?"

"And she had a party and the Whitmans didn't go?"

"So okay. Except when Whitman found out, somehow or other, those suckers always find out, whose niece she

273

was, all of a sudden comes a big pot of ivy, some damn thing, with a note. You see what I'm saying? Real crooks like Whitman piss in their pants when they make a bad mistake and send a pot of ivy to cover it up. Pretend crooks—well, we don't make mistakes."

"Johnny Roman—" God, she saw what he meant about a pot of ivy.

"That wasn't a mistake. And relax, you didn't make a mistake bringing it up, okay?"

"But, Lou, it wasn't a mistake?"

"Not for the man who ordered it. Not from his viewpoint. Now from my viewpoint—" He looked at his watch. "Want some lunch?"

"If I can have the same dessert I had last time," she said, and took his face in her hands and kissed him. Then— "Damn. I don't mean to sound like that."

"You sound fine," he said. "And your eyes are exactly the same color as my niece's."

He was so kind, so kind and gentle. He went very slowly—it seemed an eternity of feeling, of warming— from the time they got into bed before he entered her. And when he did, she could feel herself meeting him, really meeting him, felt it for perhaps the third time in her life. When it was over, she knew she was crying against his shoulder, and she turned her head into the pillow so he wouldn't see. She heard him get off the bed, heard soft sounds as he dressed, heard him go into the living room, closing the door behind him. And then the small sound of the telephone, a ring that was muffled by the thick door, and then a low steady murmur that was Lou talking.

She stretched, finally dozed, woke to hear Lou's voice. Was he still on the phone? This was a business trip, after all; she just hoped to God it was some of his lesser businesses. She hadn't let herself admit what Lou had said. People just didn't admit they were into drugs, prostitution, the rackets, extortion, and then go make love like anyone else. Like anyone else? Not like anyone else. Like no one else she'd ever been with. She had never, in her whole life, made love before.

Lou's voice rose. It didn't sound angry, it sounded worse than that, it sounded as though Lou owned the person at the other end of the line, and that if that person didn't do what he was told, Lou would toss him away like so much trash.

"You damn well will," that heavy voice said. And then there was a silence, and Lou came back into the bedroom, rubbing the back of his neck with one large hand. He came over to the bed and picked up her hand, kissed the inside of it. "Put something fancy on, doll. Some people are coming over in a while for drinks. And then I'll take you some place fine for dinner. Okay?"

"Lou? Jerry was talking once that something happened at one of the plants. One man died, two others crippled — he'd won the lawsuit, I don't know, they couldn't prove he was negligent."

"So?"

"So he was saying that night that he was. Except — 'I don't call it negligence. I call it not spending money the damn goverment says to to save some trash hide.'"

"So?"

"I just thought of that. And about the pot of ivy."

"You gonna send old George a pot of ivy?"

"No."

"Fuck George, that it?"

"No. Never again." And knew that it was true.

CHAPTER SEVENTEEN

The people turned out to be four men and one woman, a silent blonde whose hair was piled into an impossible height on her head. The woman seemed almost comatose. She sat holding a glass that she rarely drank from and offered nothing of her own volition. The four men got Lou in a corner and whispered urgently. Marguerite couldn't hear them, but she could see the way the worry left their faces and spread to Lou's. She could see that there was some problem they were trying to solve, and whatever the solution was, it wasn't a happy one, because when Lou finally said, loud enough so that she did hear him, "That's what we'll do, then," he sounded final, only final, and not at all relieved to have the thing settled.

They came back to the women then, and made small talk—every once in a while a man would poke the blond woman on her arm and say, "Tell Lou about the baby, Marie. Lou wants to hear." And the woman would open her mouth, and amazingly, words would come out, amazing because she looked so mechanical that Marguerite thought some kind of metallic tune would be more appropriate. She was afraid they would all have dinner together, but after a while the men got up, and the woman's husband went to her, and pulled her to her feet, and they left.

"What in the world was the matter with that woman, Lou?" she asked when they were gone.

"Just a goddamn dumb blonde. Married above herself." Lou was restless. He was watching the sun slip down to the other side of the world, his heavy hands kneading the deep-red-and-blue plaid draperies. "Husband started out a runner, and turns out to have brains. So she's out of her class. It happens." He turned and looked at her. "How about you, baby? You out of your class?"

"I don't think I have one," she said.

Miraculously, the lines in his face smoothed as the drapery fabric smoothed, released from the tight hold of his hand. "God, she's starting the philosophy crap," he said, but he was smiling, and she went out to dinner at a place "almost good enough for you, doll," as though to her very first prom.

And later, back in the room, she pulled the draperies at the window back and looked at the city below her and thought that Cissy and Phyllis would like Lou. He was exactly the kind of man they admired. Why hadn't she married someone like Lou?

"Lou, is there a Mrs. Armitage?"

"You think you'd be here if there were?"

She looked at him. He was serious, she could see that he was serious. "You mean if you had a wife, you wouldn't have me with you?"

"That's right."

"But suppose—oh, suppose you were tired of her, or you liked someone else, or—"

"Manny didn't get rid of Marie."

"Who?"

"The blonde."

"Oh."

"Some things you don't do, you know?"

"I've done them." Her voice was low, she hoped it was low enough to slide into the thick carpet, the thick draperies, not be heard.

"Ah, shit. You haven't done anything. There wasn't anything there to be done to, you know? You've just been playing adolescent, baby. You must have had one of those Texas Baptist families. Poor God, he doesn't always get to choose his friends."

"What?"

"Come on, Marguerite, you're no dummy. I mean, somebody's done a number on you. Or a couple of somebodies. Here you are, all equipped to have a hell of a good time in bed, and you've been talked out of it. But all the while, somebody else is having his hell of a good time—and yours, too."

She knew that if she could stay, could just stay and believe what Lou said, then she did have the key to the gate in the fairy garden wall, there really were giants chasing her, she had been right, and there really was a prince ready to lop the giant's head off—or pay to have it done.

"Tell me, Lou, tell me—"

He came to her and took her hands. "Doll, I don't think I'm ever going have to tell you anything about any of this again."

So then she did have a good time, the best time in bed

279

she had ever had. She came twice, the first time was a glory, the second a surprise that she'd never have thought possible. When they finally stopped, she lay against him and touched his skin with the tip of her tongue, his skin tasted a little of salt and warm under her tongue. She felt soft and slow and easy and she slept.

She woke to sunlight, to the sound of an electric razor, to peace.

Lou poked his head around the bathroom door. "What do you eat, an egg, what?"

"Orange juice. An omelet. Lots of coffee."

He went to the phone and ordered. My God, he even makes ordering breakfast sound absolutely essential. She closed the bathroom door behind her, staring at her face as she brushed her teeth. What had she done to deserve being here? She thought of the men she'd been with since she and Grace had started the game.

"I want to tell you about it—my sleeping around," she said, pouring more coffee into their cups.

"Up to you."

"I—I never slept with anyone until I married George. I really didn't. And after that—I just didn't. Until I met Grace."

"What, Grace had a friend?"

"What? No, it wasn't that, it was—" She listened to herself tell him about the game. How normal she made it sound, how ordinary, as though they were any two housewives, coming up with a new hobby to pass time.

"Poor baby," Lou said. He gave her a cigarette and held his lighter to it. "And you fell for it."

"I can't explain it, Lou, I—"

"Sure you can explain it. You wanted in with Grace and her crowd, you had a toehold, this looked like a long step

280

up the ladder. What you didn't know was that that bitch was already screwing everything in town. This game she made up—it was just to get you hooked."

"Grace already—"

"Sure. She was with Johnny Roman a lot last year. That's when I first got to know her."

"Did you—" She stopped. If Lou had slept with Grace, she didn't want to know it.

"No. Not me. Not that she didn't try. She'd get Johnny to bring her up to the office. Then she'd stick out her tits and try to gouge me with those big brown eyes. She's a lot of woman. But she's also crazier than a bedbug, and I wasn't having any."

"Why would she get me involved? If she were already— sleeping around, why the act that it was something new?" She thought of Grace, her terrible assurance, her terrible bitchiness. "I'm scared, Lou. I'm scared."

"Finally beginning to get some sense. Stay away from that woman, Marguerite. She's poison, she really is. Didn't you ever wonder why the great Grace Whitman had time for someone like you?"

"We got along well. We had fun together—" Her voice struggled to get past the nausea in her throat. She sipped some water and pushed the taste of omelet and buttered toast back down. "Anyway, what do you mean, someone like me? I'm as good as she is, don't give me that."

"You know what I mean. And don't lie to yourself. You're not as good as she is." He waited, blew out a stream of smoke that caught in the air between them and, for one instant, veiled his face. He got up, came around the table, and stood over her. His hands came under her elbows, pulling her up to face him. "You're a hell of a lot better. And don't you ever forget it."

Then she cried. Cried against the soft tie silk of his robe, wetting the small circles of scarlet so that they deepened and stood out against the dark blue ground of the robe like tiny wet eyes. She could feel his hand patting her, it made her cry harder, all the tears she had ever swallowed on so many nights of living with George were being let loose now. "I think I'll cry all day," she thought. She stopped, of course. Stopped when her throat was raw and tired, her eyes strained with tears.

"Jesus," Lou said. "What did I say?"

"You're too good to me, Lou. You really are."

"You cry when people are good to you?"

"I must."

"So how wet will my shoulder get if I send you to Sakowitz' today?"

"I don't want you to buy me anything."

"Why not?"

"I don't know. I just don't."

"It makes you feel kept?"

"Maybe."

"And maybe I just feel like buying something pretty for a hell of a woman I know."

The phone rang, pulling Lou's attention from her. She braided the ends of her robe belt and sat listening to him. He sounded angry: somebody named Rosie had done something, or hadn't done something, she couldn't tell which, but whatever it was, it made Lou mad as hell.

"Christ," he said, hanging up. "Want something done, you damn well need to do it yourself. Look, something's come up. I got to go out for a while. You want to shop, get your hair done, what?"

"Lou, I'm able to amuse myself. I'm not a baby; you don't have to look out for me."

"But that's just what I want to do, Marguerite. I want to look out for you, okay?"

"All of a sudden I want to tell you the story of my life," she said, and laughed.

"So okay, we'll exchange stories over dinner. You might change your mind about shopping. I'll put some money in your purse."

After Lou had gone she opened her purse and counted the hundred dollar bills he's tucked down next to her compact. Six of them. Six hundred dollars to blow. She waited for the thrill that usually chased her into her clothes and out of the house to the shops whenever George gave her some unexpected money. But she didn't want to spend Lou's money, she didn't want there to be any money involved. She could sleep in his bed, eat the food he paid for, drink his champagne, his liquor. But people traveling together shared those things—that was expected. Six hundred dollar tips were not. Unless she bought something for him. Just for him.

That pleased her. She dressed and left the hotel, walking the few blocks over to Sakowitz.' She knew what she wanted; she hardly had to look. She recognized the dress as soon as she saw it, she had somehow known it would be there. It was white, simply cut—almost Grecian in its flowing lines. It was caught at the waist with a narrow woven belt, a thin strand of gold twisted in with the white. She would ask Lou if they could have dinner sent up to the suite; she would wear the dress, she would pile her hair high on her head, she would tell Lou that the dress was for him alone, she would never wear it for anyone else. "Like a schoolgirl," she thought, turning before the dressing-room mirror, watching the long fall of white around her legs. It was in that moment that she

283

knew she was in love with Lou Armitage.

The afternoon seemed long; it seemed longer because she couldn't get away from Lou. How could she be in love with Lou? She was being silly, ridiculous. Lou didn't want her to be in love with him—as for that, she didn't want to be in love with him, either. At one point she almost paced and left. She even called the airport to see about flights, but hung up as the Delta man was telling her.

She thought of being in love with George. She didn't really believe you could be in love with two men at once. If she loved George, she didn't love Lou; if she loved Lou, she didn't love George.

She thought about George. Had they even seen each other, really looked at each other, known each other the way she and Lou did? Or had they been a prize for each other, the promised goody, the reward for effort, or for ambition, or for pride.

She had been pliant in George's hands, but she knew that she never would be again. Not in his, not in anyone's. She felt invincible. To hell with Grace and her scruffy games. When she got back, she'd beg off. No, not beg off. Just be off. Tell Grace she had more to do with her time than screw around with a bunch of lonely or sad or restless or bored or whatever old men. Now that she'd been with Lou, she couldn't imagine being with anyone else. She felt a small curling inside her at the thought of having anyone else touch her.

So what in the hell would she do about George? And for the first time, the word divorce came into her mind. Divorce. Why not? Why ever not? George had what he wanted; he didn't need her anymore. If he ever had. He could find someone else to sleep with him. To suck him. God, how marvelous never to have to do with any part of

George again. Alone at the table high above Houston, she laughed. The two men sitting across from her turned and looked at her, their looks stayed on her longer than casual curiosity warranted. She looked the younger one in the eye, forced his gaze downward, back to his plate. She laughed again. How nice to know what you could do, when you no longer had to do it.

She thought of Alan and Sue. Would Lou want them? And then she had to laugh at herself, first thinking of divorce, then already leaping ahead, having herself married to Lou. As though he had asked her. He had to ask her—he had to. It was what she had been waiting for all this time, all these ridiculous years; standing on the Bakers' patio she had felt his strength, had known she could crawl inside it and be safe.

A change would be good for Alan and Sue. She knew that she didn't like them very much. She loved them—well, she tried to love them. Had loved them when they were small, when they had been tucked into second-hand twin beds in a nursery with curtains she'd made herself. But the years had turned them into the kind of children she had been afraid of, when she herself was a child. Maybe she had done that to them. With a sudden clarity she saw herself dressing for the interview with the principal at the private school. The questions she had asked, questions about education and children's learning and the right technique for the right child. Questions she had asked as though she really cared about the answers. When the truth was that she would have sent them to the school if they'd been taught by Hottentots. Because the Bakers' children went there. And the Whitmans'. And everyone's.

She drank more coffee, staring into the pale brown

liquid in the cup as though it held an image of the very foolish woman she had been. Had been, she could say that, because now she could see all those silly, silly and ridiculous reasons she had given herself—and George—for each step taken, each choice made. At least the school really was a fine school. At least there was that. She might have filled her children's heads with a lot of spun-sugar silliness, but at least something else had been put into their heads, too. And they were bright. They could change, could stop their snobbery and their arrogance, could even become the children she had thought they would be all those years ago when she and Polly and their babies used to sit out in the straggly backyard on Stephen Street and talk and dream and think happily of the wonders that lay ahead.

Well, the wonders hadn't been so wonderful after all. She supposed she realized now what an absolute shit of a place the world could be—imagine that she had actually bothered to be pleased because some woman was impressed by the labels on her clothes, the obvious quality of her shoes. Whereas Lou—he hadn't cared for any of that. Not in a way that mattered. He liked her to look good, she knew that. But still, it was different with Lou. When she dressed to go out with George, she had the feeling of being his accessory for the evening. If no one made a comment about her dress, George would work the conversation around to it. "I'm working extra hard these days," he would say, leaning on someone's mantel with a drink in one hand in a pose that she would swear he had practiced. "I've got a wife who thinks all she has to do is push a button and the money machine will turn on to pay for dresses like the one she's got on tonight." And then they all would laugh, because it was understood in that crowd that you fussed about not having money only when you really had it. George's complaints were taken as being funny—only Marguerite knew how much George enjoyed the game, enjoyed having her to display.

She felt tears in her eyes and turned her head away to hide them. She was feeling hurt, a deeply penetrating hurt that caught at her and seemed to force her back in her chair. The litter of her lunch lay around her, the half-eaten asparagus, the picked-at chicken salad. She lit a cigarette and tried to inhale the smoke down past the hurt, but the smoke caught there. She choked and raised the glass of water to her mouth.

She knew now why George had married her. Of course, he didn't want Dorothy Hyland, with her money to hold on to. Even for all of her crazy worship of George, Dorothy could have gotten away. When George began to play his little games, she could have left. Whereas Marguerite—of course, he knew she couldn't leave him. She could barely type. And the two babies they'd had so fast. She remembered asking him to wait. But he wanted babies, he'd convinced her that she did, too. Of course, he wanted babies. How could a wife who could barely type get a job to support herself and two babies?

And after that—the way he'd given in to the things she wanted, always holding out just long enough so that when he did finally give in, it was as though it were against his will. When all the time he'd wanted the same thing. Without the responsibility of saying so. The lot, the house, the club membership—it would be only a matter of weeks before he bought the $65,000 lot near Grace and Jerry. And then he would collect from her, collect in all those little invidious ways that she had never been able to hold out against. That she had, in fact, not even seen for what

287

they were.

Dr. Forrester was damn well right. There wasn't much caring in her life. Or hadn't been. George. George doing nothing more or less than playing some kind of game with her life. And her being idiot enough to go along with it.

She felt an excitement rising in her like the lift of an express elevator. Of course, that was it. It was why she'd done all those things, gone along with Grace. Of course. That simple. And then the excitement slowed to a stop, leaving her feeling caught and baseless. She felt shame, a terrible shame that covered her, bowed her down. How could she have? Like a common streetwalker. Whatever fancy names she and Grace used for it. A common streetwalker. She had no right to talk about George, George and his games. When all the time, she was doing what she'd done.

The waiter was hovering, she looked at her watch and saw that it was almost two-thirty. She scrawled the room number on the lunch check, wrote "Mrs. Lou Armitage" under it. Lou wouldn't care, he must have registered them that way. Anyway, she wanted to see how it looked. It looked good.

CHAPTER EIGHTEEN

Upstairs, the suite still empty, she found that shame was a difficult companion. She couldn't seem to talk herself out of it; the white dress, hanging on the back of the closet door, seemed ostentatious and bold. Who did she think she was fooling, anyway? Lou Armitage knew what she was; hadn't he taken her to bed the second time they'd had lunch? So what was different about this? Except that it had to be different, it just had to be.

She forced herself to undress, to pull on a robe and sit at the dressing table creaming her face, then to lie down and rest, listening for the click of the key in the door so that she could run into the bathroom, hide that greasy-white face from Lou. At the end of an hour, he still hadn't come. She got up and ran hot water in the tub, added the bath salts she always brought with her, locked the door, and slid into the foaming warmth. But when she'd finished, and was back in the bedroom pulling on pantyhose, fastening her bra, slipping her feet into tall white sandals, he still hadn't come. She dropped the dress over her head, felt how right it was, slim, soft, with a sheen like the sheen of her own bare skin.

And then she waited, waited with a slowly sipped drink in her hand, waited in such anxiety that when he finally came she threw herself against his chest and caught at him, her words unintelligible, only the anguish coming through.

"Hey, what's going on, hey, Marguerite, what's got you so upset?"

He pushed her gently from him, held her by the arms just in front of him.

"I thought you weren't coming—that you'd, I don't know, that you'd left. I thought I was alone." She watched him as she said the words, saw him being touched by them.

"I don't do things like that, Marguerite. You should know, I don't do things like that."

"I thought maybe you would—with me."

"Especially not with you. Okay? You're too pretty to think I'd leave you, you know that." He went to the bar and began making drinks.

"Is that all?" she said.

"All?"

"You say I'm too pretty to leave. Is that all?"

"You want an Old Fashioned, plain bourbon, what?"

"An Old Fashioned. Lou, don't evade what I'm saying. I want to know."

"What do you want to know?"

"Whether I'm here just because I'm pretty."

"Isn't that enough?" But his eyes, large, sparked with the light of the dying sun, said that wasn't all. Said something else she could hardly believe. He handed her

her drink, wrapped in a small square napkin. The napkin had the hotel's name on it. She had a crazy impulse to take it off the drink and fold it away for a souvenir, a souvenir like the crushed roses and carnations of her high school corsages, memories of another time, another place.

"Can I say something?"

"Whatever you want."

"You might not think I'm a very honest woman. I'm going to lie to George about this trip, you know that. And I know you know I've been—well, sleeping around. I know you know that. So you might not think you can trust what I say. And maybe it doesn't matter to you, anyway—if I'm here just because I'm pretty, a kind of trophy, like I've been for George, then I probably ought to keep my mouth shut."

"Go on." He was watching her intently; when she'd said that about George a different quality came into his eyes, something she couldn't quite define.

"Anyway—all right, I'll say it fast. I love you, Lou. It's—it's why I came with you. I want you to know that." The distance between them was wide, a cold, windswept landscape to try to move across. She felt the urgency to move toward him, but she stood there, the glass lifted halfway to her lips, her eyes looking out the window at the light-bright horizon.

"I think that's true, Marguerite. In fact, you might say I've been counting on that being true." He was sitting on the sofa. He patted the cushion next to him, then stood, and held out his hand. His face was tense; as she watched, the tension broke, he smiled and came toward her, hand still outstretched. "I won't ask you why. I might not want to know that. And you probably couldn't tell me anyway."

She felt the coldness from his glass as the hand holding

it went around her; she put her own glass down, straightened up in his arms, laid her head against him and closed her eyes. Why this feeling of being home, why this feeling of safety when she was standing in another man's room in a city far from home, preparing to lie to her husband, having already committed adultery—she should be frightened, she should be more frightened than ever in her life, instead of feeling this ridiculous and totally inappropriate peace.

"I know something now," she said. "Something I always thought was fake, silly—something I thought I'd never say to any man."

"Okay."

"I want children with you, Lou." She said it softly, barely turned her head from him so that the words drifted slowly like the small chill from the ice in the cold glass, and like the chill were then warmed on his soft breath. "Alan and Sue—it's a shame, I don't even like them very much. I guess I love them. I don't want anything to happen to them. I do everything I can to take care of them." She thought of the procession of maids there'd been in the last few years, the times she'd thrown her shoes in wretched anger because the maid hadn't shown up and she'd a party, a lunch, a modeling job. "No, that's not true. I've been a rotten mother, and they're rotten kids, just what you'd expect. They're spoiled and sassy, and when I used to try to correct them, George would tell me to leave them alone, and later, I saw that Grace's kids, everybody's kids, were the same way, just exactly the same way, until I thought it went with being rich. And then it only bothered me because I didn't feel rich inside." She stopped, caught on the sharp and piercing point of what she'd said. "Lou, do you know that's true? In these last few years, when I've had just about everything I've wanted, I've never felt rich inside. And now I do."

"That's not feeling rich. That's feeling loved."

This can't be happening now; I'm thirty-two years old, I'm supposed to be worrying about wrinkles beginning and my stomach getting flabby, and watching my diet, and getting lots of sleep. I feel sixteen, only I never felt this way when I was sixteen, I was too busy being Miss Everything so when I went to college the sororities would notice me.

"This is the happiest time in my whole life," she said. "I want to know every single thing about you, I want to know when you were born, and where, and did you like school, and how did you get so rich, and why do you love me, especially I want to know that—why do you love me?"

"Well," he said, his arm in the summer silk suit, soft and heavy and warm and cool on her shoulder, "well," he said, slipping his feet out of his shoes and putting his feet up on the coffee table, "my mother's favorite saint was St. Louis, King of France. You believe that? I was named for a king, a king from the wrong country."

"There's no wrong country for you, Lou."

"So when I was little, the kids called me 'king,' only not to be nice, you know? They'd seen that crazy picture Mama had, him being crowned, Jesus! So I crowned a lot of heads myself and then they started calling me Lou."

She hadn't known he had that sense of the funny, the ridiculous. How glorious, all she still didn't know! She put her feet up, too, slid her stockinged feet across his silken ones, until they moved to one another and made love, they did not fuck, they made love.

"Fuck is a dirty word," she said when they went to shower.

And the next day, even though he had to make two calls, hand over the receiver, sitting with his back to the glass wall that protected his box from the rest of the crowd in the Astrodome, he took her to see the Astros win, and they ate hot dogs served on a silver platter and drank imported beer. And he took off his coat and loosened his tie and cussed the umpire and carried on "just like a normal human being" she told him, and that maybe was the biggest miracle of all.

"Is it going all right?" she asked that night as they lay in bed. Lou liked old movies. She did, too, and they kept the TV tuned to the old movie channel, watching or not, chiming in with the dialogue, laughing ahead of the jokes.

"What?" He was watching Humphrey Bogart light Ingrid Bergman's cigarette; God, was there any better way to spend an evening than watching *Casablanca* with Lou?

"Your—work."

"Chess game. All I can handle is my side."

"Then it's going fine," she said, and when they left for New Orleans the next day, she did tuck souvenir matches and napkins into her suitcase, because whatever lay ahead of them, a time of great peace and love and closeness lay behind them, and that would sweep them forward, would move them past all the foolishness that George would come up with, move them into the bright land that lay just ahead of them, and that they would reach, because they were strong and right and would persevere.

So all the way to the hotel in New Orleans, she sat close to Lou and held his hand, stroking the inside of his palm with her fingers, thinking now she felt married for the first time in her life, felt she belonged in the same bed with this man every night for the rest of their lives.

Then they were at the hotel, and they stepped into the

elevator, and the walls of the elevator rose steep and smooth around her; the elevator rose steeply and smoothly in its shaft. The silk of her dress was smooth. It fell against her lightly; it barely touched her panties, her bra. She wanted to laugh and clap people on the back and tell them about Lou. She wanted to hug Lou and kiss him. She reached for his hand, and at first he frowned, almost as though he hadn't noticed what hand it was. But then he smiled, and they rode to the floor where the pool was, and the car stopped, and they got out.

She liked the suite. It didn't have a phone jack in the bathroom, but it did have a bidet. Hell, who wanted to talk on the damn phone?

Now she walked around the living room. She had kicked off her shoes and the pile of the shag rug rose under her stockinged feet. She liked to begin to feel slowly, to arouse the soles of her feet with the tickling carpet, to then take off her dress and let the air from the ducts blow over her bare skin. Sometimes she took a brush from her purse, and brushed her hair with long, slow strokes while Lou watched her.

"You're the only woman I know who does her hair before she gets in the sack," Lou said.

"I'm not doing my hair. I'm getting ready." The brush would move through her hair, touching down at the base of her neck. It would move lightly over her skin, the nerves under her skin becoming slowly awake, and then the slow light movement would travel throughout her body, so that when she put down the brush and went to the bed, she would be ready for Lou's hands.

He moved to her, and she stood while he undid the buttons at the front of her dress and let it slide to her feet. She hurried then, moving ahead of him, her fingers fumbling at the hooks on her bra, tugging it away from her, feeling her breasts fall forward. Her hands reached the top of her pants before his did, she pulled them down and kicked out of them.

It was like the first time; it was always like the first time. She felt a wash of feeling over her; his eyes were part of her skin, they were everywhere, her skin was everywhere, the wash of feeling was everywhere.

"I think it's begun to rain," she said, and moved just ahead of his hands. She went to the french door leading out to the screened patio and pulled back one of the weighted red draperies. Rain slanted from the sky, and it led her eye to the walk just outside the door. She looked at what stood there, and began to scream. On the sidewalk was a man, a man she'd never seen, yet she recognized him, thought she recognized him, until she realized that she recognized, not the man, but the way he made her feel. It was the night terror of her childhood. It was the cold terror of all her fears of the dark, the unknown, the terrible. Because he had a gun in his hand, and even as she looked at him, before she could yet give voice to the scream that was surely rising in her throat, he had moved forward and thrust open the long french window and come into the room with the gun aimed at Lou.

She felt herself pushed, felt herself falling against the lamp table next to the chaise lounge, caught at something to break her fall, and still fell, fell hearing a small sound that she thought might be her knee striking the rug, only her knee hadn't touched yet. And then the hot tearing of something ripping into her, the quick contact with the floor, the startled look at the man, who was moving to the inside door, quickly, oh so quickly, while Lou—while Lou lay on the bed where he had fallen, a neat hole in the middle of his forehead and the black-red blood streaking down over his quiet face.

The scream came then; as she heard it, she knew that it would be the longest scream of her life, that probably that scream would echo inside of her and around her for as long as she lived, because though what she screamed was Lou's name, she knew that he was dead, and that she screamed his name not for him to hear her, but for the whole world to know her grief.

Blood was on her, too, it caressed the white flesh of her stomach as it glided slowly down her body from that silly hole just below her ribs—she had been shot, she and Lou had both been shot, only she had to put some clothes on, my God, we're shot, Lou's dead, my God.

And then the people coming in, coming in the French doors and from the hall, the first a woman who screamed, too, until the man with her said, "That's no good. Find something to cover this woman." And the woman did find a coat, it was Lou's. And there was nothing else, since their bags hadn't even been brought up.

There were too many people—someone was on the phone and a bellhop was there—but there were too many people. If they had come to mourn it might have been different, but they weren't mourning. They didn't know Lou, they didn't know her, they came only to see the dead and the dying.

She felt death in her, heavy, leaden. It weighted her so that she could barely struggle to the bed, and the people put out arms, hands, to stop her, but she moved, she somehow got to the bed, got to where Lou was lying, and bent over him, holding her wound, holding his head, feeling that if her blood could somehow mingle with his, they could both still be saved.

She heard a thin scream still. She knew that she was not screaming, that she had stopped when all these people had crowded in. But she also knew that it was her own scream that she had heard, like a watch that had been broken and stopped by a bullet. The thing in her that could cut off the sound of the scream had been broken and stopped by a bullet, and she died with the scream in her ears.

CHAPTER NINETEEN

"He could have gone to the funeral. The bastard could have done that."

"But he didn't. Don't make it worse for yourself. Leave him out of it."

"Cissy, I can't stand it. Marguerite, my God, my little girl—"

"I know. I know. A shitty damn thing to happen."

"And now this. One afternoon he's given me to clear her things out. How can I? He shouldn't ask me. He should do it himself, or get that maid, that Lora Mae. How can I touch her clothes? Cissy, I'm not up to this. I keep thinking, it's all my fault, I put it all in her head. How did I know, how did I know it would come to this?"

Cissy went to the dressing table, poured bourbon in a glass, added ice, a squirt of water. She carried it across the room to Phyllis, handed it to her, stood over her while she drank. "Okay. About the clothes. I asked Lorenzo to go out with me and take care of them. You can stay here, all right?"

"Nothing will ever be all right again. You know, Cissy, I used to believe it. I used to think, when Marguerite would write and tell me about all she was doing, the country club, the parties. And I'd come to see her, she was beautiful, wasn't she beautiful, Cissy, wasn't she? And I'd think, there, she made it, even if she did grow up fatherless and with a mother who worked in a two-bit restaurant, she made it. And now it's gone—she's gone—and I'll never believe in anything again."

Grace Whitman, reading another article about it in the morning paper, turned a pale face to her husband. "This thing has made me sick, Jerry. I want to get away. Take me to Nice—or some place new, some place we've never been."

"I know she was a good friend of yours. But she had it coming, didn't she? Living the way she did?"

"But, Jerry, she was only thirty-two. My age. Imagine, Jerry. If it had been me."

"You'd never get yourself into such a fix, Grace. Not in a million years."

She shivered, the small shiver of a person who has heard a lie and cannot correct it. "Of course, that's right. I never would."

"Caught in a hotel room. A cheap whore."

"I don't want to talk about it, Jerry. Or think about it. We'll take a nice trip, I'll buy some new clothes, throw a party—it doesn't pay to dwell on things, I mean, nothing we can say can change it, right?"

"Right," said Jerry Whitman, and he sipped cold orange juice and watched with pleasure the way the light from the window shone on his wife's smooth blond hair.

300

EXPENSIVE PLEASURES
By Stephen Lewis

PRICE: $2.95

LB929

CATEGORY: Novel

WHAT HAPPENS WHEN A WOMAN'S *EVERY* FANTASY COMES TRUE?

Cara fulfilled her wildest dreams as a superstar model. But she wanted more, and indulged in one more fantasy—to succeed as a fashion designer. Her inspired designs and transcontinental romances carried her to the apex of the fashion industry and high society. But behind her public smile hid the private pain of lovers lost in a world of diamond-studded decadence, sexual abandon, and betrayal. Soon, everyone wore her designer jeans and envied her extravagant lifestyle. But would all her fantasies come true? Would the high risks be worth those EXPENSIVE PLEASURES....A sizzling novel from the author of THE REGULARS and THE BEST SELLERS.

THE REAPING

An ancient superstition reaches out, catching
you in a net of horror and suspense

The Reaping

LEISURE
1035
$2.50

BERNARD TAYLOR

"Taylor works wizardry again here."
—PUBLISHERS WEEKLY

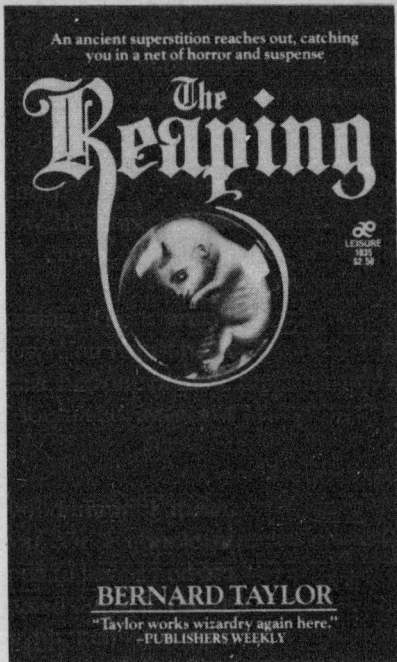

He was hired to paint the
portrait of a young woman at
Woolvercombe Mansion, but Tom
Rigby didn't know she was after
more than a painting. He wondered
about the identities of the strange
inhabitants of the house and the
bizarre events that began to
happen. And suddenly he was
catapulted into a rendezvous with
terror and violence, as the power of
the supernatural wielded its
horrifying spell!

By
Bernard
Taylor

CATEGORY:
Occult
PRICE: $2.50
0-8439-1035-6

THE INSTITUTE

By
James M.
Cain

PRICE: $2.95
0-8439-1034-8
CATEGORY:
Novel

The brilliant career of James M. Cain, the celebrated author of "The Postman Always Rings Twice," "Mildred Pierce" and "Double Indemnity," reaches a shattering climax in this power-triangle of love, lust and greed.

When Professor Lloyd Palmer seeks financial backing from wealthy Richard Garrett, he meets and falls in love with Garrett's seductive wife.

SEND TO: **LEISURE BOOKS**
P.O. Box 511, Murry Hill Station
New York, N.Y. 10156-0511

Please send the titles:

Quantity	Book Number	Price
_____	_____	_____
_____	_____	_____
_____	_____	_____
_____	_____	_____
_____	_____	_____

In the event we are out of stock on any of your
selections, please list alternate titles below.

_____	_____	_____
_____	_____	_____
_____	_____	_____
_____	_____	_____

Postage/Handling_____

I enclose_____

FOR U.S. ORDERS, add 75¢ for the first book and 25¢ for
each additional book to cover cost of postage and handling.
Buy five or more copies and we will pay for shipping. Sorry,
no. C.O.D.'s.

FOR ORDERS SENT OUTSIDE THE U.S.A., add $1.00
for the first book and 50¢ for each additional book. PAY BY
foreign draft or money order drawn on a U.S. bank, payable
in U.S. ($) dollars.

☐ Please send me a free catalog.

NAME _____

(Please print)

ADDRESS _____

CITY _____ STATE _____ ZIP_____

Allow Four Weeks for Delivery